THE TRUTH SAYER

MARCH OF THE OWLMEN

SALLY PRUE

OXFORD
UNIVERSITY PRESS

OXFORD
UNIVERSITY PRESS

Great Clarendon Street, Oxford OX2 6DP

Oxford University Press is a department of the University of Oxford.
It furthers the University's objective of excellence in research, scholarship,
and education by publishing worldwide in

Oxford New York

Auckland Cape Town Dar es Salaam Hong Kong Karachi
Kuala Lumpur Madrid Melbourne Mexico City Nairobi
New Delhi Shanghai Taipei Toronto

With offices in

Argentina Austria Brazil Chile Czech Republic France Greece
Guatemala Hungary Italy Japan Poland Portugal Singapore
South Korea Switzerland Thailand Turkey Ukraine Vietnam

Oxford is a registered trade mark of Oxford University Press
in the UK and in certain other countries

First published 2008
First published in this edition 2009

British Library Cataloguing in Publication Data

Data available

ISBN: 978-0-19-275578-0

3 5 7 9 10 8 6 4 2

Typeset in Sabon by TnQ Books and Journals Pvt. Ltd.,
Chennai, India

Printed in Great Britain by CPI Cox & Wyman, Reading, Berkshire

Paper used in the production of this book is a natural,
recyclable product made from wood grown in sustainable forests.
The manufacturing process conforms to the environmental
regulations of the country of origin.

For Alison Evans

The Mirelands

Pella moved stealthily towards the flames.

Here was a door, but it had not been closed properly. Pella pushed at it and the shimmering flame-patterns, orange and pink and rippling, widened before her.

'Pella! Pella!'

That was Mother calling. Pella slipped quietly through the door and amongst the cold streamers of fire.

'Who is it?'

There was a great scarlet bed amongst the flames, and on it lay a figure. It was so wrinkled and still that it was as if the dead had spoken.

Pella stuck out her tongue at it to see what would happen—but then something seized her. Pella let out a squawk of outrage and found herself kicking and struggling under a strong white arm.

The figure on the bed gave a chuckle that petered out into a series of tiny gasping coughs.

'Bad girl!' scolded the woman who held Pella. 'Bad girl, to be so disrespectful to the magistra. When I tell your mother, you'll be whipped.'

Pella squirmed anxiously, but the woman only clamped Pella even more firmly round her round middle.

'I shall send for someone to take the child away, magistra,' the woman said.

Pella gave up struggling at once. She was very young, but she was far from powerless, and she knew it.

She lifted her chin and smiled at the ancient woman on the bed. She showed her tiny pearls of teeth and held out her chubby arms.

And the old woman smiled too, a little, and Pella was swept up by some great invisible power and carried through the air onto the scarlet satin of the bed cover.

'Nice magistra,' said Pella, crawling closer, though the old woman smelled sour and her limbs were almost as cold as the marble of the walls. 'Nice *kind* magistra.'

The magistra chuckled again, but the other lady, the angry grabby lady, sniffed.

'The child will tire you, magistra,' she said. 'Let me send for her mother.'

The magistra's breath whistled through her sunken lips. 'Go and tell the woman her child is safe,' she whispered.

'But Great One—'

'She comforts me, Dorcis. Go, go.'

It was pretty here, with all the coloured streamers shimmering and turning like a fiery stream. But it was still very cold.

A gnarled hand twitched weakly and Pella, aware of her danger (for outside Mother's voice sounded very cross) put her own small soft one into it.

'It is years since I held anyone's hand,' said the old woman, her voice hardly more than the creaking of a branch. 'I have been alone, alone, for a long time.'

'I shall stay here for ever,' promised Pella.

'A friend as the light fails,' whispered the magistra.

But then the bony fingers twitched again and gripped Pella's hand very tightly—and the magistra began to shake. Pella tried to wriggle her hand free, for the trembling was making her feel as if she'd been dropped into a cup of the fizzy stomach-medicine that Grandfather used to take.

But the old woman's grip was like iron, and now Pella's whole body was shaking and squirming like a litter of wildcats. Even her eyeballs were quivering and squiggling until she was afraid they might pop right out of her head.

'Stop it!' she squealed.

She jerked and struggled and at last she managed to get her hand out of the magistra's grip, but as she did the light from the fire-streamers gave a great searing flash and went out.

Pella blinked round at the dimness and was afraid. She looked at the old woman, but the magistra didn't seem to be angry. The magistra lay, quite peacefully, and her eyes were as quiet as those of the furry dead springers that Grandfather used to bring home for supper.

Dead.

The word fell into Pella's heart with such a thud (*dead,* like Grandfather, and Trun, and . . .) that she screamed. And the sound rang round and round the room, her head, the shrine, the whole valley, perhaps, like the cries of the owls that followed the columns of wicked bandits. Someone was coming, running, running fast.

'Magistra!'

Dorcis's face was so frightened and appalled that Pella knew something terrible had happened.

'Go away!' Pella shouted, in terror, to Dorcis, and Mother, and everyone else who wanted to hurt her. 'Go away, go away, go away!'

And then, with a terrible cry like someone being stabbed with a spear, Dorcis stumbled back a few paces—and the wall opened behind her, and she fell into the darkness beyond.

1

The House of Truth

The boys were sitting on their mats with their backs straight and their eyes closed and they were supposed to be concentrating. The Lord Caul, their teacher, had put a large cake on the schoolroom floor in front of them.

'Some kind person has sent us this,' he'd told them, as he settled his long limbs down on his mat at the front of the class. 'This lesson I want you to use your powers to find out what's gone into making it. And if you manage to work it all out,' Caul had gone on, for although he made the boys work hard he was still quite young and far from mean, 'I'll give you the cake to share between you.'

It had taken Nian about a second to check out the cake, even going as far back as the quiet country garden where the currants had been grown. But then Nian was the Truth Sayer, who could open passageways to other worlds, and he was by far the most powerful person in the House of Truth (and that included all the Lords) so this sort of thing was as easy as breathing for him.

It was bound to take the other boys ages, though, so

Nian let his mind wander. His powers were changing and growing all the time, and he needed time to keep track of what was happening to them. It was a bit like watching the patterns made by oil on water: green, mauve, brightest blue, squirming and curling . . .

. . . and then, all in an instant, it had changed. A new streak had slid into the picture and was growing, black as soot, sending out tentacles deep into the brightness and leaving trails as cold as . . .

Someone nudged Nian, and the whole vision vanished into broad daylight. Something was happening out in the corridor, too. Nian had been too intent to notice it, but Hani, beside him, could never concentrate on anything for more than a couple of minutes. The best *Hani* could do was to rock backwards and forwards slightly and make the effort not to hum. And *that* nearly killed him.

There were people coming down the wide white corridor towards the schoolroom door. That really was something unusual, because *nothing* happened in the House during the Hours of Thought, nothing at all. The whole place was designed so that nothing could happen. The Lords needed the time and space to Think, they said.

By now all the boys were listening to the approaching footsteps, though the Lord Caul, who did most of their teaching, was still floating in a sea of Thought.

It was most likely a new pupil arriving. Someone with powers, like the rest of them.

The door handle turned, and the pupils of the House of Truth hastily re-straightened their backs and re-closed their eyes. They could see well enough with their eyes closed, anyway, and they were supposed to be concentrating so hard that an earthquake wouldn't disturb them, let alone a footfall.

'My friends,' said the Lord Tarq's voice, quietly. And at that everyone joyfully abandoned any pretence of working and got respectfully to their feet.

Tarq, who was in charge of all the boys in the House, was a little man, and so old that the skin stretched over his skull was as dull and soft as hartskin. And, yes, there was a boy with him: a boy really shockingly thin, and clothed in filthy rags.

The boy gave one swift, glittering glance around, but stayed warily in the shelter of the doorway.

'Here is a new companion for you,' said Tarq, in his quiet voice. 'His name is Keer. I have brought him here so you may bid him welcome.'

The boys shuffled their feet and mumbled things, but Keer only hunched his shoulders as if their gaze stung him. Nian felt a moment's pity for Keer as Tarq led the boy away to find a uniform. Keer looked three-quarters starved, and his scrawny wrists were weepy with sores.

Nian wondered how a boy like Keer, plainly so poor and friendless, could have found his way to the House.

Nian spent so long wondering it that he forgot all about the black edge of evil that he'd felt enter the House.

'Very well,' said the Lord Caul, grudgingly, an hour later. 'I suppose that will have to do. Put the cake in your box, Emmec, and you can share it round later.'

Everyone gave sighs of relief and let their spines relax. Nian could search the cake in a second, but it was a really gruelling struggle for the others to work out anything about it at all. They all had powers, and each of them had their own natural talents for different things, but their powers were trivial compared to Nian's.

'May we go out, Lord?' asked Alin, as Hani worked his shoulders round in circles to get his circulation going again.

But Caul only looked irritated.

'You can hardly suppose you've earned a break,' he said. 'You should have got that cake problem solved in half the time. You've been fidgeting and day-dreaming most of the afternoon.'

Everyone went quiet with suspense and dismay. The sunshine outside had conjured up so much energy inside them that it had spilled out of their bodies and was practically pushing the walls out.

'Your parents sent you here to follow the paths of Truth with discipline and humility . . . ' began Caul, yet again; then his voice trailed away in a sigh. 'Oh, be off with you,' he said. 'Go and run about until you're tired, for Truth's sake. But just keep away from the building work, do you hear?'

There was the usual scrum in the doorway as they all tried to get out at once, but they were careful not to make too much noise. Disturbing either of the Lords Rago or Grodan might well be enough to get them sent back to the schoolroom.

They slipped along the corridor and out into the garden, and then they let themselves go mad. They pelted along the paths between the bramble patches, they swung on branches, they leapt over logs, they turned cartwheels, they wrestled and climbed and rolled.

'I hope the new boy's getting settled in all right,' said Derig, kindly, at last, as they flopped on the ground to watch the building work. It was six months since Nian had travelled to another world and caused the great earthquakes that had tumbled a large section of the House into ruin, but despite the fact that Ranger, the new master builder, had been running up and down for most of that time as busy and agitated as a tiger-bee, the site had only just been cleared.

Alin snorted.

'The beggar?' he said, contemptuously. 'Tarq's probably still trying to get him clean.' Alin's father was a rich lawyer, and he liked people to remember it.

'Poor old Keer,' said Emmec, good-humouredly. 'He doesn't know what he's in for, in this place.'

'He'll go mad,' predicted Hani, pleased. 'He'll start foaming at the mouth with boredom, and we'll have to sit on him to stop him bashing his brains out on the walls.'

'Sounds more like you,' said Alin.

In front of them, a group of fat men in red tunics were trudging along carrying a huge beam of wood.

'It will be hard for him,' said Gow, who was fundamentally serious and clever. 'He won't be used to following rules and routines.'

'I suppose, if he's been a beggar, he won't be home-sick, though,' said Derig, rather wistfully.

'He'll be jolly grateful to be clothed and fed,' said Alin, pulling up a blade of grass and stretching it carefully between his thumbs. He blew hard, and got quite a good honking squeal out of it—but instead of the noise tailing off, it got louder, and deeper, until it had swelled into a raspberry of such loudness and glorious magnificence that it shivered the curving white walls of the House and set their dinners vibrating within them.

In front of them, the fat men leapt like grossly fat goats and dropped the beam. The boys felt the dull thump of it hitting the ground, and a moment later the very fattest man let out a howl that could be heard even over the dying echoes of the Great Raspberry, and began to hop about, clutching his toe, in a way that reminded Nian of the Sirrom dancers that visited the village at home.

The boys fell about laughing.

'Who made it do that?' asked Hani, weeping tears of mirth.

'Not me,' gasped Alin. 'Nian, was it—'

The men in red were looking round wildly in all directions—and the boys belatedly remembered how bad-tempered these men, the Tarhun, were. And how strong.

'*Grot!*' gasped Emmec, beside Nian. '*Scarper!*' And the boys scrambled to their feet and fled.

The Tarhun were pot-bellied layabouts, but they could run. Nian dodged down a path that took him

10

towards the most tangled part of the garden. He ducked under branches and jumped the treacherous brambles that lay waiting to snare his legs, and close behind him the earth shook under the weight of several charging Tarhun.

And then there was a squeak of terror, and a hoarse cry of rage and triumph, and the pounding feet stopped.

They'd caught someone. Nian waited, his heart thumping in his chest.

Who was it?

'*I'll break your bogging neck!*' bawled a deep voice.

'But—but—but it wasn't me!' quavered someone.

Derig.

Nian sighed. Derig had been sent away by his father in the hope that life in the House of Truth would toughen him up, but it was showing no signs of working. Derig was never going to be tough; it'd taken several weeks just for him to begin to be cheerful, in a hopeful, mouse-ish sort of way. And even now he still sometimes cried himself to sleep.

Nian couldn't abandon Derig to be beaten up by the Tarhun. He turned and jogged back along the path.

He soon found them. Rage and terror surrounded them in gouts of scarlet and ice.

'I'm going to give you such a going-over, you little piece of *grot*,' a huge figure was saying.

'Ranger!' said Nian, sharply enough.

The fat men glanced back over their beefy red shoulders, and someone muttered the words *Truth Sayer*. The Tarhun who had got hold of Derig paused while

11

everyone remembered that Nian was the most power-ful person in the place, who had opened a passageway between the worlds, and who had brought the walls of the House tumbling down around them. And then the Tarhun reluctantly opened the fist that was hold-ing Derig in the air.

Derig dropped, stumbled, and ducked swiftly under a fat red elbow to scoot to Nian's side.

They all stood and glared at each other. Then the Tarhun who had dropped Derig (Ranger, it was, the master builder, who was always fizzing with busyness) threw up his hands in exasperation.

'I know, I know, Truth Sayer,' he muttered, bitterly. 'Violence isn't the solution, crisis-resolving skills, ambassadors for the House, protectors of gifted youth, blah blah blah blah blah . . . and never mind that I'm in agony from a broken bogging toe!'

There came from the group of Tarhun a rumbling that might have meant anything. But Reeklet definitely mumbled:

'Violence has always worked all right for *me*,' and someone else said something that contained the word *traditional*.

Nian had to admit they had a point. When you lived in the House of Truth with all those pottery old Lords, violence and action did become quite dazzlingly attrac-tive. Especially when you had the power to walk the worlds, or fight half an army. Nian sighed.

'It's tough, isn't it,' he agreed. 'Your lives are much harder than when you just had to go around cheating and kidnapping boys.'

There was a general sigh at that.

'The good old days,' murmured Reeklet, wistfully.

'I'm sure the little piece of grot's broken my toe,' grunted Ranger, keeping doggedly to the point. 'Little bogger, making a racket like that right in our earholes when we're engaged in skilled construction work.'

'But . . . it *wasn't* me,' quavered Derig, his dark eyes wide with apprehension.

'I know,' said Nian, reassuringly, for Derig had to be as brave as he possibly could be just to get from one day to the next, without doing risky things like playing practical jokes.

'It's enough to distract anyone,' agreed Ranger's cousin Snorer, self-righteously. 'Surprising none of us had a heart-attack.'

Nian, very bravely, used his powers to have a look inside Ranger's fetid boot, and winced. The bone wasn't broken, but the toe was throbbing horribly, and it was swelling by the minute.

'I'm really sorry about your toe, Ranger,' said Nian. 'And, look, I'll cure it for you if you like.'

Ranger hesitated, but then nodded.

'Well, that would be a help, Truth Sayer,' he said. 'Because we've got to get these beams shifted before the weather breaks, and I'll need to be hopping back and forth supervising.'

'But of course it's too much to expect an *apology*, isn't it,' said Reeklet, bitterly. Reeklet was probably the most bitter and twisted of the Tarhun, with a moustache to match, and he was always moaning. 'We're only *Tarhun*, after all.'

13

Nian sighed again. He was the youngest of the boys in the House, and the smallest, too; but he was the Truth Sayer. The Truth Sayer, who'd been responsible for destroying the way of life of the Tarhun and Lords in the House of Truth, and a considerable proportion of the actual House, as well. The Truth Sayer, who was supposed to be the wisest person the world had ever known.

Nian kept trying to forget it, but it was impossible. 'Emmec,' he said. And Emmec emerged reluctantly from behind a tree trunk.

Nian waited.

'It was just a joke,' Emmec explained. 'I didn't think about it making you all jump. I'm really sorry, Ranger, especially when you're so busy.'

Ranger grunted, but seemed appeased.

'Rest for a couple of hours,' Nian, the Truth Sayer, told him. 'Your toe'll be quite better by supper-time.'

The Tarhun bowed as well as their paunches allowed, and lumbered back towards the building site.

'Come on,' said Alin, from up a tree. 'Let's go and have a game of pockle.'

'Yeah!' said Hani. 'Yoooooo-NITed! Come *on*, *United*!'

But for Nian the afternoon was spoiled.

2

The days were long on the mountain of the House of Truth, but dusk, when it came, advanced swiftly. The Great Sun would slide behind the glassy mountains, and in ten minutes darkness had descended on the House.

This meant that getting ready for bed was always done in a hurry and a rush. The boys would stay in the pool until the last possible minute, and then there'd be a mad jostling to be on their sleeping mats before it was quite dark.

There were no lamps or candles in the House. Any boy who needed to get up in the night was expected to use his powers to find his way. This was fine if all you were doing was visiting the latrines, but it was a nuisance if you were trying to find your toothstick, or hold a dice tournament.

They'd had to give up on the dice: once their powers were switched on they found that the tumbling of the numbers made them cross-eyed and nauseated.

Derig was generally the last of the boys to be ready. Derig was so sweet-natured that he always let the others go first, and the rest of the boys had found the new boy Keer a sleeping mat, and a place to put it, and were settling themselves down to sleep while Derig was still pottering back from the latrines.

His yelp of fright bounced round the white walls of the corridor and startled them.

'He's probably met Rago,' joked Hani, getting up to find out what was going on. The Lord Rago was the eldest inhabitant of the House, and could be relied upon to be crotchety and fault-finding.

Nian said nothing. He had caught something from Derig's mind: some edge of blackness, of evil, of danger . . .

'What happened?' demanded Emmec, as Derig arrived panting from the blue dusk of the corridor and cannoned into Hani.

'Someone's drawn a horrible great big owl-thing on the corridor wall,' Derig said breathlessly. 'I thought it was real for a moment.'

'Struth,' said Alin, throwing off his cover. 'Who did that? The Lords will go bogging berserk!'

The thing was only too clearly visible, even in the settling dusk.

'Grotting pits,' breathed Hani, and even he was really shocked.

It had been drawn in finger-thick black lines. It had more or less the shape of a man, though it was narrower in the waist than any man, but it had the head of an owl. The eyes stared spitefully over a neatly hooked beak, and round the face the thing had a feathery mane a little like a wolf's.

'The Lords will go mad,' said Gow, who was the

tallest, eldest, and cleverest of the boys, rubbing nervously at the side of his nose. 'They'll have us fasting and working from dawn till dusk.'

'And that's if Grodan doesn't freeze us to death with sarcasm,' said Emmec, for the Lord Grodan had little time either for the boys or for the new ways of Thought that Nian had brought to the House.

'Who did it?' demanded Alin, looking round at the rest.

Nian was puzzled. Usually he knew straight away who had done things, just as this afternoon he'd known who'd amplified the grass-squeaker. He tried to call the culprit to mind, but he found himself struck with a chill that somehow also had the acrid smell of metal, of mildew, of destruction.

'I don't think any of us could have done this,' said Derig, very troubled. 'Except Nian, of course.'

Keer hadn't followed them into the corridor; he was lurking behind them in the doorway of the sleeping room. The others exchanged questioning glances; surely an uneducated, untrained beggar couldn't have conjured up this thing, for, as they could feel in their bones, it was something very very powerful.

The shadow of Keer watched them. But it said nothing.

'*No!*'

Nian twitched and fell out of a dream where he was soaring through the azure air with a troupe of translucent butterflies.

'*No! No! DON'T!*'

Nian reluctantly opened his eyes. The darkness of the sleeping room was filled with a tepid smog of sleep and muttered cursing.

'Derig, shut up,' groaned Alin. Then, when there was no reply, he said it louder. '*Derig!*'

The figure on Derig's mat jolted and twisted and began to speak quite loudly, but without any proper words.

Hani pulled his cover over his ears, waited for a tense moment, and then flopped over onto his back.

'For bog's sake,' he said, aggrieved. 'Nian, shut him up, can't you?'

Nian sat himself up blearily. He'd thought he and Derig had found a way to stop Derig having these bad dreams. Derig had a talent for picking up anything scary—even an attack on a fly by a spider—and then waking everyone up with it.

Nian hunched his cover round his shoulders. He had got pretty practised in easing Derig out of bad dreams, and all he had to do now was rest a foot against Derig and sort of feel soothing.

But this time—*ow!*—something like a bee-sting shot through Nian's foot as soon as he touched Derig. Nian snatched his foot away, rubbed it irritably, and tried again.

Ow!

Nian, properly awake, now, sent healing powers down his leg and on into Derig. It got rid of the stinging, but . . .

'No,' muttered Derig, his head turning from side to side. 'Not me. *Goway!*'

Keer's voice snarled from the corner.

'What the pits is he on about?'

'Nothing,' answered Emmec's voice, fed-up. 'Just a dream. Nian'll sort him out. Go to sleep.'

'*Goway. Goway. Goway!*'

Nian, worried, moved his thoughts close to Derig.

Derig, he thought. *It's Nian. It's all right. It's just a dream.*

But it wasn't. There was a sudden wave of cold crashing through him, and a great shriek like the cry of a bird ringing through his skull—and one of Derig's dreams had never done that.

Nian, the Truth Sayer, gritted his teeth and bent his will against whatever it was. Derig's mind was filled with jagged blackness, but slowly Nian managed to push it back, back, and out of Derig's mind.

The other boys were breathing quietly again. Nian was the Truth Sayer: it was easy for him to sort out any problem. They could leave him to it.

Nian sat shivering in the night. It took quite a long time until he had erected enough barriers of power to make sure that Derig would sleep really peacefully again.

And then at last Nian himself could lie down, and try to banish that chilling more-than-dream from his own mind, so that he himself could get to sleep.

In the pink light of dawn the figure on the wall seemed even bigger and uglier than ever. Alin rubbed his thumb over the black lines and checked to see if any of the colour had come off.

'How's it been done?' he asked.

The lines were as sharp-edged as ink, but they did not have the orange sheen that ink has.

'We'd better get it cleaned off,' said Derig, nervously. 'If one of the Lords sees it we'll be in terrible trouble.'

'But we didn't do it,' said Hani. 'They'll know it wasn't me, anyway. I'm miles too stupid to make anything like that.'

Nian tried again to find out who'd drawn it—but his mind hit such a wall of black-cold spite that he could only wince away.

However the thing had got there, it was evil, and it was best got rid of.

'I'll get a bucket and a scrubbing brush,' he said.

They must have worn away a finger's width of bristles between them, but they made absolutely no impression at all on the black lines of the owlman.

'But what can we do?' asked Derig, in dismay.

Emmec frowned thoughtfully. He was the practical one amongst the boys, and he was always messing about with magnets and chemicals and bits of wood.

'We might be able to dissolve the marks,' he suggested. 'With alcohol, perhaps. The Tarhun have got loads of beer and brandy and stuff over in the Outer House.'

'Which they won't let you have,' pointed out Alin.

Above their heads owlman's eyes sparked with malice.

Derig shivered.

'The thing's foul,' he said. 'I had horrible dreams last night.'

'About owls?' asked Gow, with more than usual interest.

'About the Lords,' suggested Hani, with a snigger.

But Derig shook his head.

'It was about knives,' he said; it was clear that he was puzzled by this, but also disturbed.

Alin shrugged, and turned away.

'Well, if we can't get rid of it, we'd best start eating,' he said.

And that was good sense, for if the boys caused trouble they were likely to be rewarded with a missed meal: it wasn't so much a punishment, as that the Lords genuinely believed that fasting was good for their minds.

Nian was bolting his fourth piece of toast when a cracked screech of outrage announced that the Lord Rago had discovered the owlman.

Rago was as bad-tempered as a viper on a griddle at the best of times, and by the time he reached the boys there was practically steam coming out of his ears.

'This is an outrage!' he burst out, almost dancing with rage. 'An outrage, do you hear?'

They got up and bowed, though for some reason they were all struck with an insane urge to giggle. They kept their eyes firmly on the stone of the floor in case they should set each other off.

'What is the *meaning* of it?' demanded Rago, his voice shooting up an octave in exasperation. 'What is the meaning of that horrible scrawl? This is the House of Truth, do you understand? It has remained unsullied for a thousand years—until the recent disaster, at least.'

Nian made a face. Rago had not forgiven him for causing so much damage to the House—or for destroying the source of so much of the Lords' powers, either.

Rago's face screwed itself up into a thousand peevish wrinkles.

'Boys!' he spat. 'Uncontrolled boys, loose about the House! I knew it would be a disaster from the start!'

They did laugh once he had stormed off, but their laughter had a hysterical edge to it.

'What do you think they'll do to us?' asked Gow, at last.

There was a pause while they all thought about it.

'Well, I'm not taking the blame!' spat a voice from the corner. It startled them, because Keer had hardly opened his mouth till then. 'I'm telling them it was all you lot!'

The others looked at each other.

'It's all right,' explained Derig, kindly. 'They won't torture us, or shut us up in the dark or anything.'

'They'll just make us *think*,' agreed Emmec. 'For hours and hours.'

They all sighed.

'But I still don't see why we should *all* suffer,' muttered Alin. 'Are you sure you don't know who did it, Nian?'

'I don't even know who *could* have done it,' he replied. 'I'm not even sure *I* could have.'

'Come off it!' said Hani. 'You're the Truth Sayer. You can do anything.'

Nian shrugged. It was true his powers were about a hundred times greater than theirs, but he didn't want to get his mind messed up with anything like that owlman.

'But if it wasn't one of us . . . ' began Emmec.

'One of the Lords must have gone totally bonkers,' suggested Hani. 'I mean, most of them are halfway there already.'

But Gow shook his head.

'None of the Lords would have done it,' he said. 'They love this place. They aren't going to start drawing monsters on the walls.'

'But then it must have been one of us,' pointed out Alin, with inescapable logic. 'That thing's taken real power.'

'Well, don't look at me,' said Hani. 'I told you, I'm miles too stupid.'

'And it's not just the amount of power you'd need,' said Emmec, shuddering, 'or even how you'd make it. That's dark stuff, that owlman is. Hey, Nian, what's it made of?'

Nian called on his powers to look at the owlman again. He let his mind dive into it. At first it seemed all just darkness, but then he caught a gleam of something: an edge, a knife, sharp and slashing and . . .

. . . he ducked, and just managed to heave himself back into the outside world before the blade cut into him. He stood and panted with shock. Yes, there was evil there. A lust for harm, for blood, for death.

The others were staring at him, and on Derig's face he saw a horror that echoed his own.

23

'Nian?' said Alin, impatiently, as if he were not saying it for the first time. 'Have you gone deaf or something? What's up?'

'I don't know,' said Nian, still shocked.

'But you're the Truth Sayer,' said Derig, bewildered and shaken. 'You always understand things.'

Nian frowned. Surely that owlman could not have been made by anyone in the House. It was hard to understand how it could have been made by anyone human at all.

'Not about the owlman,' he said slowly. 'I don't understand anything about the owlman at all.'

The Mirelands

Pella stood at her window and looked down over the blustering grass.

There were figures trudging along by the shining trail of the stream. They were bent under the weight of their bundles, and their bare feet showed white with cold.

Beside Pella, Dorcis compressed her lips.

'Branto's been busy, by the look of it,' she commented, grimly.

'Like the total moron he is,' said Pella. 'Do we have to keep taking in all these women?'

'They've got nowhere else to go,' said Dorcis. 'Their homes will have been burnt and their men killed. Finding sanctuary in the shrine's all they can do.'

Pella shrugged, and turned away from the long window and plonked herself down in front of her mirror. Her rosy face looked at itself consideringly in the mirror.

'The word is that Branto is still heading this way,' Dorcis said.

Pella snorted.

'Branto would never be mad enough to attack the

shrine,' she said. 'I'd blast him into a thousand pieces. No I wouldn't. I'd tie his bowels into knots and then slice them up like sausages.'

Dorcis's cold grey eyes stared at Pella through the dimness of the mirror. Pella had been the magistra, the wielder of power, for ten years—but she was still only a girl.

'Branto will have his army with him,' Dorcis said. 'Do you think you'll be able to kill them all, magistra?'

Pella scowled at Dorcis's reflection, but she made no reply.

3

The Lord Caul was waiting for them when the boys traipsed reluctantly into the schoolroom. He looked them over distastefully and read them a long lecture about:

    a) the Glorious Traditions of the House;

    b) the Responsibilities of Possessing Powers; and,

    c) Living Together.

They ended up with an extra period of Thought instead of a dinner hour. They would have felt much angrier about this if there'd been any believable reason for the owlman's appearance, except that one of them was responsible.

Alin took the first opportunity to take Nian aside. 'That Keer,' he said. 'He looks a squirt, but how powerful is he?'

Nian couldn't pretend the question hadn't occurred to him.

'Not powerful enough to have made the owlman,' he said, shortly.

'But he might have brought it here,' Alin pointed out. 'If he's been a beggar he's probably friends with every crook in the city!'

'So what?' said Nian. '*Who* doesn't matter, Alin. What matters is *why.*'

'Nian,' said Derig, a little later. 'That owlman . . . it's only a picture, isn't it? So no one needs to be afraid.'

'Not when you've got Nian around,' said Hani, lightly. 'Nothing can get past the Truth Sayer without being exploded into a million pieces. *Boom! Ker-pow!*'

And Nian felt even lonelier than before.

The morning was enlivened by the sounds of various of the Lords trying to get the owlman off the wall.

Ker-thump!

Aaaargh!

'Oh, struth, that was the Lord Firn,' said Caul, distracted. 'Perhaps I'd better go and see . . . oh! You'd better come in and sit down, Lord . . . yes, yes, I expect we'll be able to make your eyebrows grow back.'

And, later, the almost equally entertaining sounds of Tarhun Ranger trying to get rid of it.

Ssssscrrrrapy-scrapy-scrapy-scrapy scrape.

Yscrapy-scrape.

Yscrapy-scrape . . . ohhhhhhhh BOGGIT!

But having to miss dinner was hard.

'Especially as it's not my fault,' said Hani, still put out by the injustice of it.

'Nor mine,' said Alin, throwing a black look at Keer.

'Told you,' spat Keer, from the corner. 'Wasn't me.'

'Just concentrate on your powers as hard as you can,' advised Derig, kindly. 'You don't notice how hungry you are, then.'

The boys sighed heavily, sat down, and tried to ignore the scents of food that were wafting down the corridor. The House's food was prepared in the Outer House by Snerk, the Tarhun cook, in a kitchen of complex, magnificent, and fascinating filth. Despite this, the boys made a point of sneaking across to visit Snerk as often as they could, because, whatever germs and dirt were in it, Snerk's cooking was a towering masterpiece of succulence and flavour.

Nian sat, with a thick brown vision of taste-bud enrapturing gravy teasing the edges of his mind, and tried not to think about Other Worlds. All he had to do was walk up to the square statue in the middle of the garden, and in just a few minutes he could be having dinner in a completely unknown world . . .

. . . except that of course he couldn't. No matter how he itched to go up to the statue in the garden and force open a link between the worlds, the risks of world-travel were much too great. If he got stuck in the wrong world for more than a couple of days then the strain that would put on the whole world-system would swiftly lead to that world and this one pulling each other to pieces.

The Lords had spent a lot of time talking to Nian about this, and he agreed completely; but knowing that there were other worlds only a few minutes away sometimes made him so restless and curious that he nearly went mad.

Most of the time there were enough things in this world to keep him busy. Pockle, for instance . . . and if he got too low or frustrated then Hani would make

29

him laugh, or Derig would be sympathetic, until he'd hauled himself back to normal again.

The Lords of the House of Truth tended to be so deep in Thought that they hardly noticed the food in front of them, but even the Lords couldn't fail to notice the stew that day. For one thing it was giving off a purple, tear-inducing vapour; for another, it was an unmissably bright blue; and, thirdly, it was *furry*.

The Lord Rago's cries of outrage reached the boys as they sat, upright and empty, in the schoolroom. Effortlessly, the boys tuned in their powers so they could hear what was going on. They didn't eavesdrop very often, but this sounded too good to miss.

'Look at it!' the Lord Rago was demanding. 'What does the Tarhun think he's doing, serving us this? I am a Lord of Truth, not a starved dung-rat!'

'This . . . this fur upon it,' quavered a voice. That was Firn, the librarian. 'Do you think that perhaps some poor animal has . . . *drowned*?'

There was a silence, and the boys held their breaths. It was just possible that the Lords might notice them listening, and the last thing they needed was more trouble.

There was a clatter as several of the Lords put down their spoons.

'No. This is not truly fur,' said Tarq, at last, with some relief. 'It is some sort of . . . mould, perhaps.'

'Aye,' agreed Grodan, grimly. 'But it's poisonous, whatever it is.'

'Poisonous?' whispered Hani, in the schoolroom. 'Come off it, who'd want to poison anyone?'

'Perhaps . . . perhaps it isn't really poison,' said Derig, whose soft heart made it hard for him to think ill of anyone. 'Perhaps it's something that's got into the stew by mistake. Like a few toadstools, or a scorpion or two, poor things.'

'It's a miracle it hasn't happened before,' said Alin, darkly. 'That kitchen's completely squalid, and Snerk's the filthiest thing in it. They can't even keep a ferret because the place is so smelly the poor things keep running away.'

'They don't need a ferret,' Emmec pointed out. 'Even dung-rats won't go anywhere near Snerk. There are traps all over the place, but I've never seen one with anything in it.'

'I had a pet dung-rat, once,' said Hani, wistfully. 'Until my mother found it.'

'Shh!' said Gow.

They all listened, not with their ears, but with the powers that swam inside them.

'But what can we expect?' Rago was asking, in a shrill squall of irritation. 'Those Tarhun idiots! They seem quite incapable of repairing the walls, let alone preparing food fit for human consumption.'

'And he hasn't seen Snerk's kitchen,' murmured Emmec. For the Lord Rago never left the Inner House—had not left it for over eighty years, and had declared his intention of never doing so.

Now the Lord Grodan was speaking.

'It is odd,' he commented, in a voice as smooth and deadly as a snake's tongue, 'that this has happened when the pupils are missing the meal.'

31

'Oh, but surely none of the boys would be involved,' said Caul, very shocked.

'No, we have no reason to blame the boys,' agreed Tarq, quietly. 'But we must certainly investigate the kitchens.'

'Well, I'm not going!' snapped Rago. 'This House is chaotic enough to send me distracted as it is.'

There was a pause.

'It will be best if the Truth Sayer goes,' said Tarq, at last. 'He will see furthest.'

'And he must look for quicksilver,' said Grodan. 'That's the source of this poison. I just hope the boy has discipline enough to make a thorough search.'

But Rago made a sound like an infuriated goat.

'The Truth Sayer, the Truth Sayer!' he cried. 'The boy who destroyed the work of our lives! That boy—'

But then suddenly Nian didn't want to hear any more. Grodan had always resented him, and Rago was a miserable, vicious old man who seldom had a good word to say about anyone, and Nian certainly didn't want to hear what either of them thought about him.

A prickling wave of interference had drowned out the Lords' voices before Nian had even realized he was causing it.

'Sorry,' he said, hastily damping it down as the other boys clapped their hands to their painful ears. 'Sorry. I didn't mean to.'

Keer sat sullenly scratching at his sores while the others shook the mind-buzzing out of their heads.

'I'll tell you what,' said Emmec, when he'd stopped

massaging his ears. 'The Lords are in too much of a bother to notice what we're doing. Let's have that cake we were studying yesterday.'

It only took Emmec a couple of minutes to slip along the corridor to his box, but he came back agitated and angry and empty-handed.

'It's gone!' he said. 'The cake was there in my box this morning, but now it's gone!'

Everyone looked over towards the corner.

'It wasn't me!' spat Keer.

But Nian, the Truth Sayer, sighed.

'Yes it was,' he said.

Emmec took an angry step towards him, but Nian said: 'Leave him alone, Emmec.'

'But—'

'I said, leave him!'

'What can you expect?' jeered Alin, from the side-lines. 'You'll never find a beggar who isn't a thief. And worse!'

'He's not a beggar, he's a pupil of the House, just the same as us!' snapped Nian, but as he said it he was wondering why on earth he was trying to stop a quarrel when what he really wanted was a proper fight where he could let himself go, where he could use the mighty powers that were coiled up inside him instead of always having to be the Truth Sayer: the sensible, quiet, wise, forward-looking, thoughtful, and peace-loving Truth Sayer.

'Keer,' Nian went on, as calmly as he could. 'There's no need for you to steal. There's enough for everyone, and we always share, anyway. If you've stolen anything else you must give it back, and you've got to promise not to do it again.'

Keer shot him a look of pure hatred.

'I won't steal, then,' he muttered. 'All right?'

'But that's too late for the cake,' said Hani, regretfully, as Emmec cast himself sourly back on his mat.

Just for an instant Nian came close to doing something big. Earth-shakingly, wall-topplingly big. He just would have felt so much better for it.

He would also have felt better if he'd thought that Keer's promise was worth even a little more than the air of which it was made.

The Mirelands

The public rooms of the shrine were full of shivering and terrified refugees. Dorcis seemed to get pleasure from telling Pella every time a new lot arrived.

'Well,' snapped Pella, clutching one of her stuffed animals to her. 'If they don't like it, they must go somewhere else, that's all.'

'I'm sure they would if they could, magistra,' said Dorcis, drily. 'Especially with Branto on his way.'

Pella scowled at Dorcis, who was looking even more annoyingly than usual like one of the statues that held up the roof of the great hall: grey-eyed and large-limbed and highly tragic.

'If he so much as shows his face—'

'—oh, he won't be as foolish as that,' agreed Dorcis. 'He'll send his army in first, naturally. They have catapults for throwing rocks. Very difficult to combat.'

'No they're not. I'll explode them. I can do that.'

Dorcis pursed her lips.

'There will be a lot of men,' she said.

'So?' said Pella, obstinately. 'I'm the magistra. I'll send an army of homicidal springers after them. They won't get far with their kneecaps bitten off.'

But Dorcis only looked more than ever as if she'd been carved out of marble by someone with stomach ache.

'Will you?' she asked. 'Are you certain that will be enough? Think of the danger to yourself, personally.'

Pella shrugged.

Dorcis paused for a few moments and then took a deep breath.

'Pella, I studied with the old magistra for many years before she chose you as her successor. If you were to lend your powers to me, just for this time of emergency—'

Pella threw her stuffed animal hard at Dorcis's sandalled feet. It went through the air with a screech, and Dorcis only just managed to jump back out of the way before it hit the floor and burst into a hundred flaming fragments.

'No!' snarled Pella, her face red. '*I* am the magistra. *I* have the powers. The magistra did not choose you. She chose *me*!'

4

Everything seemed calm when Caul looked in at the schoolroom door, but the anger inside was making the air taste sour.

'I need you to come with me, Truth Sayer,' Caul said. 'The Lord Rago will be here in a minute to supervise the rest of you.'

The other boys exchanged appalled glances. There were exercises in Thought so difficult and dull that you could practically hear your brain disintegrating into dust as you struggled to do them, and this was the sort of task Rago usually set them.

'Sorry, you lot,' said Caul, apologetically. 'But it's an emergency.'

Caul and Nian hurried along the corridor and past the black outline of the owlman.

'I expect you were all listening to what happened at the Lords' dinner time,' Caul said.

'Some of it,' admitted Nian.

'Do you know who was responsible for the poison?'

Nian shook his head. Usually pieces of knowledge would appear in his mind like birds perched in the trees. But this time there was absolutely nothing.

Caul pushed open a door. Until six months ago a Lord would never leave the Inner House of the House of Truth until he was dead, but things were different, now. Caul led the way along the path towards the Outer House. A squad of Tarhun led by Ranger were prowling along carrying spades. Ranger was still limping hugely—but that, as Nian knew even before he checked, was being done entirely for effect.

Tarhun Snorer was on reception duty in the Outer House. Snorer led Nian and Caul along the strip of grubby lumber-room that passed for a corridor. There were no windows, here, and the louvres of the occasional ventilator had long since been shrouded with cobwebs and grime.

The stink told Nian when they were approaching the kitchen. It was a powerful stink, though warm and comfortable, like . . . yes, a bit like the compost heap at home. It was the smell of things that had been rotting so long they'd lost their own individual scents and settled into an indistinct warm brownness.

'Here we are, Lords,' announced Snorer, stopping by a large door. For a moment Nian thought he'd got dots before the eyes, but when he looked again he saw that the door was covered with hundreds and hundreds of small copper flies. They kept making little jerking runs at each other, and then zooming off in an agitated buzz before landing to start all over again.

Caul had hardly seen the suns in the seven and a half years since he'd entered the House, so he was hardly able to get any paler; but there was something about his expression that suggested that he would have done, if he could.

'This is the kitchen?' he asked, aghast.

'Yes, Lord,' said Snorer, fondly. 'A temple to excellence, we like to think.'

'Where the Lords' food is prepared?'

'Yes, Lord. Since the recent . . . er . . . *catastrophe* the Tarhun have taken on all the catering for the House, including all hospitality and tourism. We've acquired quite a reputation.'

Caul took a deep unsteady breath, choked on a fly, and then suddenly laughed.

'Ah well,' he said. 'I suppose ten thousand flies can't be wrong.'

The kitchen was as big as a room in the ring-shaped Outer House could be. That made it about fifteen spans deep, and perhaps forty wide—though the little windows were so covered in soft layers of soot that the side walls disappeared into the gloom.

Right in front of them someone had dumped a huge sack-like mound of something in a chair, from which two white things protruded to rest on the scarred surface of the table. The white things were divided at the tops into . . . toes.

Caul's pallor had taken on a green tinge. He cleared his throat, but the mound only sighed and settled deeper into its slumber. Behind them, Snorer's shadow shifted.

'He needs his rest, does Snerk,' he explained,

earnestly, in a hoarse whisper. 'The afternoon teas will be starting soon.'

'Afternoon teas?' echoed Caul, in fascinated horror. Snorer nodded, a little shy, but proud.

'Going very well, are the afternoon teas,' he told them. 'Stands to reason. The tourists have to climb halfway up the mountain to get here, don't they. I mean, the inn's right down by the river, so it's not surprising they're desperate for a nice cup of tea and a slice of homemade by the time they get here.'

Caul stared appalled at the rusty oven door set into the wall by the reeking fireplace.

'He makes *cakes*, in here?'

Snorer shifted from one huge foot to the other. 'Well, I'm not really involved in the *haute cuisine* side of the operation, much,' he admitted. 'I'm more security and welcome. I'm not sure we've got the actual *cakes* going, yet, to tell the truth, but we're doing very well with the biscuits. Yes, the old biscuits are proving very popular.'

Caul looked round the room and shuddered. 'Biscuits,' he whispered, palely.

'Squashed fly biscuits,' said Nian. And laughed.

All the members of the Tarhun were large, but Snerk was a mountain, if there had ever been a mountain that had never known a shower. His first reaction on being woken up was to grope for the meat cleaver that had been at hand on the table, but Snorer, thoughtfully, had hidden it high on a shelf behind a pile of dung-rat traps.

'Wurrr-wurrrr,' growled Snerk, from behind a bloodshot eye. 'Wurrr. Durrrrr. Wojawurrrr?'

Beside Snerk, Caul looked more heron-like and scholarly than ever.

'We are here on a matter of great seriousness,' he said.

'Murrrrr,' rumbled Snerk, the sound magnified by the great fatty caverns of his belly. 'Murrrrrrr. Boggoff!'

Once you'd been in Snerk's kitchen for a while the smell began to get to you. It wasn't so much that it was pungent, especially, as that it didn't seem to leave much room for oxygen. Nian found himself beginning to feel a bit dizzy.

Snerk shifted himself round on his chair and seemed to be trying to open his other eye.

'Gurrrr,' he said.

'Of great seriousness,' repeated Caul, spikily. 'The Lords' dinner today was poisoned.'

Snorer looked really shocked.

'But old Snerk would never *poison* anyone,' he said. 'Why, he's sensitive, Snerk is. A genius. Dedicated to his art.'

There appeared to be some rags hung up in a corner amongst the garlands of fat round haggises, but when Nian looked at them more carefully he realized that they were actually spit-swifts.

'But not,' observed Caul, waspishly, 'to hygiene.'

Nian had always made a point of not Thinking about the contents of the various sacks that were left slumped against the walls, or what actually made up the patchwork of stains that encrusted Snerk's

41

enormous belly. But now, tentatively, Nian let his mind explore the place. It took some courage. There was a pale nest of earwigs in the cutlery drawer, and a band of point-snouted weevils in the flour barrel. And, over there, in that sack, were hundreds upon hundreds of oat-lice, chewing their way quietly through the contents and depositing a pale powder of frass in their wakes. Nian hastily banished all memories of the oat porridge he'd eaten since he'd come to the House, and pushed his mind deeper through the damp air of the place. He didn't know what he was looking for, but he was pretty sure he would know if he found it.

An expression of deep shock passed over Snorer's bulgy face.

'Cleanliness isn't everything, Lord,' he said, stoutly. 'You don't get a fine ripe full-bodied taste with *cleanliness*. Have you ever wondered why the Tarhun are so strong and healthy? That's through eating well, that is. Eating heartily. We've got Snerk to thank for that.'

'Gurrrrr,' Snerk said, darkly, his words sending fat-waves of almost tidal proportions surging through his body. 'Snurrrrr . . . humph. Snurr-humph! Humph.'

'It's certainly likely to weed out the weaklings,' said Caul, irritably, 'but unfortunately many of the Lords are old and frail.'

'Murrrrr,' snarled Snerk, glaring at them. 'Gurrrrr!'

'I fear that *kill or cure* isn't good enough, Snerk,' snapped Caul.

Snorer heaved a regretful sigh.

'Well, you can say what you like, but Snerk's roasts

are lovely,' he said. 'Red, and bloody . . . you'd think the meat was killed that minute, you would. Yes, there's no one can make more of a brace of moles than Snerk, here. And the gravy . . . ooh, it practically makes you weep. A batch of sweetroot chips smothered in green gravy, with a mug of slug beer to wash it all down, and you have nothing left to ask for, Lord. Nothing!'

Nian sent his mind round the room again, searching, not for vermin, now, but for malice and cunning and poison. His mind went right round the room, even snagging on the tiny brain of the blue beetle readying itself for an attack on a millipede that was curled up under a loaf of hairy bread.

Nothing else. Nothing at all. There was filth and decay aplenty, but it was all *peaceful* filth.

'Be that as it may,' Caul was saying, severely, 'the dinner today was lethal. If the poison hadn't made the food go blue there might have been a death.'

Snerk scowled until his face was as corrugated as a drain toad's.

'Gurrrrr,' he said. 'Gurrrrr! Nurrrrr-nurrrrr. Nurrrrr.'

Nian sent his mind round the room once more to make certain. But it was all clear. And there was no sign at all of quicksilver.

'The poison didn't come from here,' he announced.

Caul turned to him quickly.

'Are you sure?'

Nian nodded. 'There's *nothing* like that at all, anywhere.'

Caul knitted his brows.

'How about something accidental? Something . . . something decaying in a canister, perhaps, or a toad-stool falling into a pan?'

This wasn't as far-fetched as it sounded, for there were indeed a cluster of pale fungoid things like dead fingers growing out of the soft wood of the mantel-piece.

Nian shook his head.

'No,' he said. 'This place is . . . it sounds mad, but it's *wholesome,* somehow.'

'That's right,' agreed Snorer, nodding round with approval. 'All good clean dirt, this is. And Snerk, here: he's the master.'

There were footsteps outside, and the room was dimmed further by another bulky red-clad figure.

'First tourists are here, Master Snerk,' he announced. 'Pot of tea for two and a plate of biscuits.'

'Gurrrrrr,' said Snerk, and reached for his fly swat.

Caul shuddered delicately.

'We'd better leave you to get on, then, Snerk,' he said.

'That's right,' said Snorer. 'No time to hang about, not if you're a member of the Tarhun, nowa-days. What with the Lords, and the Tourists, *and* hav-ing to rebuild half of both the grotting Houses! It's a good thing we've got a master builder like my cousin Ranger to direct us, but it's still wearing us down to the bone, it is.'

Caul and Nian edged their way cautiously past the Tarhun waiter's bulging belly.

44

'Mind the frills on my apron!' he growled. 'They took me half the bogging morning to iron!'

'The poison,' said Nian, suddenly, as they walked back. 'It came from within the Inner House.'

'Up a bit! Up a bit!' Ranger was calling from somewhere round the corner—and then there was a huge shattering crash that made Nian and Caul wince.

Caul walked on a little way before he answered.

'I think so too. But you say you don't know who was behind it?'

Nian thought of saying something about Keer, but there was no reason to connect Keer with this, any more than there was any reason to connect him with the owlman.

'No,' he said, slowly. 'I have tried to find out. But I just don't know.'

'Same here—and I've got quite good at identifying culprits since I've been teaching you lot. Could Derig help? He's got a talent for picking up what other people are feeling.'

Nian tried not to think about just how disturbed and frightened Derig had been.

'Derig can feel things,' he agreed. 'But I don't think he really *knows* anything about this.'

'Hm. And it could have been done by anyone, couldn't it? He wouldn't even have had to have been in the same place as the food. Not if he used his powers.'

'No . . . but he'd have needed the quicksilver. Where

on earth has that come from? And as well as that, this is something . . . something evil, Caul.'

They stood and regarded each other.

'It couldn't possibly have been one of the Lords,' Caul said, but without much confidence.

'Then who was it?' asked Nian. 'Do you really think one of the boys could have done it? *Could* have done it?'

Caul shrugged.

'Their powers are growing all the time, and in all sorts of directions. Anyway, could one of the Lords? We've very little power left since you destroyed the wreaths of Thought, Nian.'

That was true, too. Except . . .

'You have power, Caul,' said Nian. 'Your powers have come back, haven't they? And they're stronger than they ever were before.'

Caul hesitated, and then nodded.

'I think it's because I'm young,' he said. 'I'm not twenty yet, and so my mind was never so set in the ways of the House. I still seem to be growing, too. It's much harder for the others.'

'So it must have been you, then,' said Nian, lightly, and still not mentioning Keer.

Caul gave a reluctant half-grin. 'Or you, Nian.'

Nian considered this.

'That's not the sort of thing I'm good at,' he said. 'I'm good at healing, and growing things, and travelling into other worlds, and seeing deep into things—'

'—and pulling down walls—'

'—but, even if I could have got hold of some

46

quicksilver, if I was going to poison someone I'd make sure the poison wasn't blue and furry.'

'And if it did turn out that way,' said Caul, 'you'd throw it all away and try again.'

Nian frowned at the stones of the path.

'So that means we're looking for someone extremely clever and evil and devious, but at the same time unbelievably stupid.'

'That seems about the long and short of it,' Caul sighed.

'So what do we do?'

Caul shrugged.

'Hope the poisoner doesn't get any cleverer,' he said. 'Search our food before we eat it. That's all there is to do.'

Wait and see. Keep to the well-trodden paths. Live in hope. That was the way the Lords thought, especially now most of their powers had been taken from them. But it got them nowhere, nowhere at all.

Nian was suddenly overtaken by a huge wave of frustration. He was so full of power that sometimes he felt as if he were going to explode. His mind kept returning to the statue in the middle of the garden which was his route to a million other worlds—but using his powers for that or anything else (like finding the poisoner) always seemed to be forbidden, or impossible.

But they needed to do something. Now. First there had been the owlman, and now this poison. There was danger in the House and it had to be searched out and stopped. There was evil and they had to attack it. Hit it hard.

There was a burst of irritable shouting from somewhere along the long curve of the corridor, and a small fireball fizzed towards them and burst against a white wall.

Caul sighed again.

'I think the Lord Rago has been trying to teach the control of clouds again,' he said. 'Honestly, he should know that's just asking for trouble as far as Emmec and Derig are concerned. I think I'd better go and take over before Rago goes up in smoke. Are you coming?'

Lessons were a waste of time for Nian, and they both knew it: he was miles more powerful than Caul, or Tarq, or any of the Lords.

But at least they were company.

Nian went along.

5

'Oh, for truth's sake,' said Caul, a couple of hours later, when Derig, still shaky with nerves from being bawled at by Rago, had lost concentration and managed to conjure up a small but aggressive skunk that made its presence felt quite eye-wateringly before Nian could stop laughing enough to send it home again. 'Go away for half an hour and let off some energy, the lot of you.'

The other boys looked up hopefully from their slates. 'Can we, Lord?' asked Emmec. 'Right out into the garden?'

Caul hesitated, and then sighed.

'Oh, I suppose so. You've been in most of the day, after all. You're certainly doing no good here, you're as fidgety as dizzybugs. Just don't make too much of a racket, all right, and whatever you do be careful not to eat anything.'

The boys slipped out of the schoolroom and along the corridor away from the owlman.

'I thought we were going to have a whole day without being able to play pockle,' said Hani, diving into a cupboard by the garden door. 'But we've got time for fifteen minutes each way, at least. Catch!'

Hani threw Emmec an egg-shaped pine cone. 'I'll take a spare cone with us just in case,' he went on. 'Keer, have a flipper. Hang on, not this one: Emmec's been trying out his home-made flipper oil on that one and it's gone all sticky and rancid.'

'But pliable,' said Emmec, as they went out into the sun.

On the far side of the garden there was a clearing where the grass had been well trampled, and more or less at each end of it there was a tree with what might have been a squirrel's drey hanging from one of the lower branches.

'There's seven of us, now Keer's come,' said Hani. 'What shall we do? Keer, have you played much pockle?'

'Nah. Waste of time,' said Keer. The others rolled their eyes in disbelief.

'But you're from the city,' pointed out Alin, exasperated. 'You must have played pockle! You must have seen it played loads of times in the street, anyway.'

'Suppose so,' admitted Keer, with ill-grace. 'Can't say I see the point of it, though.'

Emmec and Alin looked disgusted, but Hani's face was lit with enthusiasm.

'Hey, let's play Shield Finals,' he said. 'Me and Derig and Emmec'll be United and you lot can be City.'

'Waste of effort,' said Keer.

'It'll be all right,' said Derig, encouragingly. 'You'll soon get the hang of it.'

'Bet we still win, even against four of you,' said Hani, practising strokes with his flipper.

'No chance,' said Alin. 'But I'll tell you what, just so the whole thing isn't totally one-sided, you can have first flip-off. We play Amateur Rules, all right, Keer? Two sides to a game, at least two flips to a catch, no forward throwing, and a touch-down is a free throw. *Come on, United!*'

Pockle was a game of the cities and the plains, but it was good fun. Nian hadn't been playing long enough to be much good, yet, and his reach was small, but it was tremendous to be able to run and jump and use his speed and wits. He couldn't use his mental powers really properly in case he accidentally destroyed a mountain or something, or went and got stuck in the wrong world and put an end to a couple of universes, but at pockle he could use his physical powers to the full.

He was so absorbed in the game he didn't notice the group of Tourists until he went for a flip he couldn't quite reach and sent the pock out of play and into a heap of rubble.

'*Nian*,' groaned Alin, who always really needed to win.

'It's rolled right under that flat stone that looks like one of Grodan's ears,' called Hani, who always knew where things were without even thinking about it.

Nian jogged over to retrieve the pock. It was beginning to ooze resin a bit, but it would last for a few more games as long as no one went and trod on it.

'*Yes, the one with the pock*,' someone was saying as he made his way back. Bulls-Eye, that was, who was perhaps the laziest and most cowardly of all the Tarhun.

51

'Him? He's the Truth Sayer?'

'Saved my life. Rescued me when I got sucked into another world, he did. Saved the whole world.'

'Oh . . . he's not very good at pockle, is he?'

Nian tossed the pock to Emmec and tried not to mind. After all, it wasn't as if he didn't *know* he wasn't very good at pockle. That was one of the reasons he enjoyed it so much. He was the Truth Sayer, and he spent his whole life being careful and thoughtful and cautious. Pockle was the one time when he could forget all that.

The easiest toss in the world came his way, and he fluffed it. He mistimed his stroke, sent the cone up vertically, and actually managed to hit himself on the head with it.

The others fell about laughing.

'Foul!' called Emmec, when he had breath.

Nian laughed, too, but he couldn't help but be aware of the crowd of tourists behind him. He could have found out what they were saying, if he'd wanted to. But he didn't want to.

He carried on playing, but out of the corner of his eye he could see that the crowd had got bigger. Alin and Hani were loving the attention: Hani was ducking and running, and Alin was shouting frenzied instructions.

Then Alin intercepted a pass, flipped it high, and Gow, easily the tallest, sent it over Derig's head and on to Keer.

It was obvious that Keer had never played pockle before in his life. He twitched, swung petulantly at the pock, and it bounced off his fingers and forward.

52

'Foul!' shouted Hani, Emmec, and Derig, all together.

Emmec's free throw went to Derig, who flipped to Hani, who, at home on the pockle ground as he never was in the House, tipped a beautiful shot high and true straight into the drey to make it one–nil.

Hani chucked his flipper into the air, threw himself onto his knees in a triumphant skid, and made noises like a swing-gibbon. The Tourists provided a slight splatter of applause.

Nian checked the suns. His team had got another ten minutes to get the equalizer. The Tourists had settled down to watch the rest of the game, even though they'd be lucky, now, to get back to the inn before dark.

Alin, with a determined set to his face, was flipping off. He was strong, though not especially fast, and he hated losing. Mind you, Nian hated losing, too—but with pockle he'd pretty much got used to it.

The pock went straight to Keer, who swiped out vaguely and sent the pock more or less to Gow, whose long arms allowed him to pass back to Alin. Nian dodged under Emmec's elbow and ran up the ground, but Gow had charged round Hani, as ungainly but unstoppable as a marsh-ox, and was in a perfect position to receive Alin's return pass. He struck it hard and the cone went straight and fast across the ground.

'Catch!' yelled Alin.

All Nian had to do was catch the cone and then toss it back to Gow, who could set Alin up to equalize. Anyone could do it.

The pock came towards Nian, spinning in the air, and tumbling just slightly as the air caught it. Nian concentrated so hard on it that it seemed to slow down, and he had all the time in the world to close his fingers round it, be sure of it, and then toss it back precisely to where Gow was waiting.

Gow had a look of shock on his face, but he reacted instinctively. His long arm reached out and then the cone was flying to Alin, who tipped it skilfully up and into the depths of the drey.

Over by the wall, the Tourists were applauding with enthusiasm, but on the pockle ground everything had changed. Everything had gone cold. Nian looked round, puzzled: it wasn't so surprising that Hani and Derig and Emmec were a bit fed up, but Gow and Alin were as stony-faced as the others.

Of them all, only Keer seemed unmoved.

Alin walked over to Emmec and held out his hand.

'Your game,' he said, shortly, even though he had just scored the equalizer. 'Well played.'

And then he turned on his heel and walked determinedly off the ground and back towards the House.

The Mirelands

Pella's room was full of furry stuffed animals—springers, most of them. She caught the springers easily enough, slicing her powers through the air like the owls that haunted the hills. The springers always died before she could get them back to her, but they were soft to hold until they stiffened; and then her shrine women took out the meat, and stuffed them, and made them new button eyes.

And then, with her powers, Pella would make them come back to life again, a little.

Pella could make almost anything come to life—shadows, springers, knives—although of course it was not really life, because she could only get them to do certain things. Sometimes it was hard to control them at all. The first shadow-man she'd brought alive had strangled Vanna; it would have strangled Pella, too, had she not managed to fry it with her powers.

Behind her, Pella could feel the draught of the rift in her wall. It was tiny, hardly more than a crack, but somehow Pella knew (though she couldn't see it or feel it) that it led to Somewhere Else; that through the tiny rift in the stones of the wall there was somewhere vast and dark, and beyond that . . .

If Branto was coming, then she must be ready to escape, and she would have to make sure she was escaping to somewhere safe.

The rift was much too small for her to get through, but it could be worn wider, she was sure, like water wears away the bank of a stream.

Pella held up her hands, which were ringed on each finger with circlets of quicksilver and diamonds.

Against the wall, the lamp cast a long shadow that seemed to be tipped with a hooked beak.

6

No one spoke to Nian all that evening. Even when they were on their sleeping mats no one said anything, and this was the time, when the rule was for silence, that they were naturally most inclined to talk. But that night, silence fell with the lesser sun.

Nian lay on his mat, looking through the high window at the tiny green glow-worms on the holm-tree, and puzzled over what had gone wrong.

It had been something that had happened during the pockle game. He'd messed up that catch, of course—but then he was always messing up catches. He was fast, and not generally clumsy, but there was something about pockle that confused him. Perhaps it was being part of a team that did it: having so many minds about him all intent on the same thing, but from literally so many different perspectives. Or perhaps he was just naturally bad at it. Just because he was the Truth Sayer, it didn't mean that he was going to be good at everything. No one expected him to be able to play the pipes, or juggle, for instance.

But in any case it hadn't been the missed cone that had changed everything, but the caught one. Nian remembered the way the cone had spun so sweetly into his hand, and then the way his fingers had curled round it and swung it away again to Gow.

Those passes had led to the pock. The equalizer.

So why had Alin, who'd scored it, been the angriest of them all?

It took Nian a long time to get to sleep. And when he did, as so often since he'd come back to the House of Truth, he dreamed of walking up to the statue in the centre of the garden and making a passageway, as only he, the Truth Sayer, could, into a forbidden world.

If Derig also had dreams that night, Nian did not hear them.

Nian had forgotten about the pockle game by morning—but the others hadn't. They avoided his eyes. Even Derig wouldn't look at him, and Derig was the softest-hearted person you could meet. Why, Derig even shook out his clothes before he put them on in case an earwig had gone to sleep in them and, outside lesson-time, only used his powers for things like protecting birds' nests and being nice to people.

The House of Truth was always filled with silence. The House was so vast, and the silence had been there so long, that you could never overcome it, quite. It made a sort of weight that you had to push your voice through, so that often you ended up sort of sliding your words underneath it in a whisper.

But that morning there weren't even any whispers.

The Lord Rago ate his breakfast with the boys to make sure nothing was poisoned, but the silence amongst them was so complete that he astonished himself by being unable to find any fault with any of them.

The Lord Tarq supervised their morning's lessons in History and Scrollcraft and Lore. Tarq didn't teach Thought any more, for his powers were small, now, though he took a careful interest in the boys' progress. Tarq's lessons weren't exactly thrilling, because there was next to no chance of anyone calling up a shower of stink newts or a sword-swallower, but the boys found that the hours they spent with Tarq went reasonably quickly. And afterwards, they sometimes even found themselves arguing about what he had said.

But that morning the old man's voice failed to charm them. They sat, and they listened, but the room was cluttered with ugly blocks of resentment.

Tarq must have noticed it, but he didn't say anything until the lesson was ended, and then, when he said *Farewell, my friends,* he only stressed the word *friends* a little more than usual.

'What shall we do?' asked Hani, when Tarq had gone, but he spoke without any of his usual half-witted enthusiasm. They all looked at Alin, who usually decided, but he had sat himself back down on the floor and was glowering at the heap of slates.

Derig opened his mouth, but then only kicked gently and sadly at one of the scroll stands.

'We ought to do *something*,' said Emmec, half-angrily. He hated wasting time when he could be doing things or making things. 'We've got lessons again in half an hour.'

'We could . . . ' began Gow. But then his voice trailed away hopelessly.

Nian looked round at them. Keer was scornful and suspicious, but the rest were just miserable. Really, deeply, miserable, as if everything that made their lives worth living had been spoiled. And he didn't understand it.

Not understanding had been happening to Nian too much lately. It made him agitated, confused, angry, resentful.

'What's *wrong*?' he demanded, hugely frustrated.

The others shifted moodily, but no one answered.

'What is it?' Nian went on. 'I haven't done anything!'

But still no one would look at him.

'But I *haven't*!' said Nian, though the whining edge to his voice appalled him.

Alin looked up at him, then.

'You cheated,' he said, in a flat, steady voice.

'No I didn't,' said Nian, very quickly. 'I wouldn't. When?'

The others were scared, now, and a little excited.

'You *know* I wouldn't!' Nian went on, more excited than any of them.

Gow hunched his bony shoulders.

'We saw you, Nian.' He was almost apologetic. 'We all did.'

They were all embarrassed and uneasy, but only Alin would meet Nian's eye.

'When?' Nian demanded; then suddenly, with a sickening draught of pure horror, he knew when.

'When we were playing pockle,' said Alin. 'You used your powers to take that catch.'

'*No I didn't!*' said Nian, too loudly, because just somewhere, vaguely, he was remembering how the whole world had slowed down as the cone had tumbled through the air towards him, so he had all the time in the world . . .

'*I didn't!*' Nian repeated, more loudly still, to scare away the horrible knowledge that it was true.

Derig was looking troubled.

'I'm sure you didn't mean to,' he piped up, anxiously. 'I mean, you're the Truth Sayer, aren't you, so you're different from us, so—'

'No I'm *not!*'

Nian found he'd almost shouted it. And he would prove it to them, too. He would prove that he was one of them, that being the Truth Sayer made no difference at all. What could he do?

Anything: almost anything. Call up a whirlwind to blow them right round the corridor, a blizzard to freeze them, even a swarm of bees (there was one in that stoneberry tree on the other side of the garden, he could sense the vibrating of each of the fifteen thousand bees) to throw them into panic, to chase and sting . . .

But there were so many things in his head, now: fear and anger and panic and shame and the constant, constant, constant, constant lure of the statue in the garden that would lead to a new world where everything was unspoiled, that he couldn't think at all.

'I didn't,' he said.

Alin got up.

'We all saw, Nian,' he said.

And so it must be true. Their powers were puny, compared with his, but they would not be mistaken about that.

Nian tried to find a way out of the disgrace, of the cheating and the lying, but there was no way out at all. So he hit Alin.

It was the only thing he could think of to do.

Nian had seen dogs fight—circling and snarling, and nipping in to snap—and at fairs he'd seen men wrestle with dignity and wit and grace. But this . . . well, if anything, it was like trying to fight a marsh-ox: stupidly, humiliatingly futile. Afterwards, Nian could remember struggling as hard as he could, but at the same time he'd never really worked out quite what he was trying to do.

The first thing he was sure of was when someone pulled him to his feet (so they must have been rolling about on the floor) and it was then, when there was suddenly silence around him, that he realized they must have been making quite a lot of noise.

He shook himself, to settle all the various bits of himself back into their right places. Nothing fell off. Alin was over there, red in the face, chest heaving, wiping away a trail of blood from a cut eyebrow onto his sleeve. And now Nian came to think about it, there was something making its way ticklishly down his upper lip from his nose.

It was odd, but Nian couldn't actually remember what they'd been fighting about.

Someone cuffed him just sharply enough to get his attention.

'The rest of you pick up all this mess these two idiots have made,' said the Lord Grodan (where had he come from?) casting a dry and withering eye over the room. 'And you two had better go and explain yourselves to the Lord Tarq.'

Tarq was the mildest and gentlest of men, but in his way he was powerful. He listened patiently until he understood what had happened, and then, when he'd made sure Alin wasn't much hurt, he sent him back to class.

There was, of course, little that Tarq could do to Nian. He was a frail old man who had lost most of his powers, and Nian was the Truth Sayer, who could destroy the whole world if he wanted to. They both understood this quite clearly.

'I shall try to find ways of helping you, my friend,' said Tarq, when they were alone. 'Do the other boys make your life here difficult?'

Nian shook his head.

'It was all a mistake,' he said. 'None of us understood.'

'I see. Do you need my help with explaining?'

'I don't know,' said Nian, who hadn't even thought about explaining until then.

'Well, come back to me if you do,' said Tarq. 'Oh, and Nian!' Nian looked back from the doorway.

'Being powerful is a burden,' he said. 'You understand that very well, of course. But we must remember, my friend, that to be powerless can be more of a burden still.'

'Good fight,' said Derig, shyly, when lessons were ended for the day and habit was taking them along the corridor away from the owlman and out into the garden.

'Yeah,' agreed Emmec, with a sigh of satisfaction. 'We've not had a proper fight since I came to the House.'

'What did Tarq do to you?' asked Hani, with ghoulish interest.

For a moment Nian was tempted to say, grandly, *nothing*.

'He said I had to explain what happened,' he told them. 'You know, about the game.'

Everyone carried on walking.

'Caul's already said some stuff,' ventured Gow. 'About your powers being really deep inside you, like your hearing or something.'

'Yeah,' blurted out Alin, awkwardly. 'And how they're changing all the time. Mind you, it's like that for us, too. I'm never quite sure what mine are going to do next, despite all this Thought and stuff.'

'I don't even know I'm using mine, sometimes,' explained Nian. 'They sort of creep up like a cloud-lynx.'

'Only not so spotty,' suggested Hani.

'And slightly less likely to eat people,' pointed out Emmec.

Everyone grinned, except Keer, who was walking a little way away, as usual, and casting suspicious glances all round.

'We'll have to have special rules,' suggested Alin. 'Anyone using their powers gives a flipped penalty to the other side.'

They considered this, and nodded, and everything was all right again.

They stole a few stones from the building site to make an enemy fort, and practised exploding it using their powers until it was time to go in.

Nian remembered something as he was going to sleep that night.

I don't know I'm using them, he'd said.

But if that was true, then what else might he have done, and not realized?

Only things he wanted to do, surely, like being good at pockle. He didn't want to poison the Lords, or scrawl evil monsters all over the walls.

But then, who did?

Who did, who had the power to do it?

He rolled himself tightly in his cover. The night seemed cold.

'*More*,' groaned Derig, in the night. '*Not more, not more!*'

He stopped as soon as Nian touched him, and seemed to pass into more tranquil sleep.

More?

Nian tried not to think about it.

The next morning, after another dismal Rago-supervised breakfast, Gow was the first into the school-room. Gow was the cleverest of the boys, and found his studies hugely exciting, though of course he'd never have dreamed of saying so.

He found the room wrecked.

The boys, jostling in the doorway, viewed the mess with mind-boggled dismay.

'But who could have done it?' asked Derig, at last, deeply shocked.

'Bogging pits,' said Hani, a bit scared; and when they looked at each other they found that they were all a bit scared, except Keer, who seemed to be regarding the destruction with detached and cynical pleasure.

Nian searched for the culprit using his powers, but all he found, yet again, was darkness.

'But how *could* this have been done?' asked Emmec, the practical one. 'Even if one of us had *wanted* to do it, how could it have been done?'

Alin stepped carefully into the room. He picked up something that looked like a skewer.

'Look at this,' he said. 'It's a bit of one of the scroll stands.'

'Bogging struth,' breathed Hani, awe-struck. 'But that was solid wood!'

'Bronzewood,' agreed Alin, grimly. 'Hundreds of years old, and hard as iron. Really valuable.'

The others stepped into the room too, as cautiously and delicately as herons.

'It's all been smashed to matchwood,' said Gow, appalled.

'No,' said Nian, his voice grating. 'Not smashed. Look at the edges: it's all been cut.'

Derig looked, wide-eyed and shaken.

'You mean someone's done it with an axe?'

'Nah,' said Keer, from near the doorway. 'We would have heard an axe. I reckon one of those old Lords must really have gone round the twist.'

Emmec squatted down and poked at the matchstick-sized splinters that were heaped about on the floor.

'This hasn't been done by someone mad,' he said. 'This has been done with skill. And surely none of the Lords . . .'

But Gow shook his head.

'Anyone might have done it if he'd found the right way of using his powers,' he pointed out.

'But not this,' said Alin, suddenly angry. 'Look at it! If one of us had wanted to wreck the schoolroom we'd have jumped on the scroll stands, or smashed the inkwells or something. At least, that's what I would have done. I've wanted to, sometimes. But look!' He picked up a thing like a small tile, but with a square hole in the middle.

'What the pits is that?' asked Hani, mystified.

'It's a horizontal slice of an inkwell. See? But who, for truth's sake, would think of cutting it up like this?

67

And how the grotting pits would you do it, if you did?'

Nian took it. The cut surface was as smooth as butter, but the edges were razor-sharp. He ran his mind through it. Yes, here was a trail of . . . of something sliver-thin and cold, and dark. His mind slipped along it, but slammed into a wall almost straight away. He winced, and dragged himself away up the almost impossible slope back into the schoolroom.

'I couldn't have done this,' he said, trying not to sound shaken.

But that was not quite the truth. He might have done it, if he'd taken enough thought and care about it; if he'd set out to destroy everything, the whole contents of the room, in the most complete and efficient manner.

And now he understood what Emmec had been saying. This had been done carefully. Not in temper, nor even in anger. This had been done by a hatred cold and clear enough to slice everything in the room—*everything*—into neat strips no more than a quarter of a finger wide.

'It looks as if it's been done with a knife,' said Hani, as he stirred the wreckage with his toe. 'But what sort of knife could cut through all this?'

'That's not the important thing,' Alin pointed out. 'It's the mind that did it that worries me.'

Derig shivered, and took a sideways step towards Nian. 'But who would *want* to do this?' he asked.

Keer watched them from the doorway.

'A maniac,' he said, with contempt. 'Someone totally

mad. Mind you, you're all bonkers, you are. Crazy as spring hoppits, the lot of you. Bogging pits, I'd be better off starving in the city, I would.'

'Not a maniac,' said Nian, to no one in particular, trying to hold on to what he had felt in that freezing black wall. 'Not a madman. This was done by someone evil.'

And, suddenly angry, he threw down the slice of inkwell that he still held in his hand.

It landed edge on, and drove itself deep into the stone flags of the floor beside the small splattering of brown dots that were made of Alin's blood.

The Mirelands

Pella made sure her door was closed tight.

No one must know what she was doing. If anyone knew she was going to escape then they would try anything to keep her powers in the world. They might tell Branto, so he attacked at once, before she was ready to leave. Then she'd be forced to fight him even though he had a whole army with him. Or Dorcis would say, yet again, *Give me your powers and then Branto won't want you.*

But Pella knew what happened to people who had no powers. She had seen it for herself. Men like Branto came. And then, like Grandfather and Trun, you were dead. No wonder Dorcis wanted Pella's power so much.

But Dorcis would never have it. Never.

Pella held up her bejewelled arms to cast another shadow, and let the memory of Grandfather's death solidify with the shape. Once the shadow had hollowed itself out she sent the owlman marching away on long scissor legs after the others: hunter, sharp-beaked, formed for battle against whatever alien creatures might live on the other side of the rift. And as each owlman passed through, the rift yawned wider.

She couldn't follow them yet. The owlmen were vicious, knife-sharp. She'd made them so they would hide on the walls until the moment, two days away, when she would have sent enough of them to be sure their attack would make the new world completely safe for her.

Enough to wipe clear a city.

She had to wait until they had killed everything, and after that she had to wait until time had dissolved them, for they would attack anyone they saw.

She had to stay here until the other place was safe.

Pella conjured up shadow after sharp shadow on her bedroom wall.

7

Caul went quite white and still when he saw the damage to the schoolroom. Nian had expected him to rage, but he only ordered them back to their sleeping room, and strode away.

'And guess who's going to get blamed again,' said Emmec, bitterly, as they trudged back along the corridor.

'The same people as got blamed for the owlman,' growled Alin.

The owlman was as black as ever, despite all the Lords' attempts to get rid of it.

'So what will they do to us this time?' asked Keer, his voice sneering and his eyes never still.

But none of them knew. Tarq was pupil-master, but he never really punished anyone. Caul did snap and rant a bit, but never in a very concentrated sort of way.

'Tarq will be upset,' said Derig, very sad, for the old man had always made the boys' progress and welfare his priority.

They sat themselves down on their rolled-up sleeping mats and waited, listening.

* * *

Tarq came at last. He was an old man, and in his bewilderment and hurt he seemed as frail as thistle seed. He did not seem to want to look at any of them. Instead he stood, with one hand on the door frame as if for support, and he spoke.

'You have all seen the damage to the schoolroom,' he began, not angry at all, but grief-stricken. 'And there can no longer be any doubt that there is a great evil come amongst us.'

He paused here, as if finding the breath for speech was difficult.

'My first concern, of course, is for your safety,' he went on. 'So, from now on, the rule of the House is that none of you must ever be alone.'

'Are you all right?' Nian asked Derig, quietly, when Tarq had gone away. Derig absorbed people's feelings like marish-weed, and Nian wasn't surprised to see Derig pink and floundering.

Derig did his best to smile.

'It's just the shock,' he explained. 'I'm not very good when people are surprised by stuff.'

Nian looked around and wondered how many surprises there were to come.

'We'll be all right,' he said.

'I know,' Derig assured him, bravely. 'Everything's fine as long as we're all together.'

The day, having started badly, proceeded to get worse. The schoolroom was unusable, so the boys were issued with a scrubbing brush and bucket each, and given the task of scrubbing the corridor floor. '*Repetitive tasks are useful for refining and focusing your powers,*' the Lord Grodan told them, drily.

'It's not *fair*,' whispered Hani; but one of the Lords was supervising them at all times, and the Lord Rago, for one, was plainly *itching* to kick somebody, so there was nothing to do but to get on with it. After the first ten minutes or so their knees grew numb from the coldness of the stone floor, and soon after that their minds grew numb with boredom.

They were given a break every half hour, and Caul even allowed them to sit together and have a moan.

'My fingers have gone all wrinkly,' said Derig, sadly, as they sat leaning against the small wooden boxes that contained everything they'd brought with them from the outside world.

Alin cast a resentful glance in the direction of the Lords' Council Chamber, where an agitated meeting seemed to be taking place.

'I don't see why this lot keep going around calling themselves Lords and bossing us about,' he said. 'They aren't Lords of anything. They can't even protect the House, can they? All this stuff going on, and they haven't a clue. I mean, none of them is a tenth as powerful as you, Nian. I'm not even sure if some of them are as powerful as *me*.'

Nian tried to explain.

'They might not be, at the moment,' he agreed. 'Nearly all their powers were destroyed—'

'By you,' put in Hani, with satisfaction.

'—well, yes,' admitted Nian. 'And because they've spent most of their lives sort of travelling in the wrong direction, most of them are still struggling to get back to where they started.'

Gow rubbed hard at his beaky nose.

'And after all, even Nian doesn't understand what's going on,' he said.

Derig shuddered.

'I don't think I want to understand,' he said. 'Especially not about that owlman. It's really scary.'

The others hesitated.

'I know what Derig means,' admitted Gow. 'I know it's stupid, but I don't go near it if I can help it. Especially at night.'

'Ranger tried painting over it yesterday,' said Emmec. 'It was quite funny, really, because it was as if . . . as if the lines were made of space, somehow: the paint just vanished into it.' He shook his head in bafflement. 'I've been thinking and thinking about it, but I just can't even work out what it is, let alone how it's been done.'

'Hey, Nian, you couldn't tear it down like you brought down the Council Chamber roof, could you?' asked Hani, hopefully.

Nian shook his head.

'No,' he said. 'I can't. Because . . . because it's sort of *not there*. I mean, it is there, but it's not that sort of thing.'

'But look,' said Alin, urgently, 'we can't expect the Lords to sort it out. All they do is Think, and Thinking isn't going to work.'

'Why not?' asked Gow, with a frown.

'Because if it *was,* then Nian would have had the

whole thing worked out in less time than it takes the Lords to sneeze,' said Alin. 'We've got to go at it a different way.'

They all looked at one another. 'What way?' asked Emmec.

Alin took a deep breath.

'We start from the fact that all this has only started since Keer arrived in the House,' he said.

Keer bared his teeth like a cornered dog.

'Bogger!' he hissed. 'That's right, pin it on me, won't you?'

'Why not? You've already proved you're a liar and a thief.'

The others shifted in their places.

'But . . . he only took some cake, Alin,' pointed out Derig, uneasily.

'Thieving's thieving.'

That didn't convince any of them. Alin's family was rich, but the others knew the threat of hunger was a powerful one.

'You can't really think Keer could have done any of this stuff,' pointed out Gow.

Alin snorted derisively.

'Of course not. But he might have an accomplice.'

Keer jabbed his fingers spitefully towards their eyes.

'Listen to *him*, won't you,' he spat, in disgust. 'Listen to the lawyer's son.'

'No,' said Derig, distressed. 'It's not like that at all.'

'Keer—' began Nian, but words were spurting from Keer in a squally stream.

'I mean, the trouble's not caused by the *powerful*

76

one, is it? The cheat, the destroyer. It's all *never mind, never mind, poor little Nian,* isn't it.'

Nian glanced round at the others, but their faces were shadowed with suspicion, and none of them would meet his eye.

Quick footsteps approached round the curve of the corridor.

'All right,' said Caul. 'You boys have obviously got your energy back. You'd better get to work again.'

By supper-time every part of their bodies ached. They had tried kneeling, crouching, sitting, even lying on the stone floor as they worked their way along the endless corridor, but every joint was protesting bitterly at its ill-use.

Their minds were as miserable as their bodies. The boys had always squabbled and scrapped and insulted each other, but never beyond the point where a quarrel cleared the air. Life in the House was tough: it demanded strength of body and mind. They'd always relied on each other, and made allowances for bouts of boredom, strain, stupidity, and homesickness.

But now, the easy comradeship was broken.

A preoccupied and frail Tarq supervised their time in the pool and preparations for sleep, and then Caul came and installed an invisible dome of safety around them to protect them from poisoners and maniacs with knives.

'Don't try to leave the dome,' he warned them. 'You're safest here with the others even if the dome doesn't work.'

'Even if it doesn't work?' echoed Derig, quaveringly.

Caul shrugged, and sighed.

'It's hard to know how effective it'll be. After all, we don't really know what we're trying to keep out. If you really *have* to leave the room, then you'd better wake the Truth Sayer, but, from the look of you, you'll sleep like logs all night.'

'I don't want to be stuck in here with this lot with their accusations,' snarled Keer, from his mat. 'Bogging snobs!'

If anything, Caul looked even more tired than the rest of them. He ignored the hiss from Alin, and the glares of the rest.

'Derig, look after Keer, will you?' he said. 'Now get to sleep. Goodnight.'

There was silence until Caul's footsteps had died away. 'You grotting little . . .' began Alin, dangerously.

'Oh, don't, Alin,' pleaded Derig. 'Not now.'

'No, don't,' said Emmec, yawning. 'I need to sleep. I can hardly hold my bogging eyes open.'

'Just no one snore,' said Gow, settling his long body down on his mat. 'Please, no one snore.'

'Housework, eh?' murmured Hani, pulling up his cover. 'Struth, women must be bogging tough.'

And, despite everything, Nian felt them all smile.

Nian slept unstirringly until he was awakened by someone screaming. He knew at once that something terrible was happening, but for a while he was still so enmeshed in sleep that he wasn't sure if it was real or not.

'Struth!' said someone, beside him.

'What the bogging pits . . . ' said someone else.

A bit of extra black darkness moved and twitched and turned into Alin's silhouette.

'Quick,' he said. 'Someone's—'

There was a hollow *boinngg* as Alin's head hit the dome of safety that Caul had rigged up round them, and he fell back, clutching his head.

'Bog!' he said, between rage and confusion.

Nian would have laughed, except that something so awful was happening that claws of fear were squeezing their way through his belly.

He sat up, and turned on his powers, and at once the darkness withdrew. He found himself surrounded by half a dozen faces with blinking, startled expressions.

'What the pits is going on?' asked Hani, his voice still slurred with sleep.

Derig's eyes were pools of black horror in his white face. '*Knives,*' he whispered. '*Knives, all round—*'

There was another scream, and Alin slammed his fist on the dome that surrounded them.

'Nian, I can't get out,' he yelled, in frustration. Nian pushed himself to his knees. He still wasn't completely awake, but the dome was nothing—a tissue of power. He swiped it away with a flick of a finger.

The darkness stooped closer for a second as he diverted his powers, but then sprang back into moon-pale speckles.

'Come on!' said Alin, as he dived for the door; and Nian, still partly asleep, plunged after him.

That way: there was something red and jagged and clashing where usually there was only paleness and tranquillity. Alin set off at a run through the shadows that could still be sensed even though their powers turned the whole world into a shifting of pale shapes, and Nian followed him.

An image slashed through Nian's mind: a dark striding shape that somehow wasn't quite a man, and a crimson glow like fire.

Except that fire was never crimson. So it must be something else. Something terribly important.

Nian ran on.

Another image tore through his mind: scissors, nearly as high as the ceiling, and striding, striding. There was a fleeting second when the scissors swung round on one pointed toe and took a swift stiff step towards him—and the blast of cold they brought with it nearly knocked Nian sideways into the wall.

Alin's bare feet were thudding away along the stone flags they had scrubbed the day before. Nian recovered his balance and pelted along in his wake.

But now Alin was slowing, stopping, panting. 'Lost it,' he gasped. 'Which way, Nian?'

For everything had changed. The slashes of crimson, darkness, arches, swiftness, had all gone, vanished. Nian leant one hand on the wall to support himself and let his mind search.

There. It was there, there, though he could hardly bear to look—a mound of softness, pain, crimson wounded, still-alive but not wishing for anything but that the agony . . .

Nian drew a gasping breath, for the crimson was of course of course of course the crimson of blood.

'Where?' demanded Alin. 'Where, Nian?'

Nian forced his feet into the last direction they wanted to go.

Grodan was on the floor just outside the door to his cell. He was curled, limp, though he kept twitching and making horrible sounds like an animal. The splattered trail of blood led back to his mat: he had been attacked in his sleep, then.

Alin was on his knees beside Grodan, swearing and swearing.

There was so much blood. Nian held his breath against the stench of it.

'Nian,' said Alin.

Nian heard the word, but he was too busy trying to believe that Grodan's body wasn't there to take any notice of it.

'Nian!' said Alin, more sharply. 'Nian, he isn't dead! Nian, do something!'

No, Nian wanted to say. *I don't want to look at him in case I have nightmares for ever and ever. I'm only young, and I'm afraid. It isn't fair!*

He lifted his foot to take a step away . . . but somehow he ended up closer.

There was too much blood to see how Grodan was hurt, but that place, there, where a great clot of blood was all matted into the hairs of Grodan's arm, trailed into a long thin line, as if Grodan had been slashed with a blade.

'I can't see,' Nian muttered.

Alin got to his feet at once. There were other sounds in the House, now. People were coming, coming to help, though none of them would be able to do very much. No one except Nian, who wished with his whole heart that he had never come to this awful place.

'I'll get water,' said Alin, and ran off.

There were people coming. They would be shocked and frightened and they would need Nian's help.

Nian's knees gave way.

While he was there, kneeling, he began to heal the long thin cut on Grodan's arm.

That night there was something close to chaos in the House of Truth. It was so bad that for a while there wasn't even space for Nian to tend to Grodan.

Incredibly, it was the Lord Rago who did most to help. He used what strength remained in his skinny old body to cuff away anyone who was crying, or asking questions, or, indeed, just making the place look untidy. He sent them off to brew sweet herb tea and be quiet.

Then Rago stood a little way away, a gnarled shape by the wall, and guarded Nian's back. It was the very darkest part of the night, and the House was full of chilly draughts, even on that last day of summer.

Nian was doing things he'd never done before. The Lord Grodan's body was covered with knife-slashes, and some of them were deep, had cut through flesh and muscle and even bone. Nian honestly didn't dare think about how much pain Grodan was in.

Nian started from the trailing end of one slash and

worked carefully, a finger's width at a time. That wasn't the best way to work, because there might be—certainly were—more dangerous injuries, but at least it was a start.

It didn't help that Nian was tired, but something else was making it hard, too. It took a while for Nian to understand what it was. Grodan was resisting him. This confused Nian until he finally realized that Grodan was wishing to die.

'What's the matter?' demanded Rago, testily, behind him.

It was hard to put the thought into words, but Rago had snapped the idea up before Nian had more than drawn breath.

'Fool!' he spat. 'Coward! Does he call himself a Lord of Truth? Continue!'

Nian felt a spurt of anger.

'He's making it difficult,' he said.

'Rubbish! He has hardly had the powers of a newborn mouselet since you came along.'

Nian felt an urge to call up a whirlwind to blow Rago right out of the House and off a precipice, but he hadn't the power to spare. He carried on, using the energy his anger gave him; perhaps Grodan was angry too, for he was no longer concentrating nearly so carefully on foiling what Nian was trying to do.

At some point Nian realized that someone had cleaned away the blood from Grodan's wounds; later still, he realized that it had been done by Alin and Caul between them.

There were two empty beakers beside him, and he

could taste herb tea in his mouth. He rather thought that it had been Derig that had brought them, and that Emmec had come with him, for courage and company.

Nian had come to the worst wound, now, that sliced deep into Grodan's scrawny belly. Nian carried on, little by little, matching flesh to flesh and muscle to muscle, every tiny part.

Grodan was no longer fighting him, for he had slid down the long slope into unconsciousness, but now Nian was almost spent. He set his mind to do the next small task—but the elastic ends of the blood vessel he was trying to join sprang back, out of the control of his will, and began to send out little pulsing jets of scarlet blood again.

Nian sat and watched the blood obscuring what he had done, and had not the will left to do anything about it.

'Humph!' Rago was still watching him. 'Well, if that is the best you can do, then that must do, I suppose.'

Nian leant back against the cold wall.

Rago was poking out his scrawny neck over Grodan's body.

'He seems to be steady,' he admitted. 'And I daresay the new blood will soon clot. He'll probably do for now, Truth Sayer.'

'Yes,' whispered Nian, letting his head slide down the wall.

Rago sniffed.

'No stamina,' he rasped. 'In my day boys came here to learn, and learn they did, and every hour of their waking lives, too. There was none of this dancing around after pine cones, or sniggering in corners.'

Nian closed his eyes. The floor was cold and extremely hard, and there was a spreading stain across it that smelt of quicksilver, but finding somewhere more comfortable to sleep was out of the question.

'Take the Lord Grodan, here,' Rago was saying, irritably. 'When he came to the House, nigh on forty years ago it would be—yes, for I was just around my half-century—his promise was evident straight away. I taught him. I thought that perhaps he would have a talent for controlling the skies, as I did, but no, he soon fell into the way of healing. Yes, that was the way his mind tended. And it was hard to regret, for later he was able to cure me of the stone.'

Rago's harsh voice seemed almost to soften, to sound almost polite, towards the end of that speech; that was what convinced Nian that he must be asleep.

He slept.

The Mirelands

'Branto's men are setting up camp,' reported Dorcis, at the window.

'I know,' said Pella, sprawled on the bedcover (which was pink, now, and no longer the scarlet of flames). Dorcis turned a pale face on her.

'He will soon be in a position to attack.'

A fleeting expression of doubt might have passed over Pella's round face, but the dead springer in her arms turned its glassy eyes on Dorcis and snarled.

'He's an idiot,' Pella snapped. 'How dare he threaten me?'

Dorcis shrugged, and turned back to the window. 'Probably because he has an army at his back, magistra.'

'Branto shall never even lay eyes on me. Not if he sits there for a hundred years.'

Dorcis pulled aside a pink swag of the curtain to peer out.

'His men are erecting a catapult,' she observed. 'I do not see how we are going to avoid people getting hurt.'

'So? I am magistra,' said Pella, dismissively. 'I shall heal them.'

Dorcis turned right round, then, and stood, a long column of darkness against the window behind her.

'Your powers are not enough to deal with this,' she said.

Pella clutched the springer even more tightly to her pink bodice. The draught from the rift between the worlds was running icy fingers round her neck. It was much wider, now, but still not nearly wide enough.

'You don't know much about my powers,' she said, as scornfully as she could.

Dorcis's mouth contracted with anger.

'I know everything about your powers!' she almost snarled.

Pella buried her face in the cold fur of the springer, and made no reply.

8

The Lord Grodan was the very worst patient the world had to offer.

Possibly, the very worst patient *any* of the worlds had to offer.

He was: ungrateful, impatient, restless, sarcastic, big-headed, untrusting.

There were other words that came to Nian's mind, but those were mostly designed to relieve his feelings. He did his best to be calm. By noon Grodan was well enough to tell him to go away.

'Truth Sayer!' he said, when Nian was at the door. Nian turned back, half expecting some words of gratitude, some recognition that Nian had worked half the night to save his life.

'There will be no need for you to return,' Grodan announced.

'But you aren't completely healed yet, Lord,' said Nian, very nicely and respectfully, considering.

Grodan's eyes grew cold.

'I shall have much more confidence in my healing if my treatment is put on a sound footing,' he said. 'So I shall take over my own cure. Now go.'

Nian came within a whisker of using a word Grodan had not heard for forty years, but he bit it back and went away.

And found that, after all, he had been perhaps the most tranquil person in the House.

'How is he?' asked Derig, anxiously, as soon as Nian found the others, who were occupied sweeping up the mounds of wreckage in the schoolroom.

Nian shrugged.

'Even more bitter and twisted than usual.'

'Oh.' Emmec blinked at him. 'Well, I suppose that might be a good sign.'

'Probably,' growled Nian. 'If you want him to live it is, anyway.'

He cast himself down in a swept corner and wondered why on earth he didn't feel happier. No one else could have saved Grodan. But Nian was waiting for the next thing to happen; as if there always would be a next thing, always, and that there would always be only him to do it.

Into his mind came once again the image of the statue in the garden that marked the passageway to other worlds; but he pushed the possibility miserably away. Even if he went, he wouldn't be able to stay for long, and he was needed here.

Alin swept a pile of chinking rubbish towards the middle of the floor.

'You look as if you need a proper rest,' he said. 'Why don't you go and find your mat.'

'I'll come and sit with you,' offered Gow. 'I don't mind, I can get some Thinking done.'

'Sit with me?' echoed Nian, faintly irritated because it was less trouble than being bewildered. 'What for? Are you planning to sing me a lullaby, or what?'

Gow flushed until his freckles hardly showed.

'It's orders,' explained Hani. 'Tarq's stepped up the order about us not being alone. We even have to go to the latrines together.'

'Like girls!' said Emmec, ruefully.

Nian ran his hands over his face. He'd been with Grodan ever since the attack, and of course the reason Tarq hadn't been with Nian and Grodan was because he'd been with the other boys. He'd have been trying to make sure they were safe.

Nian looked round him properly for the first time. The room was nearly bare, now, but for the glinting pile of wreckage in the middle of the floor. Strips of hartskin blotched with old writing, skewers of bronze-wood, slivers of inkwell . . .

'Grodan was attacked by the same person who did this,' he said, almost to himself, remembering the parallel slashes in Grodan's dry skin.

Derig shivered.

'I want to go home,' he said. 'I'm sorry. I've been trying to be brave, but I really do.'

'So do bogging I,' said Hani, with feeling.

'Perhaps Tarq will send us away,' suggested Emmec. 'We could just go down as far as the inn until this is all sorted out . . .'

But Gow was shaking his bony head.

'We're needed here,' he said. 'The Lords have lost most of their powers; even without Nian, we must be nearly as strong as they are, mustn't we?'

'*Grot!*' said Alin, forcefully. 'But I only came to learn stuff! I didn't expect to have to save the bogging world!'

'Not the world,' said Nian, with a sudden sense that someone had shot an arrow through the darkness that had been befogging his brain. 'It can't be anything to do with an attack on the world. Whatever it is, it's been here too long for that. If it had come in from another world then the link it had made would be causing earthquakes by now.'

'Then . . . someone from here,' said Derig, his eyes wide with concern and apprehension. 'One of the Lords, or one of us.'

Suddenly, it was as though they were thinking straight for the first time for ages.

'No,' said Gow. 'Not necessarily. Just someone with powers.'

'But—'

'—just think, six months ago we didn't live here in the House, did we, but we still had our powers. There might be hundreds of people out there with powers they've never told anyone about. There probably are.'

Emmec nodded.

'I always thought my gramp had powers,' he admitted. 'Whenever we had a picnic we could be sure it'd always be fantastic weather.'

Hani let out a long low whistle.

'So . . . anyone, then,' he said. 'One of the Tarhun, one of the tourists . . .'

'They'd have had to get into the House,' said Derig.

'Not that difficult,' said Alin, flatly. 'Not with about a third of the walls gone.'

Gow's head was nodding slightly on his long neck, the way it did when he was thinking really hard.

'But even if someone came in from outside,' he said, 'and even if they had that sort of focused power—'

'—they'd have to be grotting bonkers and want to destroy everything in the House,' finished up Hani.

'That's a point,' said Emmec, 'why on earth would anyone want to do that? Who could be more harmless than the Lords? And what could they get out of it?'

'They killed my uncle,' said Nian, tossing one more fact into the room. And suddenly it was as if they were playing pockle, but passing ideas instead of the cone.

'Anyone might have had a relation killed by a diverted storm,' said Alin.

'—or had a friend taken away by the Tarhun—'

'—it might be someone like Grodan's father! He wouldn't have been able to get into the House until now.'

'—not *Grodan*'s father, idiot!'

'—it might be, if he didn't recognize him. Grodan would have been only about our age when he came here: he must be much, much uglier now than then.'

'Must be, might be, but probably isn't.'

'—but that still doesn't account for it,' said Gow, doggedly refusing to be diverted. 'Whoever came into the House and did all these things would leave some sort of a trail, and we'd pick it up. At least, I'm almost sure I would, and I'm *certain* Nian would be able to.'

It was as if Gow had tossed the pock high into the air; Nian watched it come, and as it came it tumbled slightly, showing off first one side and then the other.

'Can you really pick up nothing at all, Nian?' asked Alin, but not quite accusingly.

But Nian was seeing things. The culprit was someone with great powers, who had access to the House, and wanted to destroy it.

Oh, but *perhaps Keer was right*. It was someone with powers, someone whose whole life had been stolen by the House. Someone whose powers obeyed such deep parts of himself that he wasn't even always aware they were there. Someone with anger.

The others were all looking at him, breathless, anxious, appalled.

'Only blackness,' Nian whispered, though he was too afraid to look properly. 'All I can see is blackness.'

9

It was ridiculous that no one missed Keer sooner. They didn't miss him until they started dragging the wreckage from the schoolroom out to the building site so it could be used in the foundations for the new walls.

The stuff was so razor-sharp that they had to drag it on mats, which involved a lot of back-breaking waddling, even after Emmec found a way to join several mats together to make the process more efficient. It was hot work, even in the steady drizzle, and Ranger kept telling them to dump the stuff in one place, and then scratching his head and striding up and down and changing his mind.

'Where's Keer?' demanded Emmec, at last, hunching away the drip he'd just got down his neck.

Alin snorted.

'Skiving,' he said. 'Typical. Good riddance.'

But Keer still hadn't turned up by the time they sat down to their dinner.

'Smells all right,' said Gow, sniffing at his bowl of stew. 'It's the right sort of colour, anyway. Nian, what do you think?'

'It's fine,' said Nian. 'Hey, if Keer doesn't show up in the next five minutes, I'll eat his.'

'Oh no you don't,' said Hani.

'Let's share it,' said Derig. 'That's fair.'

Nian, who had never expected anything else, dipped his spoon into his fragrant stew. Snerk was a total genius.

But Derig paused with his spoon halfway to his mouth.

'It's not like Keer to miss dinner, though,' he said.

Alin scowled.

'He'll be all right. He's probably stolen someone else's.'

'But he wouldn't have needed to steal anyone else's if he'd turned up here,' pointed out Derig, mildly.

'Hm.' Gow chewed his way through a piece of caramelized rutnip. 'When was the last time anyone saw him?'

That took a bit of working out.

'He must have been at breakfast,' said Hani.

They all thought.

'I can't remember him,' admitted Derig, falteringly.

Emmec made a face.

'We were all gum-eyed because we were up in the night,' he said. 'We forgot he'd ever existed.'

'It was weirder *Nian* not being there,' said Hani. 'We were all thinking about him and Grodan. And wondering who . . . ' his voice trailed away.

Alin frowned.

'I suppose this is pretty much proof, then,' he said, grimly. 'If Keer's run away . . . '

Gow shook his head.

'It's not proof of anything,' he pointed out, with scholarly accuracy. 'We've got no proof even that he's run away.'

Derig put his bowl of stew down.

'I should have missed him,' he said, very troubled. 'Caul told me to look after him, and then I didn't even notice when he disappeared.'

'Oh, grot the bogging idiot,' growled Alin. 'I suppose we're going to have to look for him, now.'

They searched, two by two, in all the likely places, and then the unlikely ones. Alin even went cursing into the rain to check out a particular tassel-tree that always stayed dry when the wind was from the east.

'He's probably run away,' said Hani, when they met up again at last. 'I mean, usually we'd be able to find him with no trouble at all, wouldn't we?'

'He'll be more at home back in the city,' said Emmec, uneasily. 'And probably safer, too. He never seemed very happy here.'

Derig looked stricken.

'We should have *made* him happy,' he said.

Alin shrugged.

'Oh, he'll enjoy living on his wits,' he said. 'That's the sort of person he is.'

Gow rubbed the side of his nose, which was a sign that someone had said something stupid.

'Enjoy being a starving beggar?' he asked, but only experimentally.

Emmec sighed.

'We really messed up, didn't we,' he observed. 'Mind

you, Keer didn't make things easy. I sort of told myself he was best left to himself until he could get to know us. But we could at least have got his sores properly dressed.'

Nian frowned.

'Sores?' he echoed. 'What sores?'

The others gave him odd looks.

'All over his arms and legs,' said Hani, as if he was pointing out something very obvious. 'I didn't even like getting in the pool with him.'

Now Nian came to think about it, he had seen Keer's sores. Of course he had. So why, why, why had he never bothered about them? It would have been the work of a couple of moments to set them healing.

He hadn't cared. That was the truth of it. And he hadn't cared because . . .

Nian grasped the truth with a bump.

He hadn't cared about the sores that encrusted Keer's skinny body *because they had not really been there.*

10

It was not possible for the Lords to be more worried than they already were: all they could do, when they discovered that Keer was missing, was to rearrange their anxieties.

'I have been at fault,' said Tarq, more frail than ever. 'I failed to make Keer understand his value to us all, and to the House. We must send a Tarhun squad to overtake him and persuade him to return.'

'I doubt he'll be convinced,' said Caul, drily.

'I should go,' said Nian. 'I'll probably be best able to find him.'

Caul stopped pacing.

'Oh no, we can't do without you,' he said. 'Not with the House under attack. You could send a message via the Tarhun, though. Or perhaps Hani might help with locating him.'

'But you don't understand,' said Nian. 'The Tarhun won't be able to find him, and I don't think Hani will, either. You see, Keer . . . ' He paused, trying to find a way to speak the astounding, almost unbelievable truth. 'Keer . . . he can change his shape.'

Caul actually laughed.

'And you have seen a field of grazing sheep,' he said, mockingly. 'Come on, Nian, that's all fairy tales.'

'I know it is,' Nian said. 'But that doesn't mean it isn't true, does it.'

Tarq's old face had become very troubled.

'It is true that the wisest of us dwells in ignorance,' he said. 'But to have such powers among us . . . it seems almost beyond the realms of possibility.'

'And for good reason,' said Caul. 'I mean, what sort of powers would you have to have to be able to shape-change?'

Nian pulled a face.

'I've no idea,' he admitted. 'That's why it took me so long to realize that Keer . . . well, that he wasn't actually Keer.'

'Hm,' said Caul, slowly. 'Nian, have you any idea how extensive Keer's powers are? Could he be a fly on the wall, or a loaf of bread, or a knife . . .' His voice faltered away to nothing.

'I don't know that, either,' Nian said. 'I don't even know how much Keer is truly like the person we've been seeing. Those sores on his arms and legs aren't real, for a start. I think that's partly why it's been so difficult for us to like him very much: because lots of the bits we could see were fake.'

Tarq's face was grey with regret.

'So Keer is not Keer,' he said. 'And so perhaps there is no boy to pursue.'

Nian thought about that.

'I think Keer was more like himself than even he knew. I think his distrust of everyone was real.'

'But what was the point of covering himself with fake sores?' asked Caul.

'To keep people at a distance, for one thing,' said Nian. 'You'd want to do that if you'd learned not to trust people.'

'That may be so,' murmured Tarq, sadly.

'So not only is Keer quite unknown to us, but he's got peculiar powers that none of us understand, as well,' summed up Caul. 'So he could be hanging from one of the rafters disguised as a spit-swift. He might be able to do anything.'

Nian thought about Keer. About the way he always lurked in corners, in shadows.

'I don't know if Keer did any of the things that have been happening,' he said. 'They were done by someone mad, and evil, and very powerful, and Keer didn't really seem any of those things. But I don't know. He was a liar. So I really really don't know.'

11

The Tarhun were a select band of men who had been refining their skills for centuries, so that by the time Nian arrived in the House of Truth their capacity for cheating and kidnapping had reached the highest level of sophistication.

Every member of the Tarhun underwent a long training in the martial art of Pirt-Pu, so that, whether in cottage, field, or hall, he could not only fight his way out of it, but he could take a struggling adolescent with him when he went.

And then suddenly, all in a moment, this millennium of dedication was rendered useless. A large section of the House of Truth was demolished in earthquakes, and the Lords, who had always stayed in the Inner House and never, ever, left it, began to disperse.

And those Lords that stayed, woke up. For instance the Lords, who until then had survived without complaint on a diet of oatmeal, bread, and apples, started noticing the scents of roasted ox that drifted over from the Tarhun's kitchens.

Boys were no longer to be cheated and kidnapped, either. Instead, the Tarhun were to go out bringing glad tidings of the new regime in the House of Truth. The Tarhun would receive visitors, act as guides, provide refreshments. They would rebuild the fallen down bits of the House, for they were strong, practical men, and Snorer's cousin Ranger was most fortunately a master builder by trade who was willing to come and join the Tarhun and supervise the job. Cut-price, finest materials, clean up as you go, no smoking or bagpipes during working hours, all workmanship guaranteed, and starting Tuesday.

And so the Tarhun made the best of it. They introduced Pirt-Pu exhibition matches to entertain the tourists while they ate their teas (which brought with it, of course, the opportunity for a little betting on the side). And Reeklet, who, though vile and crooked, had always had a penchant for needlework, worked long and strenuous hours making aprons for those on Waiter Duty.

The building work was held up firstly by the weather, and then by shortages of oxen and seasoned timber. Snorer's cousin Ranger hurried up and down, with his leggings settling lower and lower round his haunches, and his voice climbing higher and higher with worry, as he directed the Tarhun to move blocks of stone from here to there and then back to here again, because, otherwise, they were going to be in the way of the carpenters who might possibly turn up at some point.

Still, the Tarhun told themselves that things could be worse; the wisdom of this was proved by the fact that they *did* get worse. And worse, and worse still.

The Lord's stew was poisoned. (Poisoned? How the pits could that have happened? One of those old Lords gone bonkers, that was what it was, most probably, but guess who gets the blame, eh?) Then there was an attack. Everyone was under suspicion, which the Tarhun found deeply hurtful. All right they might not have powers like the Lords, but that didn't mean they were untrustworthy. Cunning, yes; they prided themselves on their cunning, but that was something quite different. When they put on their uniform of red-dyed leather, they put on a sense of responsibility, with it.

And now they were to be nursemaids. Every Lord and all the bogging boys had to be nursemaided backwards and forwards, day and night.

It was a situation to try everybody's patience. The Lords spent most of their time sitting in empty rooms doing nothing—really, really *nothing*, not even having a quiet game of patience, or yawning, or having a scratch—which meant their Tarhun guard had to keep still, with not even a shifting of the feet or a blowing of the nose.

And as for the boys, they were terrifying. The Tarhun had watched them often enough, playing pockle or chasing each other about: fooling about, scrapping, like all boys.

But these boys, these boys had powers. Yes, boys with powers were the Tarhun's job, and yes, keeping such a boy under control was what they were trained for. It could be done, as long as there were at least three of you, for you had to keep him terrified, exhausted and with never a moment to think.

But you couldn't do that with this lot, and the little boggers knew it. Their guards' nerves were in shreds. Poor old Ranger was as edgy as a bee in a bottle at the best of times, but after his boy (Emmec, the little grotter was called) had made an invisible cloud-lynx snarl right in his ear-hole, so that in his confusion he ran straight into a door that had been open a little while before, poor old Ranger lost it.

There might have been murder done. Well, only in a manner of speaking. Probably. Ranger *did* have his hands round the boy's throat, that couldn't be denied, but the little bogger ended up with hardly a bruise on him. But on the whole it was a good job the little one, the Truth Sayer, had been around. True, he was the one who'd caused all this trouble in the first place, but you couldn't really blame him because being locked up with that lot would drive anyone crazy. The Truth Sayer was the sort of boy who might himself have grown up to be one of the Tarhun, if he'd had a bit more beef on him. A fighter, (though just lately he was stopping as many fights as he'd started).

Mind you, the power most likely had to come out of the boys somehow. Pits, when they'd made that giant fart the other day that had made them drop that beam! Boggit, but you had to laugh. No, even that Emmec wasn't really a *bad* lad.

The pressure was getting everyone down, though. Like a thunderstorm. Even the Lords were feeling it, and it was pretty plain that no progress had been made towards nailing the culprit.

Tarhun Bulls-Eye said, *Something from another world,* but he was mad on other worlds, he was, just because he'd been to one. Anyone with any sense (which let out Bulls-Eye) knew that it couldn't be anything from another world, otherwise they'd be having earth-tremors. No, whoever was poisoning and slashing and destroying was someone from here. Someone on the mountain. Perhaps a ghost, as Reeklet said, except that none of them believed in ghosts; or some bogging boggart or other, except that none of them believed in them, either. That was all just fairy tales.

What they did believe, all of them, Tarhun and boys and Lords, what they really believed, was that soon, very soon, they were all going to die.

The Mirelands

'Still watching, Pella?'

Pella turned round quickly from the window. It was Dorcis again, of course. Dorcis was the only one who'd dare to come into Pella's room without being summoned. Dorcis, who'd been trained to be magistra, and who had knowledge that even Pella sometimes needed.

Thank the skies everything was back as it should be. If Dorcis had come in a few hours ago . . .

Dorcis came and stood beside her. Her eyes were cold, but then they always were.

'Pella, I know a way you can use your power to weave injured people back together,' she said. 'Let me show you. There'll be people here needing healing soon.'

'You've showed me before. It didn't work.'

'But . . . but you were younger then.'

Pella stood for a moment and listened to the powers that the old magistra had thrust inside her. They were squirming and fighting, as usual, and she'd as easily weave with them as she'd be able to weave a basket of snakes.

The sooner Pella got Dorcis out of the room the better. Dorcis was no fool, and the last thing Pella wanted was Dorcis poking around discovering things.

'All right,' said Pella, reluctantly. 'I'll give it a go tomorrow, when I'm rested.'

The rift in Pella's wall was yawning invisibly wide, now, but Pella had to send many more owlmen through before it would be quite big enough.

They were due to come to life tomorrow.

She dismissed Dorcis, closed her curtains, and lit her lamp.

12

The schoolroom was still bare except for some moth-eaten old mats someone had found somewhere, but lessons had started again. Nian was surprised at how glad he was to sit quietly and watch his powers shifting and growing. It was like watching oil on water, except . . .

. . . and he remembered, now. That black edge of evil he'd sensed come into the House. It had arrived pretty much at the same time as Keer, and not long before the owlman had appeared. So did that mean that the evil, the owlman, and Keer were connected?

The colours squirmed and danced before his eyes. It was beautiful and fascinating, but it was different from how he remembered it because there was lots of black, now, streaking unevenly between the vivid blues and flaring pinks.

'All right,' said Caul. 'That wasn't bad at all, you lot. We'll take a break, and afterwards, as there's nothing left in here to damage, we'll have a game of mind-darts.'

The boys got up and stretched as Caul went out. Outside, the rain was lashing down, but they could hardly have gone out and enjoyed themselves anyway, not with this grim line of Tarhun watching their every move.

'Look,' Alin said to the Tarhun, patiently. 'We're just going to stand around and talk. That's all. So why don't you all go off and do whatever it is you Tarhun like to do?'

Reeklet's nasty moustache clung round his glower like one of the more poisonous sorts of caterpillar.

'Orders,' he growled.

'We'd promise not to go anywhere, or do anything,' piped up Derig, hopefully. 'We're just going to talk.'

But even Snorer, who was generally quite friendly, only folded his arms so they rested on his great mound of a belly.

'Nobody's stopping you,' he pointed out.

Everyone glared at one another. The Tarhun had been watching the boys' every move all day and they were all, boys and Tarhun, at screaming point.

'We can't go on like this,' said Emmec. 'It'll drive us all mad.'

'Yeah,' agreed Hani. 'It won't matter so much with the rest of you because you're all bonkers to start with, but it frightens me to death.'

'And it's not doing any good,' said Gow, ignoring the insult. 'That's the worst thing about it. I mean, it doesn't help us find out what's going on or who's behind it all.'

Derig raised an anxious face.

'It doesn't help find Keer, either,' he said. 'And he's been gone a whole day.'

'If he's actually gone,' said Alin, looking round. 'He might be a spider listening to everything we say.'

Emmec made a face.

'That's actually a creepier idea than living with the Tarhun,' he said. 'No offence,' he added, quickly, as a growl rose from the line of men standing at attention along the wall.

Tarhun Reeklet curled his hairy lip.

'We've sent a squad out after him,' he grunted. 'I'd never have believed we'd be sending men out looking for a shape-changing monster out of a fairy story, but I'm beginning to think anything might happen. And it's not easy, either, trudging all over the mountains looking for someone who might not look like himself—'

'—and who might not be there at all,' put in Snorer, reasonably. 'Let alone the fact that he's probably got powers enough to rip our heads off. Or that he might be lurking in any tree or in a cave, ready to stab someone or poison their bit of honest bread.'

Derig shivered.

'Just a few days ago I thought that living in the House was the scariest thing anyone could do,' he said. 'But there couldn't be anything worse than searching for someone who might jump out and attack you.'

Alin snorted.

'Oh yes there could,' he said. 'He—or it—could still be in here with us.'

Everyone checked behind them, even the Tarhun, who were against a wall.

'It's the waiting,' said Snorer, heavily. 'If we knew

what we were fighting then it wouldn't be so bad. It's the waiting for a sleeping mat to come to life and smother you, or for a sock to wrap itself round your throat.'

'I never liked the idea of being strangled,' said Derig, sadly.

Snorer turned to Nian.

'Don't you know, Truth Sayer?' he asked. 'We all thought that with your powers . . . '

'But I don't,' said Nian. 'I don't know why I don't, but I don't. I keep trying, but there's nothing that I can see.'

'You mean it's invisible?' asked Hani, in fascinated horror.

Everyone went to look behind them again, and then realized it was foolish and pretended to have been doing shoulder exercises.

Nian shook his head.

'I don't think so. Not really invisible. But I keep seeing a sort of darkness—'

'—a shadow monster!' breathed Reeklet.

'No. Not that sort of dark,' Nian told them. 'But like a shadow in that it . . . sort of . . . isn't actually there.'

The Tarhun and the boys looked around to see if any of the others had a clue what the Truth Sayer was going on about. But even Gow's face was showing no spark of intelligence—and Nian's certainly wasn't.

'That's why I don't really think the attacks have been anything to do with Keer,' Nian went on. 'Keer was certainly here. At least, bits of him were.'

111

'But . . . ' began several people, and then got no further.

Emmec heaved a sigh.

'And so what do we do?' he asked. 'We can't just sit here.'

'Just waiting to be picked off one by one,' agreed Snorer, solemnly.

'And what about Keer?' asked Hani. 'If he wasn't the attacker . . . '

'I think Keer's left,' said Nian. 'After all, even you can't find him. But I'm not sure, because if he was in another form then we might not be able to pick him up.'

Reeklet smoothed his moustache round his grim mouth.

'The boy'll be back begging,' he said. 'He's better off, isn't he? Anything's better than hanging round here with invisible monsters lurking about ready to rip your throat out.'

'Not rip,' said Nian, with a shudder. 'There was no ripping.'

'No,' said Gow, thoughtfully. 'Everything was cut, wasn't it.'

'Sliced,' said Emmec, frowning tremendously. 'Really skilfully, too.'

Derig suddenly spoke up.

'We've got to do something,' he said earnestly. 'We've got to make completely sure that Keer isn't somewhere around needing help.'

Snorer screwed up his face.

'I'm afraid it's probably too late for that,' he said,

with regret. 'The boy's been missing since last night, so—well, it's pretty obvious why you can't pick him up, isn't it?'

Everyone winced, but Derig said:

'We've still got to find him.'

Reeklet shrugged.

'A corpse will soon make its presence felt, this warm weather,' he pointed out, with a certain amount of ghoulish satisfaction, and suddenly all the boys were on their feet. There was no sitting comfortably once that dreadful word *corpse* had been uttered.

'We'll search in pairs,' said Alin. 'One pupil and one Tarhun. That's six pairs. We'll split the compass between us in alphabetical order, all right? So that's Hani, Emmec, Derig, Gow, me, and then Nian.'

Nian made sure Derig was paired up with Snorer. Snorer wasn't exactly bright, but there was a certain kindness lurking somewhere inside his huge body. Possibly. Well, Nian had never seen him actually kicking any small furry animals, anyway. Breaking their necks with his bare hands and then eating their eyeballs raw, yes, but never actually kicking them.

Nian looked round to check everyone was ready, and then plunged out into the corridor with the bulky Tarhun shadow of Reeklet at his back, to begin the search for whatever was to be found of Keer.

13

Nian realized almost at once that the search for Keer wasn't going to be successful. He needed to proceed carefully and quietly, with every one of his senses alert for the merest trace of anything that might be Keer, or might once have been him. But going round the House with a member of the Tarhun was like taking a marsh-ox for a walk. The tramp of great Tarhun feet echoed round the long curve of the corridor, and Reeklet, Nian's particular Tarhun, kept making long juicy phlegm-churning noises that completely wiped out any attempt to listen, or to think about anything that didn't involve extreme violence to members of the Tarhun.

Nian had been in the House for a year and a half, but he hadn't explored half of it. True, he and the others chased each other round the place on most rainy days, but Nian had never bothered to look behind every door. Most of the rooms were white and empty, except perhaps for a musty sleeping mat or a spider-webbed bowl, the relics of some long-dead Lord.

The place was enough, as Reeklet pointed out, to give you the willies.

'Why don't you have a sit down,' suggested Nian,

at last, his concentration ripped apart again by a sound like someone churning up slugs with sharp gravel. 'This doorway can't lead anywhere much, so I'll be back in a minute.'

But Reeklet shook his mean jowls.

'Got to keep you in sight, Lord.'

Nian wanted to brain him, but he knew that would be a feat of marksmanship far beyond even his capabilities.

'But I'm the Truth Sayer!' he snapped, exasperated. 'I'm much more likely to be able to deal with anything dangerous than you are!'

An expression of smugness and cunning settled onto Reeklet's face.

'I know, Lord,' he agreed. 'And that's why I'm not letting you out of my sight.'

Nian shrugged and plunged on. He went fast in the hope of leaving Reeklet behind, but all that happened was that his heavy footsteps and laboured breath got louder and even more irritating.

And then Nian sensed something. Something under his feet.

Not a tremor. It was nothing like a tremor—but something was certainly moving.

But how the *bog* could anything be moving down in the solid rock of the mountain?

'Keep still, can't you!' snapped Nian, to the blundering Tarhun.

Reeklet's idea of still was a long way from Nian's, but at least he was now only treading slowly from foot to foot and grunting softly like a constipated hog.

Yes, there was something down there. Perhaps a person. No, two people. And there were other things, too. It was hard to know what they were, but they were certainly nothing like a mole or a bear or any creature that you might find in a cave, but instead . . .

Nian was almost sure he had come across something like this before, but at the same time it was completely alien and strange. It was moving, but it was not alive; it was under his feet, but not actually *anywhere* at all.

He focused his powers back on the people. One of them was a member of the Tarhun—Snorer, probably—yes, Nian could sense the simmering fat hulk of him. There must be some sort of a cellar down there, and the person with him must be Derig.

And now Nian could sense Derig's unease, and the careful way he was using his powers to illuminate the cellars as he took step by cautious step. Derig's fear made a halo around him that prickled Nian's mind.

And then, completely suddenly, the fear changed: it accelerated wildly from fear to cruel shock to terror. Nian was all but thrown backwards, dwarfed with the violence of it, as, below him, Derig was slashed through with utter panic.

Nian didn't even have the wits to think about moving until, from somewhere below him, Snorer screamed.

14

Nian ran. Reeklet's heavy body was blundering after him, but Nian couldn't wait. Snorer's scream had been cut off with horrible suddenness, but Derig's terror was going on and on and on and Nian had to reach Derig before it stopped. It was desperately vital he got to Derig before it stopped.

Nian threw himself round a corner, saw a doorway, dived through it, and nearly plunged head-first down a flight of narrow steps that led down into darkness.

'Lord!' cried Reeklet behind him, in an agony of anxiety. 'Lord, wait! *Lord!*'

This must be the way. This way. Nian ran down the steps through the shifting paleness that his powers revealed to him.

Here was the bottom, but Derig—yes, here, this way, another door.

And quick, oh quick, *quick,* because Derig's fear was weakening, weakening so fast. Follow the fear before it failed and ran away into nothingness.

Reeklet was following, slow in the ground-black. 'Lord!' came his hoarse, frightened voice. 'Lord, wait!' But Nian had no time to wait.

Another door: and here was a choice of ways, but that didn't matter because the trail of the fear led him. He swerved into a rocky passageway.

Noises, now, ahead. A muffled thumping, and continual cursing. Snorer. Nian used the noise to guide him, for Derig's fear was rolling away down an ever-steeper slope. Nian flung himself round a corner, caught his shoulder on a projection of rock, stumbled, and went on, his pale power-vision and the pitch-darkness tumbling round him.

And here was a place where the walls curved away and something was coming towards him—but he could not see it, not even with his powers, so that sometimes, mostly, he could not tell it was there at all until it appeared above him again in a flash of darkness and hatred and malice.

It was striding, black, invisible; he ducked away, lost his balance, and fell on something warm.

That contact with reality, with life, gave Nian an anchor upon which to fix his scattered wits.

'It's me,' he said, to the still body beneath him. 'Derig, it's Nian! I'm here.'

But now something monstrously large was rising through the dark. Nian snatched a handful of power to throw at it—and realized in the nick of time that it was Snorer.

Nian heaved in a breath and scanned the pale blackness for the Thing, the terrifying Thing that sometimes wasn't there.

Nothing.

Could it have gone, completely gone?

Yes, but any moment might bring it back.

Nian waited, with Derig lying warm beside him and Snorer shifting and groaning and swearing by the wall. This place had been hewn out of the rock. It seemed to be completely empty except for the three of them.

Nian waited. Where had it gone, that Thing? It had struck itself into being like lightning, dazzling, but black as pitch, and vanished again as instantly and completely.

Be *ready* . . .

Nothing. Nothing.

Nothing . . .

Derig was beside him. Was he badly hurt, was he even alive? What if he were dying now, now, with Nian not helping him?

And what should Nian do if the Thing appeared again? He could send power at it, enough power to demolish the great walls of the House, but how could his power get a grip on *nothing*?

In the dark, Nian was afraid.

Reeklet was still blundering about several rooms away, the fool, and he was not even going in the right direction. Nian could have called to him, but he was afraid to draw attention to himself. Perhaps if he was very very still there was a chance . . .

'*Grot*,' muttered Snorer. '*Bogging* grot. What the bogging bogging bogging bogging grotting *pits* was that?'

It was truly a pit down here: the sort of place a Thing like that (like what?) would be powerful. Nian's heart thumped against his ribs.

119

Still nothing.

Was the Thing waiting, too, until Nian lost concentration? Would it stride across through the tumbling darkness and . . .

Derig's breath was moaning in his throat.

Be quiet, Nian wanted to say. *I need to hear!*

Snorer was lurching to his feet, now, and groping blindly over to Derig.

Nian waited with every nerve stretched.

Beside him there was the dry *snick* of a flint being struck. The blackness moved back a little, away from the tiny flame, and Nian could see his hand's sharp shadow silhouetted against the shadow-mottled rock of the floor.

'Lord!' gasped Snorer, urgently.

Nian ignored him. He could sense nothing of the striding blackness, but he had to be ready.

'Lord,' said Snorer, again, but now his voice was curiously quiet. 'Oh . . . oh *struth*.'

His mildness caught Nian's attention as none of Snorer's curses had. Snorer was reaching down to the heap in the blackness that was Derig.

'Oh, struth,' Snorer murmured. Then he went on, in a sing-song almost like a lullaby. 'Here we are, then, boy. There, boy, there, here we are. That's right, that's right, hold still, hold still, yes, you're doing everything right. You just stay there, my son, and you'll be home soon. Oh yes, yes. Home, quite soon, and as happy as a mud-skunk.'

Nian risked a moment to flick a thought at Derig, and then, stricken with panic, he hurled away all his watchfulness and snatched at every scrap of power he possessed to hold together what life there was in Derig's faintly twitching body, and to make a bandage for his throat, which had been cut.

Snorer carried Derig up the rocky stairs and out into the light.

Nian had healed Derig's cuts, but too late: much of Derig's blood lay in clotted pools in the cave below them. Derig was still breathing, though not deeply or easily or often.

Grodan arrived, silently, quite soon. He was still so weak he could hardly stand, but he wouldn't go away. He laid himself down on the floor beside Derig.

'Rest,' Nian ordered him, tersely. Derig's face was white against his mat.

'You need my help,' said Grodan, who was no longer white but a horrible stagnant yellow.

'Help? What help can you be?' muttered Nian, beyond caring. 'You've hardly strength to heal yourself.'

But Grodan was past caring, too.

'Before you came to the House I was the greatest healer the world had seen in forty years,' he snarled. 'I was laying down new lore—not that *you* would ever have the courtesy to cast your eyes over it. And now, true enough, I can do little. Well, go on, Truth Sayer! I suppose you might as well enjoy your triumph while you can. For the thing that felled me, and has almost certainly killed your friend, does not seem to be subject even to your powers.'

Nian bent low over Derig so he could feel the faint warmth of Derig's breath on his cheek.

'I know,' he said.

15

Snorer was even less clear about what had happened than Nian, for as far as he was concerned the whole thing had happened in the pitch black. He'd felt something cold enough to freeze the eyeballs off a bronze gibbon, and then the lad had let out a scream that had laid ice in the marrow of his bones. So he'd tried to find the boy. Derig. Yes, Derig. That was a valley-name. A nice lad, very quiet and thoughtful. He'd been careful Snorer hadn't gone head over heels coming down the stairs. In fact, the lad had reminded him a bit of . . . well, that was neither here nor there.

He'd tried to find the boy (and it was darker down there than a mole's chamberpot, remember), but he'd run into something like . . . sheet metal, perhaps, but not twangy like sheet metal would be. Perhaps more like a bit of cast iron, then. Bang. Just like that. Hard as rock. See, look at the bruise. Well, that staggered him, but he'd picked himself up and charged at it, but it wasn't there any more. No, he hadn't moved it, it was completely solid: he'd have had more luck trying to push the mountain over. The thing was just, literally, *not there* any more . . . he'd been lucky not to break his skull on the wall.

Then the Truth Sayer had come rushing in. Yes, the Truth Sayer must have been quite a way away when the attack happened. Yes, definitely.

And even Reeklet, who never had a good word to say about anyone if he could help it, bore witness to that.

Nian did what he could, but he wasn't sure how much there was left of Derig to save.

When Caul came to the room, later, his thin face was grim.

'I think you'd better come with me,' he said.

'What is it?'

'We've found something in the cellars. You might be able to tell us something about it.'

'Something someone's dropped?' asked Nian, thinking about clues and footsteps and feeling a second's shaft of hope.

But Caul shook his head. 'Nothing like that,' he said.

'Go, go,' urged Grodan. 'I have skill enough to keep us both alive. Go and do something useful, boy.'

Nian followed Caul down the stone steps to the cellars. There was no need to use his powers, for a lantern-bearing member of the Tarhun stood uneasily at every turning.

'Here,' said Caul, standing aside for Nian to go in first.

There were half a dozen of the Tarhun here. As Nian entered they held their lanterns high, chasing the shadows up and up to stretch thinly across the great domed roof.

And from every wall the eyes of a hundred owlmen stared at Nian with a malice as cold as death.

16

There was a crowd in the Council Chamber of the House of Truth. Everybody was there except for those Tarhun who were on guard duty, and Grodan, and Keer, and Derig.

Nian steered his mind away from Derig, and banished the small frozen expression that he knew had taken over his face. The bits of Derig's brain that were not dead would recover. Worrying would make no difference.

There were perhaps thirty of the Tarhun in the chamber, but if there had been a hundred of them they would have been no good against the owlmen. The Tarhun had brawn and pride and a tradition of fighting, but nothing to deal with this.

The Lords were taking their seats in the council circle, and the boys were settling themselves in a corner. Even Hani was sitting down quietly, without any of his usual shoving and nudging. The Tarhun were prowling along to stand in formidable lines along the top of the steps. Everyone was in place, now, except Nian. For a moment he felt all the minds around him as a quivering fog of bafflement, fear, anticipation, cowardice, dread, hope, resentment; and far away, though not nearly, nearly, nearly far enough, was the piercing malice of the things that inhabited the walls.

There were empty places in the Lords' circle, but Nian was not a Lord. He had power, far more power than any of them, but it was not the trained and disciplined power of the Lords. He could heal people, make plants grow, make paths to other worlds—but against the owlmen his powers were unwieldy and useless.

The Council Chamber was quite still, now, and Nian had never been so lonely, not ever, not even when he had first come to the House, for then, he had had some hope.

But now . . .

Half of him wanted to shout, or bring down the laboriously-mended roof. To tell them the truth, which was that he had no idea when the next attack would be, or what the owlmen were, or how they could stop them. That there was nothing, nothing, nothing he could do.

Pack up your lives, he should say. *Go somewhere where you will be* safe, *if anywhere is safe, for these things can move and I cannot stop them.*

Nian stood with his heart beating fast, but he did not have the courage to say it.

'Well?' demanded the cracked and irritable voice of the Lord Rago. 'Have we all assembled here to gawp at each other like idiots? What is to be done? Or do we sit and wait until the shadows come to slit our throats?'

That's all we can do, Nian wanted to say. *Wait for them to come through the dark.*

But instead he only said: 'I don't know.'

Rago snorted.

'Well, that's no surprise. We'd as well ask advice of a day-old chick! We must call upon our wisdom, my Lords—not that anyone can *think*, amidst this rabble!'

'Perhaps we should leave the House,' suggested Caul.

And now Firn was breaking in, fussing, as always.

'But we cannot *leave*!' he exclaimed. 'Think of the damage that was done in the schoolroom! What if the creatures attacked the library?'

And even Tarq said:

'The Lords have lived in this place for longer than anyone knows.'

'Humph!' Rago spat, with scorn. 'And so are we obliged to *die* here, then?'

Run, Nian wanted to say. *Run for your lives. Run as far and as fast as you can and hope that you are never caught. Hope that no more of the owlmen come. Hope that they do not wish to kill everything in the whole world.*

'And . . . please . . . what about Derig?' asked Emmec, blushing at his own daring in speaking.

Derig could not be moved far, but then Nian was not sure that Derig was worth saving.

Everyone was looking at him, so he tried to think, but it was like trying to eat the air, for there was nothing for his brain to work on. He was the Truth Sayer, but the owlmen weren't even *real*, some of the time, so how could he divine the Truth of something unreal? And Keer hadn't been all real, either.

'I don't know,' he said. 'I keep trying to think, but I don't know where to start.'

He looked around and found himself surrounded by a host of hopeful eyes. And he just had to get away because the weight of all that hope was enough to crush him.

'Let me go away by myself for a while,' he said. 'Perhaps if I can just walk about in the garden and think . . .'

They were disappointed, but not despairing. Nian had put that off for a little while.

'Go then, my friend,' said Tarq, quietly. 'We will wait for you.'

And Nian turned and walked away.

17

It had stopped raining, and the garden smelled of greenness and decay.

Nian had not been out there by himself for a long time: usually he was chasing away after the others to play pockle, to squabble or tussle or to watch the building work.

He had almost forgotten what it was like to be alone. At each step the air got clearer, easier, almost as if the garden was making way for him; as if the air of the House had been thick with the evil of the owlmen.

Nian made his way towards the centre of the garden. The boys did not go there much. The statue there marked the place where the garden touched the other worlds, so it wasn't somewhere to play.

Nian ducked under the still-dripping branches of a stoneberry tree and there, in front of him, through the gap where the walls had fallen down, were the green mountains. Ranger had been charging about for months organizing the rebuilding work, but the foundations for the new walls were only just now being filled in.

But now, as Nian gazed around the garden, something dark appeared, sweeping towards him. Perhaps it was only a shadow (except that there were no shadows in the damp afternoon) but Nian ducked to avoid it, found his foot slipping away from under him, and fell flat on his back onto a mound of leaf-mould before he knew what was happening.

He took in a breath to let out a yelp of protest— but the air that entered his throat was so cold that it froze the sound in his throat.

He blinked a bit, pushed himself to his feet, and looked round. The stoneberry tree was still dripping peacefully behind him, and the temperature had flowed back to warm again. Of course it had! That lungful of air had come straight from the depths of winter. It wouldn't be anything near as cold as that for months.

What the *pits* . . . ?

Tentatively, Nian extended his hand into the place where the cold had been, but now all he could find was the slight draughtiness of an early autumn afternoon.

The most likely thing, Nian decided, was that he had gone mad. Given the circumstances, that seemed quite a wise move.

He walked on again, but more cautiously.

He'd thought he was ready for anything, until out of the corner of his eye he caught a glimpse of a shape sliding out from behind a tree.

Nian flung up an arm to protect himself, but the thing moved so fast that Nian got only a confused

131

impression of darkness before the whole thing had zipped away and he was alone again in the garden.

Nian stopped to let his heart settle itself a bit, and wondered what to do. On the whole he decided he'd rather have these things coming at him from the front, rather than turn his back on them, so he got up his courage and took a careful step forward. Nothing. So he took another.

The next shadow (though it couldn't have been a shadow) went right through him, with a slash of cold like a blade of ice, and a pain in the guts as if a blade had really stabbed him . . . and then it was gone, leaving nothing behind but a bitter taste.

The next minute Nian devoted to standing absolutely still and breathing. He needed to do it while he had the chance.

He was still trying to steady himself when the next swathe of darkness came.

It swept across from the direction of the statue, and as it came it brushed all the trees and brambles of the garden out of existence. Nian found himself gazing down a black tunnel at a wide, low valley. He could see hills as grey as a skunk's back, and a snail-trail of glittering water. The cold of the place slapped violently at his face . . . and then the garden was back and he was quite safe, though a little dizzy.

Another world. That was what he'd just seen, he was sure of it—and those shadows were coming from it.

But nothing had the power to step from one world to another. Nothing and no one—except for him, the Truth Sayer.

(But how many worlds were there? A thousand, a million? And how much did he know of even his own?)

Those shadows were owlmen, or the essences of what were going to become owlmen. Nian hadn't been able to see them clearly but he was in no doubt of it. More and more owlmen, coming into this world.

Something was letting the owlmen through a passageway between their worlds, and that would have to be something mind-bogglingly powerful.

But even as he realized this, Nian felt a spark of hope, for that was what he'd been looking for, something mind-bogglingly powerful.

An image flashed through Nian's mind, as vivid as the strange world that was balanced on the other side of the statue. He saw his father's farm, the hall, the corn feast.

And a hundred owlmen striding into the candle-light, vicious and deadly and unstoppable.

Nian wrenched his mind away in horror.

He began to run towards the centre of the garden and the passageway to the owlmen's world.

It wasn't easy to keep the statue in view through the flurrying shadows which were destined to become owlmen. The owlmen-shadows had hardly any substance, but still he kept getting snagged on the scudding slashes of darkness, and they were coming at him faster and faster as he neared the statue that marked the passageway to the other worlds.

There came a point where Nian didn't think he was

going to make it, but he put his head down and threw himself forward the last few steps in a long desperate lunge.

He flung out his hand at the statue like a swimmer in a race.

But it never got there.

Instead, he fell.

Down and down, and down, tumbling head over heels as the worlds flicked momentarily round him and merged into a blur.

And he didn't know whether he had found the passageway to the place of the owlmen, or merely the edge of another world's cliff.

He fell and fell, his body hurtling towards the rocks, or the sea, or whatever was at the bottom. He caught tiny glimpses of a hundred places—deserts, cities, oceans—faster and faster until they blurred into one another. His brain was full of one long scream; then the flickering worlds got dimmer, and he plunged into a void. And he knew where he was, then, even though he was nowhere. Literally, nowhere.

Nowhere, and falling through the vast frozen chasm between the worlds.

And now here was an edge blooming in the speckled darkness: purple, sapphire, cornelian, rose . . . and now shapes, misty at first, but growing more solid as he looked.

And he knew they were the shapes of another world.

18

Something came up and hit Nian's feet. Whatever it was seemed quite soft at first, but it quickly firmed up, solidifying from dough to moorheath to a rug—yes, truly, a rug, a silken rug.

Nian had been braced for some dark place haunted by owlmen, so this was a surprise. He blinked down at the twining flowers and little birds, and he didn't know if he was more relieved or baffled or amazed.

But then he looked round, and the horror of what he saw very nearly made him step backwards into the abyss again. He was in a room unlike anything he'd ever seen or dreamed of; his stomach tightened with shock and total gut-churning revulsion.

It was . . . *pink*.

Nian, with every nerve ready to fend off an attack by razor-sharp assassins, really, genuinely, had trouble believing it. He had trouble believing that it was actually there in front of him, and even more trouble believing that anyone could possibly have *deliberately* created a room like this.

The pink walls were painted with pinker day-flowers, and the two tall windows were framed by

135

the pinkest, flounciest curtains. On the huge pink bed several frilly cushions and three small dead animals.

Nian was shuddering, both with revulsion and the stagnant bone-chilling cold of the place, when there was a movement: a fringe on one of the curtains twitched.

There was an eye regarding him. It was a cold, grey eye, sharp with suspicion and intelligence.

Nian did the only thing he could think of. He bowed.

When he stood up he found a woman had stepped out into view. She had grey hair, a strong air of tragedy and disapproval, and the graceful, powerful limbs of a statue.

She gave him one sweeping, outraged glance and then she gathered up the skirts of her grey robe and made haste for the door. Nian got a second's glimpse of a shiny marble corridor, and then she was gone, her sandalled feet clipping urgently along the glimmering floor.

And as she went she called, in a high, querulous voice:

'*Magistra! Magistra! Magistra!*'

Nian, abandoned, hesitated. His instinct was to get out of there fast, but then what did he do? This must be where the owlmen had come from. There was someone here with a huge amount of power: more power than he'd thought anyone but himself possessed.

Nian looked round the room again, and winced. He

had seen ugly rooms in another world before, but nothing anywhere near this.

There was someone hurrying back along the corridor, now.

Clacking high heels.

Quite possibly another woman, then.

Nian did his best to pull himself together. He had not had much to do with women since he'd come to the House, but he could cope with women. Of course he could.

The door was flung open with such force it crashed back into the wall and a girl stepped into the room. She was young, perhaps only a couple of years older than Nian. She had long black wiry hair, a dress that matched the curtains (Wasn't she *perishing*? Because Nian's eyeballs were practically freezing over.) and a commanding air.

She put her hands on her hips and looked at Nian as though he were something that had come down a rat's nose.

'Just what do you think you're doing in my bedroom?' she demanded. She spoke in some strange spitty language, but Nian grabbed at his powers and managed, with a bit of a scramble, to get the sense of what she was saying.

He tried to think of a good answer: his failure was only partly due to the fact that he only knew twelve words of her language.

'Er . . . just . . . in,' was the best he could do.

The girl's eyes were sharp with suspicion. Behind her the grey woman loomed watchfully.

'He must be a spy, magistra,' she said.

The girl shrugged her hefty shoulders.

'It doesn't make any difference who he is,' she announced. 'I am the magistra, and you, boy, have entered my shrine where no man is permitted. So I shall have your head chopped off.'

Nian was literally only a step away from his escape route; still, he gave up on any attempt at overcoming his instinctive dislike of her.

'*Magistra?*' he asked, and it came out even less polite than he'd intended.

The magistra looked him up and down.

'Of course. *The* magistra. Pella, twenty-fifth magistra of the shrine. The all-high and most beautiful. Obviously.'

Most beautiful was not obvious to Nian at all, for she had a round flushed face and a lot of teeth, and she was built like a member of the Tarhun.

The grey-haired woman was looking quite shocked.

'Really, magistra,' she said, '*must* we have a beheading? Just think of all the flies and mess. And that altar's in need of re-grouting, you know. The blood will get down under the flooring and we'll have plague in the shrine before you can say entrails, you mark my words.'

The magistra flounced round on her.

'I'm only being *merciful*, Dorcis!' she snapped. 'Now the silly boy's seen the glory of my countenance he's got to die, hasn't he? He'll only pine and fade away out of longing for me, otherwise. It's a kindness to him.'

Dorcis twitched an eyebrow, but the magistra took no notice.

'Go and tell the executioner!'

Dorcis sighed, and looked even more than ever like a statue to someone tragic.

'If you command it,' she said. 'But I must remind you that you've given the chief executioner job to Wiglana Squimp, and I doubt if she knows which edge of the axe to use. Still,' she went on, casting a cool eye over Nian, 'I suppose the boy's only got a skinny little neck. It'll hardly be harder than killing a grouseling.'

'Good,' said the magistra, with unforgivable smugness. 'That's settled, then.'

'Mind you,' went on Dorcis, failing to leave. 'Wiglana always *was* squeamish. You should have appointed someone from outside the shrine. Someone mindless and brutal. Goodness knows there are enough of *them* around.'

She shuddered delicately, drawing her grey robes elegantly round her.

'I'll organize an enquiry to find out how the wretched boy got in here, too, shall I? Because if Branto's found some way in—'

'—but on second thoughts, Dorcis,' said the magistra, hastily, 'why should I care if the boy suffers from the agonies of love for the rest of his life? I shall question him myself. If there's some secret way into my room we must discover it at once, and then I'll get rid of him with as little fuss as possible. After all, he might be just some humble boy seeking truth and wisdom.'

Dorcis gave the magistra an odd look.

She muttered something like *well, good luck to him!* and snatched at the great shiny knob of the door.

19

Nian stood with the abyss between the worlds behind him, watching the magistra warily. He had never heard of a magistra before, but he found he recognized one now he saw one.

This Pella had power. Nian could almost smell it coming off her, a scent like incense but with a revolting and fascinating rottenness about it.

'All right,' snapped the magistra, bouncing round to face him. 'Where have you come from?'

'From my shrine,' said Nian, carefully assembling what words he had.

'A shrine!' echoed the magistra, rather pleased. 'Good. But then I suppose that's likely, really, as it's at the other end of a passageway between the worlds. Who's it a shrine to?'

'Who to?' he echoed, puzzled.

The girl rolled her round blue eyes in scorn.

'Is there a magister or a magistra? And how many other people live there?'

Nian could have shown her the answer on his fingers, but he wasn't going to tell her anything. Despite appearances it was almost certainly this girl who had sent the owlmen. He shook his head.

The girl regarded him for a moment. And then, but without moving a finger, she somehow reached out and prodded him quite painfully in the ribs.

He pushed whatever-it-was aside indignantly, and with only the smallest effort of his powers; and the magistra let out a sharp laugh of triumph and derision.

'I thought that would make you reveal yourself,' she jeered, with quite unbearable self-satisfaction. 'So you're a magister, yourself. I thought as much.'

Nian blinked. A magister? Well, if this great clumsy girl was a magistra, then he might well be.

She raised a plump hand, and suddenly Nian was ducking away from a sphere of power that she'd sent zapping through the air at his face.

The thing was about the size of a pockle cone, and Nian had swiped it away before he'd really registered that it consisted of a pair of snapping jaw-bones set with dagger teeth.

And then two more things happened, one after the other, bam-*bam*!

The first thing was that the magistra swiped the dagger-jaws so hard with the flat of her hand that they shattered into a thousand blade-like fragments as she shot them back at Nian. And, secondly, as Nian was hurling up a wall of power to stop the grotting things before they knocked him all the way back to the House and halfway down the mountain, there was a *snick!* behind him.

It was only a tiny noise, like a key turning in a lock. A tiny, tiny noise.

And all in an instant Nian discovered that he was an idiot, a grot-head, a complete utter and totally damned fool.

This girl had powers. He'd known that. He even suspected her of sending the owlmen: the owlmen, who had attacked Grodan and Derig. There was a huge amount of power in this place, and this girl was the source of much of it. She was hugely strong, and must be hugely ruthless, too. And no fool. No fool at all.

He spun around and gazed at the pink wall behind him, at the passageway back to his own world.

But it was a passageway no longer.

His eyes could see no difference, but Nian, who was the Truth Sayer, knew for certain that Pella had barred his way home as surely as if she had filled in the passageway with blocks of stone.

20

Nian stood and gazed in horror at the pink wall of Pella's room. It had sounded as if Pella had sealed off the passageway with some sort of key, but it hadn't been anything like that at all. It would have been far better if it had been, for Nian could have broken open a lock, or melted it with a quick spurt of power. This was something much, much more complex and difficult. It was as if Pella had woven long strands of her world right through the fabric of his path home.

Nian, horrified, explored it with his powers. It was appallingly plain that trying to force it open would involve ripping the passageway itself and a large part of both the surrounding worlds to pieces.

'What did you do that for?' Nian demanded, in outrage and dismay and the wrong language.

Pella made a turning gesture with one of her hands. He didn't understand it, but it was plainly deeply insulting. 'Oh, you're terrifying me,' she said, witheringly, and before he could summon up a reply invisible ropes had slashed through the air and were coiling themselves like snagweed round his arms and legs.

Furious, he burst them apart and sent them crashing through one of the windows.

He was glad to see that Pella flinched a little as the window broke. A damp wind that managed to be even icier than the air in the room gusted in and stirred the pink flounces of the curtains.

'I shall get rid of all the shrine if I cannot go where I came from,' threatened Nian.

'Oh no you won't,' said the magistra, redder in the face than ever. 'You can try if you like, but there's no way I'm letting you go back to your world and warn them. My owlmen are going to come to life and kill your people soon, anyway, but it'll be much quicker and cleaner if the attack comes without warning. No, you shall stay here, and I shall take your shrine over, and live there happily ever after.'

Nian's insides twisted in horror.

'You cannot live in my world,' he said. 'The passageway cannot be between the worlds for ever. The passageway must . . . it must go, and we must be in our own worlds, or the worlds will go, be killed, too.'

Pella rolled her eyes even more scornfully than before. 'Surely you can think of something more likely than that,' she scoffed. 'Perhaps something to do with the bogie badgers or the sleet wraiths. Anyway, you can forget all about that. No, you're here for ever, now, like the other one.'

The other one? Nian was pretty sure he knew the answer to his next question, but he asked it anyway.

'What other one?'

Pella smiled a blood-curdling smile.

'The one who came yesterday. I should have secured the passageway then, I suppose, but it didn't occur to me that anyone might come through once the other one didn't return. I didn't know the people of *any* world could be as stupid as that. Anyway, I needed it open so that I could carry on sending owlmen through.'

'Where is the other one?' demanded Nian, through gritted teeth, refusing to be distracted.

She showed him her own teeth in a sneer. 'Can't you even do *that*?' she asked.

Nian nearly threw something else at her, but instead he searched through the place with his mind. It would have been difficult if he'd been in their own world, but here all Nian had to do was look for something that didn't fit; something that came from another world, that mixed in with this world not at all, but had a rainbow sheen around it like oil on water.

And there, there it was. Almost at his feet.

Nian, cautiously, and without taking either his eyes or his mind off Pella for a moment, squatted down and lifted up the greasy pink silk of the bedcover.

And there, bound round and round like a fly in a spider's larder, was the skinny figure of Keer.

Keer's bonds were made of knotted strands of power, but it was the work of only a few seconds to cut them. The ropes had left no marks on Keer's skin, but his face was blue with the bone-chilling cold. Nian hauled Keer into a sitting position, and Keer sat dourly and failed to look even the slightest bit grateful.

145

Nian quelled his rising sense of panic. The owlmen were terrifying and deadly, but, even worse, if he and Keer were trapped in the magistra's world for more than a couple of days then the passageway the magistra had made would make both worlds tear themselves to pieces as they tried to turn.

'Took your time, didn't you,' said Keer, dusting himself off. 'And now you're here, you've fouled up.'

Nian considered thumping Keer, but then only swore. He'd thought when he'd come here that things couldn't get any worse, and here was a mess that made the problems of the House of Truth . . .

There was a *snick-snick-snick* sound from somewhere outside and Pella suddenly made a sound like a laying hen and threw herself down beside the great bed. She landed with an *oof* on top of the two boys.

'Eergh!'

Keer and Nian hastily shifted themselves away from her cold bulk, but before Nian could ask what the pits she thought she was doing, the second of the three windows was erupting into the room in a great fountain of glass and something—some *things*—were whizzing air-scorchingly through the space which had just contained Pella's head.

By the time Nian had realized what they were, they'd punched themselves with great *thunks* deep into the wall.

21

Nian and Keer and Pella swore—at least, Nian was pretty sure that Pella was swearing. In any case, the feeling behind the words was clear enough.

The feathers on the arrows were still quivering when a shrill cry of 'Pella! *PELLA!*' went up a little way away.

The magistra swore again, more quietly, but with just as much feeling.

'Pella! Pella, are you hurt? Those *wretched* men! Pella—oh, thank the worlds!'

Dorcis hurried into the room—but was stopped in her tracks by the sight of Keer.

'Not *another* boy,' she said, turning sharp eyes on the magistra. 'Wherever has *this* one come from?'

Pella scrambled to her feet, but made quite a palaver of doing it because one of her gold spiked heels got caught in the fringe of her dress.

'Never mind the boy,' she snapped, 'it's the arrows I'm worried about. What in the Mirelands does that idiot Branto think he's doing shooting through my window?'

Dorcis drew herself up, regaining her poise.

'Magistra, Branto has thirty men, all of them skilled in bowmanship and swordsmanship and every other foul art of the terminally stupid; and this shrine is being defended by a dozen or so of your shrine women, who are together about as dangerous as a three-legged hoglet with fang-rot. What do you *suppose* is to stop them shooting at your window?'

She cast a cold glance into the large mirror that sat on a chest of drawers by the wall.

'Yes, they're down at the river,' she said, with a certain melancholy satisfaction. 'Ah yes, there's Branto himself, the great oaf, jumping up and down and hallooing like a madman. Calling them off, of course.'

Pella made an odd growling noise.

'Why does Branto have to be such a total moron!' she demanded. 'That's the worst thing about him. Apart from all the killing and pillaging.'

Nian sat up. If the shrine were under attack, then things were far more serious than even Pella and Dorcis realized. Much worse than Pella being killed—much *much* worse—one of those arrows might have killed *him*, and unless he and Keer got home then the whole of both these worlds would be pulled to pieces.

Those arrows had missed him by—how much? Perhaps five spans.

Five spans—a couple of degrees in the aim of those archers, or a breath of breeze—and the House, this shrine . . . home . . . it'd all be gone.

Nian had a horrible vision of the earth opening, of the roof timbers of his father's hall being wrenched apart. Of them falling. Falling on Miri his sister. Trapping her. Almost, he heard her screams.

(Snorer had screamed, too, when he and Derig . . .)

Nian shook all that away.

'What does Branto want?' he demanded.

Dorcis gave him a swift, curious look.

'Wherever have you come from, not to know that?' she asked, but Pella cut in.

'What do you *think* Branto wants?' she demanded. 'He's after the greatest prize there is. The most valuable, the most wonderful thing in the whole world.'

Keer suddenly started taking an interest. He poked his head out from under the bed, where he'd been since the arrival of the arrows.

'Valuable?' he echoed. 'What have you got that's so valuable?'

Nian had thought he'd given up on being surprised, but Keer's words shocked him.

'Hey, you can speak her language!' he exclaimed.

'Of course I can speak her language,' snapped Keer. 'How do you think I've managed to survive in the city since I was a baby if I couldn't do languages? What's this great prize that's so valuable, magistra?'

Pella gave Keer a look as if he'd asked something more than usually stupid.

'Valuable?' she echoed. 'Why, me, of course.'

22

Into the silence that followed Pella's words came a new sound. It started off as a faint thrumming sort of noise, but it got louder very quickly and turned into a whistling groan. Nian had no idea what it might be, but for the time being he'd pretty much given up on pleasant surprises. He threw himself back down beside the bed.

There was a floor-shuddering crash from somewhere, and then an awful waiting pause, and then a whole series of crashes and bangs and judderings. Nian felt the floor wince beneath him at every one.

Keer was muttering a long string of rude words, but here was another whistling groan that seemed to be heading straight for . . .

RrrrrrRRRRRRCHHH—UNKKKKK!

. . . that one had landed even nearer, and the first one had been too close. *Much* too close.

And, oh pits, there was an even more terrible sound—a terrible tearing noise like a cragcrow's cry.

'Magistra!' muttered Dorcis, crouched by the wall with her grey scarf pulled round her face. '*Magistra! Do* something!'

'Yes, yes, all *right*,' said Pella. She raised herself up onto her elbow and clenched a large fist. There was a straining mauve-faced pause, and then there was another large explosion, but this time somewhere quite a long way down beyond the shattered windows.

There was a pause that was filled only with echoes . . . and then, far away, bellowing.

In the shrine itself, the dust twirled down on a deep, shocked, freezing quiet.

Pella snatched up various bits of skirt and lurched clumsily to her feet.

'There,' she said, viciously. 'I've blown up their catapult.'

'And several of their men, by the sound of it,' said Dorcis, even paler than before.

Pella shrugged.

'Serves them right,' she said.

Nian got up, too. He was feeling extremely fragile, as though he might be blown to pieces at any moment.

And it was a matter of incredible importance that he was not blown to pieces.

'If I am blown up, so will this world be,' he said warningly.

'What's left of it,' said Dorcis, and even she sounded shaken. 'We'd best find out what's happened, Pella. It sounded as if someone's been hurt.'

Keer was still swearing and muttering to himself under the bed. Well, Keer would be as safe there as anywhere.

Nian slipped out into the corridor after Pella. He wasn't letting the magistra out of his sight.

The shrine of the magistra was marrow-freezingly cold, and the whole place was dim and yet gleaming, as if it was under water. Nian quietly followed along behind the reflections of Dorcis and the magistra that swam along the dove-grey marble. Everywhere there were signs of attack: some of the great polished columns had been cracked right through, so that the tops were wedged precariously a good span out of true.

The shrine proved to be a long building of wide corridors and large windows through which could be seen a horizon of grey heathy hills. Closer, there were ice-scummed streams which trickled towards the sinewy trail of lake, and over on the hillside was a group of grubby tents round which some small black figures swarmed like beetles round a corpse.

The magistra clacked purposefully along the corridor in her fancy pink dress (Why wasn't she blue with cold? Because Nian was freezing.) and then, muttering crossly all the time, she strode through a small courtyard with an ice-bulgy fountain, and up a flight of steps.

The shrine was less grand here. The marble was unpolished, and the ceiling was no longer painted with silver snowflakes. Nian began to worry that he might lose the magistra in the gloom of the windowless corridor, but then there was an unexpected slash of milky light ahead, and soon he was wheezing in a blizzard of stone dust from the ruined roof.

The magistra came to a halt, hands on her hips. Nian couldn't see her expression, but the aggressive jut of her head told him everything he needed to know. There was an alarmed squeak, and a mad rat-like scuttling, and three hummocks came into view through the gradually settling dust. They might have been bundles of cloth, except that they had hair.

'Oh, magistra,' they were saying, with their noses in the dust. 'Oh, the honour of your presence, O light of the worlds!'

The magistra wasted no time being nice to them. 'Who was injured?' she demanded.

One of the bundles raised its head a little, almost pleadingly. It belonged to a thin, timid-looking little woman with wispy white hair.

'One of your shrine-maidens, magistra,' she said, apologetically. 'She is nearly gone. We have laid her aside, and shall put her in the vaults as soon as her spirit has left her.'

'But where is she?' asked Dorcis, still surprisingly shaken.

The three bundles shifted a little, and another one raised its head, revealing itself to be a stocky woman with apprehensive eyes.

'At peace,' she said, bravely. 'She would not wish the magistra to tire herself with a cure.'

But the magistra's shoulders rose in a menacing hunch.

'*Where is she?*'

All three bundles undid themselves and stumbled to their feet. They pulled their grey robes tightly round themselves and scurried ahead of the magistra to an open doorway.

153

Two of the women hurried to turn themselves back into bundles by the wall; the third went and stood beside a bed that was placed under the window.

There was a figure on the bed.

The memory of Derig swooped down at Nian and hit him hard. But this was a woman, of course. She was alive, but her chest had been crushed.

Dorcis's breathing had gone short. She turned searchingly towards the magistra.

'I shall cure her,' announced the magistra, almost defiantly.

An expression of horror passed over the face of the woman beside the bed.

'She is in the arms of death, O magistra,' she began, with a sort of meek desperation, but the magistra ignored her. She went to the figure on the bed and Dorcis came to stand close by her side.

Nian, with his powers focused on the injured woman, had only a split second's warning as to what was coming: it was such a shock that he nearly screamed.

The magistra had a knife.

It wasn't made of metal, or even of stone—in fact, like the owlmen, some of the time it was hardly there at all—but it was sharp, and it cut deep. It sliced easily through the bruised skin.

The woman twitched as the knife entered her, and the magistra muttered as the blade skidded off a sliver of broken bone.

Dorcis was suddenly as white as the ice that edged the pool outside the window.

'Magistra,' she said, quite sharply. 'Magistra, not that way! Pella!'

And the woman standing beside them let out a heart-breaking sound, a sort of wailing moan.

Nian rallied his wits. The magistra was cutting into the injured woman's chest, and there was blood pulsing out everywhere. Nian grabbed at his powers and slid them alongside the magistra's. He'd never done anything like this before, and it was the trickiest thing: he had to slip along the magistra's shining invisible knife and pour strength into the woman so she could heal the gashes the magistra had made.

The magistra took no notice of him—perhaps she didn't even know he was doing anything—but when she stood back at last her hand was shaking a little.

'There,' she said, still defiant. 'She is whole. If she has enough life left in her then she will soon be strong.'

Nian checked this. Yes, the magistra had joined the woman's bones again, but the woman would certainly have bled to death during the healing if it hadn't been for Nian's help.

The magistra turned away, and Dorcis, ghost-faced, went with her. Nian took a grip on himself. Pella hadn't had a clue what she'd been supposed to be doing: practically all her patients must have died if that was the way she tried to heal them.

The magistra paused in the doorway.

'Have that mess in the corridor cleared up,' she said, and walked away fast.

Nian stayed behind for a moment.

'She will soon be strong,' he blurted out.

The women hardly heard him, let alone believed what he said.

'She will,' said Nian, again, earnestly. 'I am . . . I am like the magistra.'

And then Nian realized what he'd said, and he cursed. He was *not* like the magistra. Not like her at all.

'She is not now so near death,' he went on. 'Be here with her.'

He did not know the words for what he wanted to say next, so he said it in his own language, and hoped his meaning would somehow get through. 'I promise she will get better,' he said. 'I promise.'

And then, being able to do no more, he went away.

Nian caught up with the striding figure of the magistra as she stalked through the frozen air of a large hall. It was easily the grandest place he had ever seen, with twin rows of marble giants holding up the roof, and aisles paved with glittering hexagonal crystals like diamonds.

The grey-clad shrine women who lurked in the shadows stopped their whispering and knelt as the magistra passed them, touching their foreheads to the floor; stranger still, the great white lilies that shone like ice-trumpets around the marble giants' feet turned in their vases and opened mouths of hawk-gape yellow, as if to send blessings to her.

The magistra seemed hardly to notice them.

And Nian, the Truth Sayer, who had never seen anything like that happen anywhere before (thank all the worlds, because Hani and Emmec would never ever *ever* have let him live it down if it had) ran his powers over those lilies in utter amazement.

And discovered that the women were working the flowers with strings.

23

Pella was lying on her bed kicking off her stupid shoes when Nian entered her room, and Dorcis, cold and pale as a column of ice, was watching her grimly.

'You have done that poor woman no good,' she announced.

'Oh be quiet!' snapped Pella. 'And just go away, will you?'

Dorcis's eyes gleamed coldly, like the marble that surrounded her.

'Pella—'

The magistra raised herself on one elbow and shot Dorcis a look that crystallized the air between them.

'I said, go away,' she said again. She spoke quietly, but Dorcis put back her head as if Pella had slapped her.

Dorcis shut her mouth, and bowed her fine grey head, and hastened out.

The best thing, the most *satisfying* thing that Nian could think of to do was to hit Pella over the head hard and repeatedly until she undid the lock on the passageway and called off the owlmen. But there was the slight problem that Pella, though not clever, was bogging powerful. Nian might have tried it if only his own life had been at stake, but he couldn't risk his whole world. Nor, actually, this one.

Nian went cautiously to the one remaining window and looked out over the bustling purple grass. Up by the tents there was a group of men: scruffy, run-to-seed types that would have disgraced the Tarhun. Not much of an army—but perhaps if Nian made some sort of an alliance with them, and Keer, (if he fought at all), fought with Nian . . .

He turned back to the magistra.

'Why does Branto want you?' he asked, honestly curious.

She snarled at him.

'He wants to marry me so he can breed children with powers,' she said. 'It would give him power over all the Mirelands, if it worked. It won't, of course, because the magistra's power is handed down from hand to hand, but the great dunderhead's too stupid to understand. He's got a lawyer all ready to marry us.'

Nian put aside his disbelief at Branto's foolhardiness and tried to see the situation from Pella's point of view. It was difficult, because the only girl he'd ever really known well was his sister Miri, who was rather gentle and nervous and sane.

'But . . . don't you *want* to marry?' he asked.

'Not *Branto*,' spat Pella, with scorn.

Nian thought some more.

'Well, you could kill him when he comes,' he pointed out, trying to look on the bright side. 'And then you couldn't.'

159

Pella rolled her eyes.

'That would be worse, fool. Then I'd have to marry one of the others, because, if the shrine's destroyed, then I'll need somewhere to live. At least Branto is a gross idiotic moronic thug with an *army*.'

'Yes,' said Nian. 'An army is always useful. And think how good it would be to have loads of . . . loads of little ones,' said Nian, trying not to remember what a complete roof-climbing snake-charming nuisance he'd been himself when young. 'And a marrying,' he went on, persevering doggedly. 'Think how good that would be.'

Pella actually stopped to consider that.

'I suppose if I was married already, then Branto couldn't marry me,' she said, slowly. 'And there's the dress, of course.'

'That's right,' agreed Nian, with all the enthusiasm he could rake up. 'And you could choose *anybody* to marry, couldn't you, you being the magistra and all that. I mean, it'd be an honour for them.'

But Pella only snorted.

'Huh! When I live in here? You must be joking. I suppose it'd have to be the carpet-cleaning man, then, the poor trembling fool.'

'Sometimes a trembling fool is thought good for marrying,' Nian pointed out, helpfully.

'Not that one,' sighed Pella. 'I have to hide whenever he comes, for fear he'll take one look at my glorious countenance and drop dead with excitement. Still,' she went on, 'you may have a point. After all, I'm not certain that your world will suit me. It might be full of bandits or fire or magister-hunters. That's why I was careful to send the owlmen, to make sure everyone for a long way round was dead before I got there.'

'Oh, no, it wouldn't suit you,' Nian assured her. 'Not at all. My shrine is not like this. It has nothing. You would not like it at all.'

Pella sat up on the bed. She turned her blue eyes on him and inspected him closely from top to toe.

'Yes,' she said, as if she had reached a decision. 'I think you're right. I think this is going to be the best I can do. What's your name?'

'Er . . . Nian,' he admitted, but with an awful feeling that he'd given her something terribly important and very very dangerous.

She regarded him some more, rather distastefully, but then nodded, as if she'd come to a decision.

'Very well, then, Nian,' she said, and Nian could not help but flinch as her tongue curled round his name. 'Then I shall marry someone else. Yes,' she went on, with a determined flash of her bright blue eyes. 'Yes. I shall marry *you*.'

24

From beneath the magistra's bed, where he lay wrapped in a pink blanket, Keer let out a wild snigger; but Nian was too rooted to the spot with absolute horror even to consider kicking him. He stood there, in such a state of complete dismay that he couldn't even speak, let alone think of anything to save himself.

Pella didn't look all that happy, either. Her face was screwed up as if she'd been eating wince fruit.

'I suppose that at least there'll be no trouble finding bridesmaids,' she muttered.

Nian tried to rally his wits, but they wouldn't stop jumping up and down and screaming shrilly.

'I'll have to send away that woman I cured, though,' went on Pella. 'It'll be a bad omen if she dies before the ceremony.'

One of Nian's wits caught that as it flew past and seized onto it with all its might.

'Yes, I am bad omen,' he said. 'Bad to marry,' he went on, putting up his hands as if to wring the words from the air. 'And if I am here for long the worlds will fall to bits.'

'No they won't. My owlmen have been in your

world for days and nothing's happened to the worlds, has it?'

Nian stared at her in astonishment. That was true. There were at least a hundred owlmen in the House— a hundred, a *hundred*—and there had been no tremors or sign of the worlds being under strain at all.

A voice piped up gloatingly from under the bed: '*She's got you there, hasn't she?*' it said.

Nian, harassed, cast around for another argument.

'But you do not like me,' he said. 'And I am . . . an oaf,' he went on, this being the nearest word he had to *someone who is nauseated by the sight of pink, spends a lot of time thinking about pockle, and just wants to mess about with his friends while he works out what he's really supposed to be doing with his life.*

'Of *course* I don't like you,' snapped Pella, 'but there *is* only you.'

'Then . . . ' Nian cast his mind about wildly for some solution, but his mental faculties were flapping and panicking like a landed flopfish. 'Why don't you go to see Branto?' he asked. 'You could tell him you do not like him. And that you like knives very much. He will not want to marry you, then.'

Pella rolled her eyes again.

'But of course he would!' she snapped. 'If he actually *saw* me, then obviously he'd be overwhelmed by my beauty and fall so desperately in love with me that he wouldn't even care about being sliced to pieces on his wedding night.'

Nian found himself so paralysed with appalled dread at the mere mention of a wedding night that he found himself searching hopefully for a vibrating under his feet that would mark the beginning of the end of both their worlds. But there was nothing. (And why, why, *why* was there nothing? Some of the owl-men had been in the wrong world for days. What if the magistra was right, and there was nothing to stop him and Keer staying here for ever?)

A thought struck him, and in his panic he'd spoken it aloud before he'd thought about it—though actually, he was in such a panic that he might well have said it anyway.

'Keer is not so little as me,' he said. 'And he is not so much of a moron.'

There was a snarling whine from under the bed, and a tousled head poked out from beneath the satin cover to glare at him.

'You treacherous grotting cowardly . . . ' Keer began, but cowardice had never seemed so sweetly reasonable to Nian as at that moment.

'And Keer's not so much of a fool,' Nian pointed out. Pella seemed to consider.

'You may be right,' she admitted. 'Keer may be better for me. He has fewer powers than you. You might cause trouble.'

'Oh, I would,' said Nian, fervently. 'Lots and lots of trouble. I always do. Much, much more trouble than I'm good. Really, you'd not like it, magistra. I'm thinking of you.'

'Now, stop there!' said Keer, and a thin arm and leg came spider-like into view under the slippery pink flounces of the bed and out into the freezing air. 'You wouldn't like me,' Keer assured Pella. 'No one likes me. I'm terrible. Even more wretched than him. I'm the most unlikeable boy you've ever come across.'

Nian suppressed a strong urge to tell them that in that case they were made for each other.

'You're not so plaguey,' he said to Keer. 'You're . . . practical. Not like me. I was brought up soft. I'd be really annoying. All clingy.'

'Yeah,' said Keer, 'but you're posh, aren't you. Women like that.'

'I'm not posh!' retorted Nian, stung by the injustice of this. 'I'm just a farm boy, that's all. From the valleys. I've never even seen a great place. I'm just a simple yokel, that's me.'

'And I'm a *beggar*,' whined Keer. '*And* a thief and a liar and a pickpocket. Oh yes, and a coward. Completely untrustworthy, *and* proud of it. Why, I'd sell my best friend for a bit of bread, I would. And, what's more,' he ended up triumphantly, 'I've done it!'

'But . . . but you've *had* to be like that,' said Nian, unable to prevent himself sounding slightly desperate. 'I'm sure you could be like a gentleman if you tried.'

'Not with my face in this mess,' said Keer, crawling out completely from under the bed so he could show Pella, who recoiled.

And, indeed, his skin was actually bubbling like a cauldron with pus-filled spots as he spoke.

'But they're not real,' put in Nian, swiftly. 'They're just because he feels unworthy. He's overwhelmed by you, magistra.'

Keer scrambled to his feet, his teeth showing fiercely in his thin face.

'All right, then,' he said. 'But how about *this*?'

He tugged his undershirt up out of his leggings to reveal his bony ribcage and long-starved stomach.

And Nian saw, with fascinated revulsion, that there was a large bloodshot eyeball staring out from Keer's belly button.

Nian stared back at it, frozen with appalled, rapt, incredulous wonder and disgust.

And then the eye swivelled round towards Pella, and it winked.

Pella screamed.

25

Nian, his mind galloping in empty circles, had been pacing backwards and forwards for some time across the horrible little room Dorcis called her scullery. It was desperately necessary that he did something to sort out this whole terrible mess, but he had not the faintest idea where he could start. A couple of rooms away, in her bed chamber, Pella was giving orders for her wedding dress (a green dress, which made sense, as green was the colour of mourning as far as Nian was concerned). The thought of the wedding was terrible, but the thought of what the owlmen would do in the House made him want to scream and tear out his hair and explode things.

Tarq, Gow, even Snorer . . . Nian's mind winced away from the black night when Snorer would fight hopelessly against a jagged army of razor shapes that slashed and killed and had no hearts.

Soon. The magistra had said the owlmen were all going to come to life soon. When was *soon*, for grot's sake?

Nian was still pacing when Dorcis came in bearing a plate of something which looked to Nian's fevered eyes as if it had been produced by the back end of a unicorn.

'The magistra ordered me to organize the wedding feast, but I thought I'd better bring you something, first,' she said, placing the stuff on a table and beginning to slice it up.

Nian, who hadn't had anything to eat for ages, did a hasty search of the stuff—and found to his relief that it was actually made from pond-weed roots.

'At least, I suppose you *do* eat,' Dorcis went on, offering the plate to Nian and Keer. 'Be careful, it's very hot.'

'All people eat,' said Keer, grabbing a piece, juggling it to stop it burning his fingers, and then sniffing at it suspiciously.

'Oh yes, all *people* eat,' Dorcis agreed. 'But I wasn't sure you were actually people. After all, nobody's ever heard of such a thing as a boy with powers, let alone one with an eyeball in his navel.'

Dorcis had arrived so quickly in response to Pella's scream that Nian was sure she could have been no further away than the other side of the door. Nian swiftly snatched up a piece of the weedbread—and found that it was stone-cold.

Keer glared at her.

'At least an extra eyeball's harmless,' he said. 'Not like a load of homicidal knife-edged owlmen.'

Nian found himself on the end of a stare that was even icier than the weedbread.

'Owlmen?' Dorcis asked.

Explaining about the owlmen took some dogged and inventive sign-language. By the time they'd finished,

Dorcis was pacing backwards and forwards herself, her face creamy with rage.

'But the magistra can't leave the world!' she exclaimed. 'The Mirelands need her. Well, they need her power, in any case. The lands are dying, as it is.'

'She's a moron,' said Keer, through a mouthful of weedbread.

Dorcis hesitated just a little.

'Pella acquired her powers when she was hardly more than a toddler, and she sees no need either to develop her powers, or to use them to help other people. And so the Mirelands have been left entirely at the mercy of bandits like Branto. No one's safe any more. Farms are sacked, crops are burned, and Pella, quite frankly, neither knows nor cares.'

Look, Nian wanted to say. *How old do you think I am?*

'I've tried to explain to her that at this rate the whole place will soon be starving,' Dorcis went on, 'but Pella only really believes what's right in front of her nose.'

'That, and slicing people up,' said Keer, to be fair.

But Dorcis shook her head.

'Her getting the powers of the magistra was a dreadful accident. If they'd come to me, as they should have done, I'd soon have sorted Branto out. But giving Pella her powers was like giving her a tiger, and, exasperating and ill-tempered as she is, I have to admit that it's not entirely surprising the way things have turned out.'

'Well, Nian's just what she needs, then,' said Keer. 'He's really sensible, Nian is. Reliable. Trustworthy.'

Nian went to snarl something in reply to these foul insults—but here, through his mind, unbidden, was another glimpse of something that might be the future . . . the House, in darkness, with the silver of the moon lying lightly along the floors, hummocking over dark things that lay in the corridor, the council chamber, the sleeping room . . . and above them the owlmen with mindless, venomous eyes.

The last light of the day was making Dorcis's powerful arms glow like marble.

'Whatever happens, the Mirelands need the magistra's power to stay here,' she said firmly. 'If Pella had any sense at all she'd pass on her powers to someone else. Someone too old to bear children, and so of no interest to Branto. She could even choose someone trained up to be magistra.'

'Yeah, yeah,' muttered Keer. 'And guess who that would be, then. Grot, Nian, this one's even sneakier than the bogging magistra. Still,' he went on, grudgingly, 'you came up with a neat frame-up, I'll give you that.'

Nian looked at Dorcis, startled.

'You mean . . . '

'Obvious, isn't it?' said Keer. 'Come on, even *you* can't be as innocent as that, farm boy. Dorcis persuaded Branto to attack the shrine. The idea was that Pella would panic and give her powers to Dorcis.'

Dorcis stood taller than ever.

'It would have saved a lot of suffering. And I wasn't to know that Pella would be cunning and unprincipled enough to take herself off to another world. Her powers really are most peculiar and unpredictable.'

Nian started pacing again, even though it wasn't helping.

'Well, I'll tell you what *I'm* going to do,' said Keer. 'All that end-of-the-world stuff isn't showing any signs of happening, so I'm going to eat as much as I can, then thieve as much as I can lay my hands on. Most of the magistra's stuff is rubbish, but she's got a few good bits. Then I'm going to wait till it's properly dark, climb out of one of the windows, and run away.'

Nian found himself clutching madly at his hair. 'But what about the owlmen?' he asked.

Keer shrugged.

'I'm going to forget about them,' he replied. 'They won't be bothering me. You should do the same. You can pretend the owlmen all got killed by the Lords, if it makes you feel better.'

Nian opened his mouth; then all his agitation collapsed in a great sigh.

'You are a total piece of . . . of *grot,* aren't you,' he said, helplessly, and not knowing that particular insult in Mirelandic.

Keer considered.

'But I'd have been dead long ago if I'd been all honest, wouldn't I?' he said, unoffended. 'I mean, you said yourself nobody could expect me to starve if I could thieve stuff to eat. And if the constables are looking for a skinny boy, then of course I'm going to fake myself up like a fat girl, or an old woman, or a dog, if I can.'

'A dog?' echoed Nian, his curiosity caught despite the awfulness of everything.

'Yeah,' said Keer, a look almost of fondness coming over his thin face. 'A big dog, of course. You can get food quite easily if you're a dog. You rub your belly in the dust and smile.'

Nian looked at Keer, and then looked again: Keer's ears had moved up to the top of his head, and they were all pointed and hairy, with the tips folded down like those of the most endearing mongrel.

Nian, stupidly, found himself wanting to give Keer the rest of his weedbread; even Dorcis looked almost human for a moment.

And then Nian felt the faint *chink* of something falling into place in his brain.

'See?' said Keer, smugly, as his ears sank back down round his head and grew bald, pink, and rounded again. 'Works every time. People are bogging idiots,' he finished up, with thoughtful satisfaction.

But suddenly Nian's heart was pounding with excitement. Yes! Yes, of course. That was it. That was it, that was it, that was *it*!

Keer scowled at him.

'What are you looking so pleased about?' he demanded.

Nian ran through his idea again. It might work— and that was better than he'd hoped for, a plan that *might* work.

He took a deep breath and called up all his powers of persuasion.

26

'You must be bogging joking,' said Keer, incredulous-
ly. 'I'm not doing that! It's too risky. I wouldn't be able
to stay like it for more than a couple of hours, and we
might get stuck there. Then what'd happen?'

Nian shrugged, almost light-heartedly. Having a
plan, even a hoppit-brained one like this, had suddenly made him feel much less despairing about
everything.

'I expect you'd turn into a fly and abandon me to
my fate,' he said.

Keer nodded.

'Not a fly, though,' he said. 'A tiger. I'd be able to
get the pits out of there quicker. *And* bite people. If I
didn't freeze to death in the bogging cold. But I'm still
not doing it. Why should I?'

Just for a moment Nian considered talking seriously
to Keer about Saving The Worlds. And decided not to
bother.

'Money?' he asked.

Keer gave Nian a sharp look.

'I thought you Lords were too unworldly to know
about money. All right, let's see. Risking my life to save

the world,' he went on, thoughtfully. 'Two worlds. You wouldn't *expect* that to come cheap. Let's say a hundred thousand.'

'*A hundred thousand?*'

A hundred thousand was the profit from Nian's father's farm for about two hundred years.

Dorcis shook her head.

'That's plainly extortionate,' she said. 'Anyway, there's no need. All you have to do is fight the magistra. It would solve everyone's problems. You defeat her and then transfer her powers to me, and I'll open the passageway for you to go home.'

'Yeah, *if* he defeated her,' said Keer, scornfully. 'Yeah, have a go, Nian, if you fancy your chances. You never know, you *might* survive. Anyway, a hundred thousand's my offer: take it or leave it.'

'But you'd be in debt for the rest of your life,' warned Dorcis. 'And approaching Branto's camp will be dangerous. Pella sent out a flag of truce yesterday and attacked Branto's men when they went to meet it. They'll be suspicious, and quick to fire.'

'That's no problem to me,' said Keer, swiftly. 'I can turn myself into a puddle or something. And Nian can duck a few arrows.'

'A few arrows, yes,' said Dorcis, 'but not a whole camp of bandits.'

'Has to be less of a risk than the bogging magistra,' pointed out Keer. 'Well, what about it, Truth Sayer? What's more valuable? Money, or the worlds?'

'But I haven't got a hundred bogging thousand!' protested Nian.

'If you beat Pella, I give my word I will open the passageway for you. You can't trust Pella to let you return, even if you got rid of Branto. Not even if she has promised. And think of the fate of the Mirelands.'

'Oh, yeah, and you're *really* trustworthy, aren't you,' said Keer, dismissively. 'We know you're a traitor. I'll tell you what, Nian, I'll do it cut-price. I'll accept fifty. Fifty *thousand*,' he added, quickly. 'And that's my last and final offer. Cheap, when you think what's at stake,' he finished up, reasonably.

Nian personally hadn't got any money at all: even the clothes he stood up in were technically the property of the House. Fifty thousand? It was so ridiculous that he suddenly laughed.

'Done,' he said. 'I'll do what I can to find it once we're home, all right?'

'I'll see you dead if you don't,' said Keer, but without rancour, as if this were the normal formula for sealing a bargain where he came from.

'It will do you no good unless Pella agrees to open the passageway for you,' pointed out Dorcis, grimly.

But there wasn't time to worry about that.

'Well,' said Nian. 'Let's see what she says, shall we?'

Pella's room was strewn with lengths of cloth, and Pella herself was sitting in the middle of the bed holding them up against each other and bouncing with excitement.

She turned a rosy, eager face towards Nian as Dorcis, looking like a ghost with indigestion, followed him in and Keer slid along to find himself a place in the shadows.

'Look,' said Pella. 'How about this for my wedding dress? You can sew, can't you?'

'A bit,' admitted Nian, guardedly.

She beamed a large white expanse of teeth at him.

'Good. It is the bridegroom's duty to sew the bride's gown,' she explained. 'But it's all right, Dorcis can lend you a thimble.'

Nian gulped down the screaming abdabs raised by the mention of the word *bridegroom*.

'I've thought of a way to get rid of Branto,' he announced, as firmly as he could.

Pella froze with a river of glossy emerald cascading down her front.

'Without you having to bother about all these . . . arrangements,' went on Nian, feeling guilty for some ridiculous reason.

Her eyes scanned his face suspiciously.

'But . . . there is no need to get rid of Branto now,' she said. 'Anyway, the entrails have been foretelling the arrival of a good stranger for months. I thought it was just going to be the carpet-cleaning man, as usual, but you see it was really you! Why, even the woman I cured hasn't died yet. It's as if she's waiting until after the ceremony so as to give us a good start.'

She giggled a little, and her round, eager face became even rosier.

'But I've thought of a way to solve all our problems,' ploughed on Nian, grimly, ignoring Dorcis's sub-zero glare, 'so you'll be able to stay peacefully here in the shrine. And then you'll just have to undo the gate on the passageway and call the owlmen back, and then everything will be all right again for everybody.'

Pella stopped smiling.

'But that is not what I want!' she said, indignantly. 'And you were sent.'

'Well, I expect I was sent to get rid of Branto for you,' said Nian, with a desperate lunge of invention. 'I mean, you don't *like* me, do you. I'm not worthy. I'm too young. And not beautiful. And small. And stupid. And I might get more powers as I get older and be a bother. In fact, I think I would—you wouldn't believe how much trouble I've caused back in my own shrine. I'm just not adequate.'

Pella threw the green fabric down crossly.

'But no one else is, either!' she cried. 'That's the whole point. It's true you're small and young, but a wedding would be such fun. Anyway, I've been clever enough to suck you here from beyond the ends of the earth—and a magister, too, which can't *possibly* be a coincidence—and so it must be fated. I'm sure it is fated. Don't you feel fated?'

'Oh yes,' said Nian, fervently. 'No one could be feeling more fated than I do at the moment. But the really important thing is to keep you safe. And if Branto finds out you're married he'll probably destroy the whole shrine, with us in it, in a desolate fury.'

Pella snorted.

'You don't know Branto,' she said. 'He's not seen me since I was tiny. He'll have all the love-pangs of a frozen moose.'

'All right,' said Nian, desperately, 'then perhaps he'll descend on the shrine with his cohorts and pull my head off. Then he could marry you anyway, couldn't he?'

Pella sniffed.

'We could fight him off,' she declared, defiantly. 'Probably. Between the three of us.'

Nian called to mind the appalling prospect of fighting a battle with the magistra and Keer as allies. With friends like that . . .

'Oh, but you can't count on Keer,' said Nian. 'He's totally untrustworthy.'

'And a coward,' put in Keer, helpfully.

'That's right,' said Nian. 'Keer would most likely fight on Branto's side. Or on both sides, alternately, just to cause the most damage to everyone. He's like that.'

Pella looked irritated and baffled.

'But how can you get Branto to go away?' she demanded.

Nian turned to Keer.

'Show her,' he said.

Nothing moved, and yet things changed. It was most strange and mysterious, like a storm cloud ruffling a shadow across a mountainside. Pella stared at Keer, and then she gasped.

For Keer had turned into a mirror. That was how Nian saw it at first. But when Pella moved a trembling hand up to her face, the black-haired girl in the shadow of the wall kept her hand by her side. And grinned.

Pella recoiled so violently she overbalanced and

ended up bashing her head against the carved ribbons on the wooden end of her bed.

'*I do not look like that!*' she screeched.

And Nian, looking from one figure to the other, had to admit that she was right. The actual face was the same: Keer had the right round rosy face and slightly over-sized clumsiness and crinkly black hair; he'd even managed to reproduce the magistra's clothes somehow. But there was something deeply, horribly *unwhole-some* about Keer's version of the magistra. Something that made Nian think of nameless pale creatures that dragged themselves through the blackest pits . . .

He blinked, really quite shaken.

'Eeeergh!' shrieked Pella. 'He's making me think of giant slime-maggots! Stop him!'

'Errr . . . I think she's got the idea,' said Nian, weakly, and in the blink of an eye there was Keer again, still grinning.

The magistra threw herself forward onto her knees.

'How dare you?' she bellowed, picked up one of the dead animals that lay about on the bed, and chucked it at Keer's head.

It flew through the air with a howl like a gibbon and when Nian checked there was a pastry-cutter hole chomped out of the marble of the wall in the place where Keer's head had been. Nian gasped—and then saw that Keer was squatting safely on the floor looking vindictive.

'This isn't worth it, even for fifty thousand,' he muttered. 'Even if I thought I'd actually get it. That girl's a nutter.'

Keer had spoken in their own language, luckily.

'Keer wasn't trying to make himself look like you,' Nian explained to Pella, hastily, one hand up ready to shield himself from whatever she might throw next. 'He will go and see Branto—'

'—not without you, I'm not,' growled Keer, watching Pella like a hawk.

'—we will both go and see Branto,' Nian corrected himself. 'And Branto will see how beautiful you are— he'll have heard great tales about that—but at the same time he will be filled with horror and dread and pictures of giant maggots. And so then he will go away and make a nuisance of himself somewhere else, and you will be free of him.'

Pella hissed at him.

'But he will tell people horrible things about me,' she spat.

'I expect he will,' put in Dorcis, drily. 'News like that will go round the Mirelands like a springer with its tail on fire.'

'Why don't you just kill him?' demanded Pella.

'Couldn't you?' asked Nian, irritated again. 'Couldn't you throw a dead hoppit at him and bite off his face, like you just tried to do to Keer?'

'Of course I could! And I would, too, if he'd come by himself like a proper suitor. But I couldn't take them all out at once. Though, if the worst came to the worst, I'd be happy to try,' she finished up, viciously.

Then Keer spoke up:

'I can make sure people see you looking beautiful,' he offered. 'I can save the maggots for Branto.'

Pella sniffed. 'You can do that?'

'Oh yes.'

Pella paused. And then she sat back on her heels and seemed to be considering.

'It'd be dangerous,' said Dorcis. 'They're likely to be killed approaching the camp.'

Pella nodded.

'But I suppose I've got nothing to lose,' she said, at last.

Nian clenched his fists by his sides in triumph.

'We'll be back as soon as we can,' he told her, heading for the door.

Pella sniffed again.

'Nian!' she said, as he was reaching for the door knob. He looked back and saw Dorcis's face, white with anger.

'Don't be too long,' said Pella, thoughtfully. 'You've only got six hours before my owlmen attack.'

27

The night had closed down over the hills, and the painful damp chill of the evening had changed to a blood-freezing raw cold.

Keer shivered.

'What a place,' he muttered. 'Who would choose to live here? Even the hills are moaning.'

They were, too: the wicked wind was setting up a mournful vibration in the air as it skirled along the ground. Even the coarse grass was being shuddered to a plaintive rustling.

They could see lights down by the lake—the yellow swaying smudge of a lantern, or the softer glow through a tent, or a fractured reflection in the ridgy water. Occasionally a light would wink out for a moment as someone walked in front of it.

'Well,' said Keer, 'you're more at home in this bogging wilderness than me. What do we do, farm boy? Apart from turn ourselves into lizards?'

Nian felt an alarming glow of warmth from Keer's direction as Keer started to use his powers, so he hastily conjured up a rope of power and looped one end of it round Keer's neck.

It jerked at Keer's throat, and Keer had to make a huge flaring effort to turn the lizarding process round.

They stood in the dark and glared at each other. They were both panting with effort.

'You could have strangled me, you bogging maniac!' hissed Keer. 'Take this grotting thing off!'

'And trust you?' asked Nian, grimly. Keer swore at him, long and cleverly.

'Think of the money,' said Nian, and started walking down towards the lights of Branto's camp.

Keer had no choice at all but to go with him.

They were lucky in several ways: the mossy green of their uniforms blended in well with the grass of the hills; the night was dark; and the wind made enough noise to cover the noise of Keer falling over, which he did on three occasions. Nian had to make the power-rope that joined them stretchy after the first time, because Keer had nearly broken his neck.

'Bogging cretin,' muttered Keer, rubbing at it bitterly.

'Don't use that sort of language when you're the magistra,' said Nian, lying beside him on the drenched and really dangerously cold grass and watching the lights of the camp wink on and off. 'Right. We're going to have to crawl for a bit until we're in that gully.'

'Let me be a dog,' whined Keer. 'I'd be surer-footed if I was a dog. And I'd have fur to keep me warm. And no one would shoot me.'

Nian considered this.

'What do you really look like?' he asked, suddenly.

Keer gave him a flicking, sideways glance.

'You're probably the only one who knows,' he said. 'You do, don't you? You can tell which bits are real. You knew I was a fake right from the start, didn't you, Truth Sayer. Truth *See*-er.'

Nian shook his head.

'It doesn't work like that. The truth . . . '

What was it like, he wondered, this Truth that people valued so highly?

And he found he knew that already: it was like oil on water, multi-coloured and fascinating and beautiful, but continually shifting—and always, always, always ungraspable, in the end.

'You'd best stay human,' he said, at last. 'We don't want them even to *think* about shape-changing. You'll just have to manage. Come on.'

The wet grass was coarse and sharp-edged. Nian's hands were numb with cold, but he was pretty sure the grass was cutting them as he crawled along.

They reached the gully and were able to raise their heads a little. They were near enough to hear voices, now—and then the roar of a laugh. Those men were likely to shoot anything coming from the direction of the shrine, so they'd best work their way round and approach along the course of the stream. Nian could see the line of it, gleaming just faintly greyer than the hillside.

He sighed. That would involve a half-mile crawl, which would take up another thirty minutes of their precious time. And his leggings were sticking chillingly to him as it was.

'This way,' he said.

They couldn't go fast, so Keer had breath to spare to keep up a constant whining and complaining.

'Let's run away,' he said. 'We can slip out over the hill at the back.'

Nian thought wistfully about various types of violence.

'We can't do that, because of the owlmen,' he said.

Keer shrugged.

'No skin off my nose,' he said. 'Come on, it'll be all right. Think what we could do between us. We'd be rich.'

'You mean I'd end up in the gutter with your knife between my ribs,' said Nian, darkly.

'But it's all right for you!' came the answer, in a nerve-jabbing whine. 'You're *used* to being out in the bogging freezing wilderness. You lot probably roll in the wet grass for fun.'

'Oh shut up,' said Nian.

He could hear the stream, now, rushing and gurgling. He started to crawl towards it and suddenly found himself up to his elbow in miserably cold water. He recoiled and swore. He should have known: the stream had spread itself into a morass just here, and they were going to have to crawl through it to approach Branto's camp. Nian, shivering, wondered if it was possible for him to be any wetter and colder than he already was. He reluctantly decided that it was, and, crouching, forced his numb fingers to undo the lacings of his shoes.

'When we get back,' muttered Keer, bitterly, 'and

even if we bogging don't, I'm going straight back to begging, I am.'

'And thieving,' said Nian, tying his laces together so he could hang his shoes round his neck.

Keer grunted.

'Oh, I've always thieved,' he said, with a touch of fond pride. 'Right from when I could walk. *Before* I could walk. I had a scam with this woman. I used to pretend to be lost, and then pick people's pockets while they took care of me. That was a good scam, while it lasted.'

'What happened?' asked Nian.

Keer shrugged.

'One day she didn't come to claim me. Don't know why. I got stuck with this old couple for nearly a week before I got a chance to clear off. Still, the old bag had some good jewellery.'

'The water's quite deep,' Nian warned him. 'So go carefully. Feel your way with your toes.'

'I'll tell you something,' said Keer, lowering a skinny leg into the sodden, partly-frozen peat. 'I never got so bogging hungry I had to wade through the gutters when I was in the city. So I was always a grotting sight better off than this.'

The stream was cold and fast and its bed was made of sharp gravel. Nian trod carefully, flinching away from the most spiteful stones, and biting back any howls of anguish that might reach the camp.

The last bit was the worst: just when they thought they'd got across the boggiest bits they found there was another channel, a deeper one, this time. The water came up past their knees, and their leggings sucked up the icy water and soaked them to the crotch.

They climbed out at last, dripping and pinched with cold, and the bitter air skirled round them to make their misery complete.

'Oh shut up!' hissed Nian, again, savagely, to the whingeing Keer, as time ticked on towards the awakening of the owlmen, and the chilly fingers of the wind clamped themselves onto his most sensitive and delicate places.

'Shut up your bogging self,' muttered Keer. 'Do you realize we've got to go through all that again, later, on the way back to that grotting pits of a shrine?'

'Just keep your mind on the money,' snapped Nian, at the end of his patience.

'Would have charged more if I'd known I was likely to catch my death,' Keer spat. 'Can't you do something before my joints all freeze solid, Truth Sayer?'

Nian stopped in the act of trying to persuade his frozen fingers to tie his shoelaces. That wasn't the sort of thing his powers were very good at, but he could probably get their clothes a bit drier, as long as he didn't over-do it and burn them to a crisp.

'Hold still, then,' he said.

He gathered all the pitiful amounts of heat from a grohl of land around them, and concentrated it all on their shivering and wretched limbs. Instantly it was as if they were standing in front of an oven door: the material of his leggings was actually steaming around him.

Keer sniffed.

'Good job there's no moon,' he said. 'All this

steam'd show us up like anything. Make a brilliant target for an archer, we would.'

'Well, there's not,' said Nian, swiftly, but not without a dreadful pang at the thought of what he might just have done. 'Is that better, now?'

'Better,' admitted Keer. 'I'm not as dry as before I had to wade this bogging river though.'

'Then I think you'd better start looking like the magistra, all right?'

'Shall I do the maggot thing, or wait until we get to Branto?'

Nian thought about it.

'Is it easy?'

'Oh yes. I'm good at revolting. And dogs. They're my specialities.'

Nian thought some more.

'Perhaps you could do scary, but nothing anyone could pin down,' he said. 'We want everyone in the camp to understand when Branto decides to give up on the magistra, but we don't want them to panic and attack us before we get to see him. Do you think you can do that?'

Keer snorted.

'Easy,' he said. 'I'll do her exactly as she is. I can't imagine anything more scary than that.'

Nian saw his point.

'All right. Tell me when you've got your face on.'

'I'm ready.'

Nian jumped, for the voice that answered was a girl's voice, speaking Pella's language absolutely perfectly, down to the last honk.

'That's incredible,' he said, slightly grudgingly. 'You can even do the accent.'

'Of course, farm boy. You can steal from people much more easily if you can persuade them you're from their own country. I can do any accent in the world—*any* of the worlds, I reckon. And any language, too: picked up the knack when I was just a toddler, too, I did. Now, out of my way! I am the magistra, and you are less than the mud beneath my feet. And don't you forget it.'

Nian stepped aside as the figure of the magistra flounced past him. Keer was even walking like a girl.

Nian spent half a second wondering just how complete a replica Keer was; and then, shuddering a little, he fell in behind the figure of the magistra at an apparently respectful distance.

They got to within thirty reaches of the camp, and still they hadn't been challenged; but the camp was noisy, and the lamps that the men carried were hardly brighter than a committee of glow worms. A steady cold drizzle had begun to fall, and nearly everyone seemed to have taken refuge in their tents, from where could be heard the busy sounds of eating and laughter.

Nian and Keer went on more and more cautiously as they approached the fuzzy yellowness of the lanterns.

Beside him, Keer came to a halt.

'This is a grotting stupid idea,' he muttered. 'It's going to get us killed.'

189

'They wouldn't shoot a girl,' said Nian, though his heart was pounding in his chest. 'Or a boy.'

'Once someone raises the alarm then they'll all be tumbling out of their tents, and half of them will be too drunk to know what they're doing.'

Nian would have argued, except that it all sounded horribly likely.

'We can't go back,' he said, as firmly as he could, thinking of the owlmen who would soon be walking the House. 'We need to let them know we're here, but without alarming them.'

Keer sniffed.

'So? Are you going to sing to them?' he asked. Nian went to snap back some angry reply, but then something caught his eye in the darkness over on the hillside. It was a light, faint at first, but then steadying and growing clearer and brighter.

'What's that?' he whispered.

'How the pits should I know?' demanded the magistra's voice. 'Some bogging idiot in the shrine's doing it.'

'But what for?' asked Nian, wildly. 'To provide a target for the archers?'

The light winked out, then appeared again.

'It's gone,' whispered Nian. 'No it hasn't. Yes it . . . hang on!'

Beside him, the magistra's voice cursed.

'Quick,' it said. 'Put the bogging thing out! Quick!'

'But—'

'—*just do it!*'

Nian didn't understand, but he rounded up a buffet

190

of breeze and sent it over to the source of the light. It winked out, and didn't come on again.

'What was it?' he asked, softly.

'Bogging Dorcis, I should imagine,' growled Keer.

Nian frowned.

'Putting out a light so we could find our way back?' he asked, doubtfully.

The magistra's silhouette twitched irritably.

'Sending a signal to the camp saying *here be impostors*, you moron.'

Nian felt a flush of murderous rage sweep through him.

'What's she trying to do? Get us killed?'

The magistra laughed, wildly.

'Of course not. She wants us to get back safely so we can fight Pella. She's trying to make it too dangerous for us to approach the camp, so we can't make Branto go away. And then we'll *have* to fight Pella.'

The light came on again across the hillside. Nian, in a rage, blew it out again, but not before there was a shout from the camp ahead of them.

'That's done it,' muttered Keer. 'See, I told you you can't trust anyone.'

'But we're trying to help them!' wailed Nian.

'No we're not, we're trying to help *the magistra*,' Keer corrected him. 'And can you imagine how much the people in the Mirelands love *her*?'

Nian imagined it. And amidst his anger and fear he felt a shaft of something colder, like sympathy, or pity.

The light was shining again, and now it had some

slightly new look to it, as if it were shining through glass. How did Nian blow it out now?

Beside Nian, the magistra's voice was droning on.

'I bet you anything you like Dorcis is doing it,' he said. 'She's hoping you'll have to fight the magistra to get home, and then once the magistra's dead then Dorcis will take over. Obvious.'

Nian stood in the freezing darkness, torn between the fear of an arrow thudding into him, and the frustration of being tangled up with Dorcis and Pella and Keer, and so far away from everyone he loved.

And then there was a cry: a tiny, tiny cry from over on the other side of the valley that somehow pierced the darkness and the noise of the camp. And the faraway light in the shrine went out.

'I think someone's just noticed Dorcis's signalling,' said Keer, with satisfaction. 'Boggit, the magistra will tear her head off.'

More and more men were coming out of their tents. Nian wavered. Did they go back or did they risk going on? What message had Dorcis managed to get through before she was discovered?

'Well, go on, then!' muttered Keer, by Nian's side.

'Go on what?'

'Oh for grot's sake! You're the Truth Sayer, aren't you? You're the one who's got me into this with your bright bogging ideas. The one who's supposed to be saving the whole grotting world from that mad magistra over on the other side of the hill. Just *do* something!'

Several things went through Nian's mind at once.

It's not my fault I'm here.

If I just ran and ran . . .

Everyone's waiting.

(*The owlmen are waiting, too, across the valley and through the gateway. Five hours . . .*)

Don't trust anyone.

Arrows . . .

He clenched his fists on all that. Then he pushed back his shoulders, and into the silence he called, strongly, as if no arrow could ever pierce him:

'Hey, you there! Here are visitors to Captain Branto!'

The lanterns ahead of him swung sharply and a silence snapped tight throughout the invisible valley.

And then footsteps began scratching hurriedly along the path towards them under the bobbing lights.

28

The men who arrived looked more like vagabonds than fighting men.

'Who's there?' someone shouted, sharply enough; then spoiled the effect by hiccuping.

'The magistra,' answered Nian. He peered past the light of the lanterns at the men who were carrying them. Some wore lop-sided cloth caps, and some knitted helmets, and some were bare-headed save for things that might have been the pelts of animals.

Under the ragged hems of their hairy tunics their knobbly knees shone in the lamplight like so many hovering goose-eggs. And their noses looked very much the same.

Nian suppressed a peal of manic laughter.

'Where is Captain Branto?' he asked, crisply, as if he were addressing the Tarhun. As if he expected to be obeyed.

The men, in an eye-bulgy semi-circle, shifted uneasily from foot to foot. Many of them had straggling beards that hung under their chins in wild, chaotic, and mysterious abandon.

'A woman, is it, boy?' asked perhaps the hairiest of them all.

'The captain is not allowing foreign women in the camp,' said another, less hairy, but with a bonnet like a pancake sagging over his fierce button eyes.

'True, true,' said a third. 'We have our own women, boy.'

Nian felt another urge to laugh—but then he noticed the spears that the men clutched in their great knobbly hands. The spears were much cleaner than their owners. They gleamed with care and respect.

'But the captain would wish to see the magistra,' said Nian, with a gulp. 'The captain has come all this way especially to see her.'

'True, true,' said someone in the shadows. And then all the others took up the refrain. *True, true*, they chorused.

'Well,' said the hairiest one, judiciously. 'It may be that you'd best come in, then, you and the woman.'

And the figure of the magistra swept forward into the lamplight with all the dignity of a queen.

There was a low rumbling murmur from the men when they saw her. Keer had done a good job. Hair spread down past his shoulders, and even in the meagre light from the lamps his eyes sparked cold blue with contempt.

Nian, shuddering, found himself thinking about man-eating ferrets; around him the men were drawing back and clutching their tunics protectively as if *they* were thinking about man-eating ferrets, too.

Keer walked towards them and the ring of hairy

chins hastily made way for her. Nian knew for a fact that Keer was wearing the pale green tunic and leggings of a pupil of the House, but at the same time he could see the shine of the magistra's heavy skirts in the lamp-light, and he could not but admire the graceful way Keer seemed to be holding them up out of the mud.

Keer was a no-good lying thieving treacherous beggar—and proud of it—but he was earning his money now.

Two sentries, staring with eyes habitually screwed up against the bleak winds of the Mirelands, stood aside for Keer and Nian to go through the tent flap. Branto's tent was the biggest in the camp—but this was not saying much, for once you were inside you could stand upright in only about half of it. And that was if you were Nian's size.

The tent proved empty apart from a folding chair, a blanket roll, and a bit of tarred canvas on the floor. Nian looked around and wasn't sure whether to be scornful or impressed, but before he could decide there was a commotion outside and a tall man was ducking in through the tent flap. He seemed rather boisterous, in a bony sort of way, had a mop of dark wiry hair, great furry eyebrows like weasels, and a grin as wide and white as a segment of scorbfruit. Which were yellow.

Nian had sudden pang of intense sympathy for the magistra. This man made even Keer look quite a tolerable companion. Why, Keer would merely steal everything you possessed, betray you to any enemy who would pay him, and then desert you.

This bloke looked as though he would entertain you with comic songs at breakfast time.

The man was still grinning like a lunatic. Nian could only think of one explanation for this: and, as the man seemed genuinely to want to live with the magistra—even worse than that, to *marry* her—it was almost certainly the right one. The man *was* a lunatic.

'Good old Pella!' he said, and Nian discovered that the weasels jumped up and down every time he spoke. Nian tried not to stare, but it was fascinating. They wriggled and squirmed with every word.

'Haven't seen you for ages,' the man who must be Branto went on. 'Not since your naming day, actually, ha ha! And that was when you were only the size of a hoglet.'

Keer's magistra stood in dignified and terrifying silence.

'Still, nice to see you,' the man went on, with the weasels waggling and jumping all over his low forehead. 'I heard about you, you know.' He winked hugely. 'About the magistra-thing. Jolly good, eh?'

He nodded seriously fifteen times and then must have lost his train of thought, for his face brightened as he said:

'Peggary's here, you know. Do you remember Peggary? But of course you do: no one could forget her. No, once seen, never forgotten. Good old Peggary!'

The magistra's head turned sharply to Nian, who gulped a little. Peggary? Who the *pits* was Peggary? He allowed his powers to slip into Branto's brain. It was something Nian avoided doing as a rule, for it felt like spying. But actually, in this case, it felt more like being stranded in the middle of an ocean: just the same amount of vaguely swelling and pointless emptiness, with here and there the occasional whale . . . hang on, no, that wasn't a whale: it was an enormously fat girl with a topknot of thin mouselet-coloured hair and very small feet.

Her name drifted into Nian's mind as slowly as the swell of the seas around her. Yes, that was Peggary.

Nian hauled himself out of Branto's mind and engaged his vocal cords.

'The magistra hopes Peggary is in good health,' he said, politely, and Branto's weasels leapt with enthusiasm.

'Yes, oh yes!' he said. 'She's champion, now, you know. Yes, she got her wreath just last week. Tremendous to see her. Mind you, she's been training for this for years and years. Of course,' he went on, confidentially, 'I had ambitions in that direction myself, like any boy, but I soon realized it wasn't to be.' The weasels drooped a little. 'Hadn't the reactions for it. Too tall, really, too. So of course I decided to go in for pillaging. And I've done quite well, really. But Peggary . . . why, she was always a natural. You just had to watch her to know that. Poetry.'

'Poetry?' echoed Nian, in surprise, for neither Branto nor Peggary seemed quite the type for poetry. He looked a little deeper into Branto's mind again and saw something like a vigorously bubbling brown stew . . . or eels in a mire . . . yes, it was much more like eels in a mire . . . great fat eels . . . with legs . . . and yes, that one had bright blue eyes shining out of the glutinous brownness of everything.

He suddenly twigged what it was.

'Hog-fighting,' he said. 'Hog-fighting in the mire.'

Branto nodded, very pleased.

'She went through every round without a single submission,' he announced proudly. 'Won by a clear margin. No points or wrangling. Best bit of hog-wrestling I've seen in years. Yes, it gave the men a real lift, that did. They needed it, too, after coming all this way along the river. Slim pickings round here, you know.'

He stopped to scratch his head and gaze at the magistra, slightly bewildered.

'We lost three men this afternoon, when you blew up the catapult,' he said, rather reproachfully.

Keer inclined her head.

'Still,' Branto went on, more cheerfully, 'the buryings will be done tomorrow, and we'll sink a barrel or two to see them on their way to the Great Tavern, we will. Yes. And now I come to think about it, we can do the marrying at the same time. Oh, but there'll be some headaches come daybreak! Yes, a night soon forgotten, that'll be, and that's for sure.'

He looked at the magistra earnestly. She still had her veil down, but you could see the shape of her nose and get a general impression of her round face.

'And then we'll be able to breed up lots of littl'uns,' went on Branto, with a new burst of enthusiasm. 'Just like Cousin Dorcis said. Yes, they'll soon be crawling around and up to all sorts of mischief, I expect . . .

199

setting fire to the tent, and blowing people up, and all sorts.'

He laughed, though not quite as heartily as before.

'It sounds . . . dangerous,' said Nian.

Branto's weasels went nose-to-nose.

'They'll need keeping an eye on,' he admitted. 'But then, they'll have their mother for that.' His face cleared, and the weasels leapt with relief. 'Why, by the time they're a few seasons old they'll be helping with the pillaging. Oh yes, you mark my words, there won't be many as will stand and fight when they hear that Branto and his sons are on their way.'

'But . . . what if they're girls?' asked Nian, fascinated, despite everything.

Branto laughed heartily.

'Then they'll run faster and further!' he said. 'Wouldn't you?'

Nian briefly imagined several miniature versions of the magistra crawling around the place, but it was too appalling a thought to dwell on.

Then he suddenly realized something. 'Did you say *Cousin* Dorcis?' he asked. Branto nodded.

'That's right. Clever woman, Dorcis. Yes, I can just about remember when she decided to go into the shrine. Well, it was that or get married, and she said that *nothing* was better than a pillager, ha ha! And of course she did very well and got chosen as the old magistra's successor.'

'And . . . what happened?'

Branto shrugged.

'Pella's mother took her to the shrine for safety after

their place got looted. And the next thing anyone knew Pella was pulling tiaras out of thin air. Dorcis had to make do with being nursemaid. But then a few months ago Dorcis sent word to my tent and suggested that Pella would make a good bride for me. Clever, eh? I'd only really thought about Peggary as a wife, before that.' He sighed, and the weasels sagged over his little black eyes. 'Touch of class, you are, though, Pella,' he ended up, rather wistfully.

And at that the figure of the magistra took a step forward and lifted up her veil.

She was actually looking all right. Her face was a duller shade of scarlet than usual, and her teeth were probably a bit smaller. But there was something about her smile that put Nian in mind of crack-scorpions, and he was suddenly certain that if she opened her mouth she would reveal a purple tongue. A *forked* purple tongue.

Something flicked out from between the magistra's teeth, and Branto made a noise between a yelp and a hiccup and leapt backwards, his weasels beginning a terrified struggle to escape into the shelter of Branto's bushy hair.

The magistra took one long slow step closer to him, so that a glimpse of pale foot showed for a moment beneath her velvet skirts and Nian was left in no doubt at all that the foot in the delicate red sandal had no toes; it was pink and fleshy, but it was cloven like the foot of a hog.

It was only the fact that Nian knew this was an illusion that stopped him screaming.

The magistra's eyes slid slowly closed, and when they opened again Nian saw to his horror that they had the slit-pupils of a lynx; around them her black eyelashes kicked like the legs of poisoned flies.

Branto was hunched down as far back against the tent wall as possible, now, and the weasels were burying their heads in each other's necks in terror.

And then the magistra spoke. She didn't use her normal voice (which was clever, Nian realized, for this magistra might not have quite the right words for that) but instead spoke in tones that rang round the tent like a brass gong.

'Do you wish to see all my classy powers, Branto? The powers of the magistra?'

'No, no!' said Branto, almost in a yelp. 'It's just that Dorcis said—she's so clever, so I thought—'

The magistra let out a skin-freezing laugh.

'Did you dare to try to possess me?' she demanded, with her forked tongue splitting each word into an echoing chord that sent shivers of doom down Nian's back.

Branto seemed to be trying to assemble enough of his wits to get his lips moving coherently.

'Ber-ber-but all women like little ones,' he said, but he was gibbering. 'And I always dreamt,' he went on, from behind a hand that was held up ready to ward off some dreaded danger, 'of a daughter who was a her-hog-wrestler.'

The magistra hissed, a long menacing vibration that filled the tent: it was like nails on a slate or teeth on metal or scorbfruit on an ulcer. Branto sank down onto his knees, bent over with the pain of it.

'A *hog-wrestler*?' echoed the magistra in her double voice, though the hissing did not stop.

'No!' shouted Branto, with beads of sweat on his corrugated forehead. 'That was a mistake! I see it, now. I thought it would be a good idea because you were so beautiful and clever, but I didn't realize how much you'd . . . changed.'

'*Changed*? From beautiful and clever?'

'Yes!' screamed Branto.

'*What*?'

'I mean no! No. To . . . to much too beautiful and clever for me.'

Nian suddenly became aware that the figure of the magistra was shaking. It looked as if it was shaking with anger, but when he checked he found she was less solid than before. He hurriedly reached out a little power to support her, but found, with a shock, and then a shock at his shock, that she was not quite where she seemed to be. He tried again, looking more carefully, and found the reality inside the shape that Keer was projecting. Keer's magistra-shape was certainly weakening.

They had to get away quickly, before Keer was forced to let the illusion fade any more.

'Do you truly give up your desire for the magistra?' demanded Nian.

'Yes! Yes. Truly,' said Branto, wincing and shuddering. 'The men have been complaining at being stuck here in the wilderness, anyway; and the deaths this afternoon unsettled them. They would have started deserting before long, in any case.'

'And you will never return?'

Branto pushed himself slowly, still gasping, to his large feet.

'I wish I'd never come in the first place,' he groaned. 'I should never have listened to Cousin Dorcis. But the thing is, she's always been clever, and I've always been a fool. Not that I'm not a good pillager: I've got my band here, and we do very well. I mean, we have people queueing up to join us whenever we have a vacancy.'

'You must leave now, then,' said Nian. 'At once, so the magistra can see you are keeping your word. Give orders for the striking of the camp.'

Branto wiped his hands over his long face.

'Most of the men are drunk,' he said, hesitatingly. 'It won't be easy to get them to move.'

The magistra let out a scalding hiss.

'Then tell them that when day comes I shall visit a plague upon anyone left within sight of the shrine,' she said in her voice of brass. 'A plague that will make all their hair and other small pieces shrivel and drop off.'

'That should sober them up,' said Nian, approvingly.

Branto had gone the colour of cave-fungus. He edged as far away from the magistra as he could.

'I'll tell them,' he promised. 'I'll tell them. It'll be a big job, but we'll do it. If we start out now we can be halfway to the coast by daybreak. And, I'll tell you what, I'll marry Peggary as soon as I can. A nice girl, that Peggary. Always thought so, if I'm honest. Big. Strong. Capable. Laughs a lot. Hey, you should have seen her in the third round of the championship. They put her in with a great blue hog with tusks on it like a—'

'—a plague,' rapped out the magistra, viciously. 'That would put Peggary out of your reach for ever.'

Branto's large larynx bobbed up and down in a painful gulp.

'Yes, yes. Of course. Small bits. Certainly. I'll tell them. Straight away. There's no need to worry. You won't see us for dust, I can promise you.'

The magistra gave him a look that made him clutch protectively at the front of his tunic.

'Then we shall leave you,' announced the magistra.

'Good!' said Branto. 'Er . . . I mean, if that's what you want, O magistra. I'll see you out.'

Branto paused when they reached the wide chilly darkness at the edge of the camp, and, above them, a faint yellowness that must come from the shrine.

'Shall I send someone with you to see you home?' he asked. 'We wouldn't want you to get hurt before you've called off that . . . er . . . '

'You will do best to set your men to work,' spat the magistra. 'You have a long walk ahead of you.'

'Yes, of course,' said Branto, hastily. 'We will. We do. We have. So we'll be getting cracking, then, great magistra. Er . . . sorry to have troubled you, and all that. Give my love to Cousin Dorcis, if you should happen to think about it . . . er . . . perhaps not.'

The magistra raised her arms so that her long veil hung down like the wings of a great owl.

'*Go!*' she hissed, with a flick of her purple forked tongue, and Branto turned and he ran.

He was shouting as he went.

'Hey there! You men! Strike camp, strike camp, there's a curse upon us! Move, if you value your small bits!'

'Oh *grot,*' muttered Keer—for suddenly it was Keer, just Keer, beside Nian. 'We must get out of the way before any of them see me. Nian!'

Nian, who was already moving, turned back. 'What?'

'I'm going to need some help,' said Keer, and his voice was suddenly as thin as a whisper. 'That took . . . oh, *grot*!' and he had stumbled and fallen onto the ground.

Nian hastily called up his powers. Everything always looked pale when viewed using power-vision, but Keer was almost shining with whiteness.

Nian hurried back and helped Keer up, slipping an arm behind his back to support him, though not without wondering about the contents of his pockets, which would almost certainly have been picked before they reached the shrine.

'Just don't take my comb,' he muttered, as they began their stumbling way along the path.

Four hours, now, until the owlmen came to life? Keer seemed truly exhausted, but he still had the spirit to say:

'I save you and two whole bogging worlds, and you grudge me a grotting comb? Pits, and it's only a cheap bone one. You'd hardly get a couple of pieces for that from a fence.'

'My grandmother gave it to me,' growled Nian. 'And my sister sewed the cover.'

Keer slipped on a greasy tuft of grass and his foot went into the icy water up to his shin. He let out a thin howl of protest. And then he said:

'Do you have a mother, Truth Sayer?'

Nian heaved hard, and Keer's foot came unstuck from the mire with a sound like Snerk tasting soup. Mother had snorted a little when he'd unwrapped the comb. *Well*, she'd said. *The amount of use your comb gets, it should last you a lifetime.*

Nian looked up at the faint glow of the shrine. The House was a whole world away, and his mother was further away still.

'She's a long way away,' he answered, and called up his powers so he could see the black chilly water that curled through the coarse reeds along the bottom of the valley.

'She's practically always a very very long way away.'

29

The water of the stream seemed even more cruelly freezing, now, and the hill steeper. Keer stumbled and tripped, too tired to use his powers to see where he was going. Nian helped him as best he could, but generally if Keer fell over he took Nian with him.

They staggered at last over a wide bit of tussocky ground and onto the bare rock that surrounded the shrine. There were shadows flicking in one or two of the windows, but apart from that the place seemed lifeless.

'Bogging place,' muttered Keer, shrugging off Nian's supporting hand. 'Pits, what a world, eh? Dark, and freezing, and dangerous, and the only thing to do is hog-wrestling.'

'And pillaging,' pointed out Nian, a little spitefully. 'I would have thought that was right in your line.'

But Keer shook his head.

'Nah. Pillaging, that's just for morons. It's obvious, isn't it? If you're living in a place you don't want to destroy it. You want it prosperous. You need people rich enough to support you. Stands to reason. We're predators, my sort are, and we need healthy prey.'

'Like the cloud-lynx,' said Nian. Suddenly for an instant he was home, properly home, with the sun shining on the green mountains and a river of living gold moving with heavy grace from crag to crag.

A skirl of icy wind buffeted them.

'Come on,' said Keer. 'Let's go and tell the magistra she's free to stay in this pit-hole as long as she likes.'

The marble of the shrine glimmered a little even in the dark and filthy night.

'This world might still be a fantastic place, though,' said Nian, thoughtfully. 'We've only seen a tiny bit of it for a few hours.'

'Yeah, I suppose so,' agreed Keer, somewhat to Nian's surprise. 'After all, there must be places worth pillaging. It's just our grotting luck to end up with the bogging magistra. Nian!'

'What?'

'That Dorcis. Don't forget she's clever. And Pella isn't nearly as stupid as she looks, either. *Trust no one*, all right?'

Nian was suddenly desperate to get back to the House, where there were people he could trust. Really desperate. People like Tarq, and Alin.

And Derig.

'I'll remember,' was all he said, as he stepped up the shallow step between the cracked columns of the shrine.

There was a commotion going on somewhere in the shrine. Someone was ranting and screaming and furious.

'Guess who,' said Keer, as they turned towards it.

The words came echoing towards them long before they reached the door to the magistra's room.

'*I'm going to kill you!*' bellowed the magistra's voice, and then she followed this up with a wide range of insults.

Keer blew out his lips.

'Just like a fishwife,' he said, with grudging respect. 'Grot, I've hardly heard a *fishwife* use language like that! Right. So the magistra is in a foaming mad frenzy, and she's a complete maniac at the best of times, so we're going to run away over the hills and make ourselves a new life, right?'

'Wrong,' said Nian, still heading for the source of all the screaming as the time of the owlmen ticked ever on. Three hours, now?

'You know she'll kill us, don't you,' said Keer. 'Once she's finished tearing Dorcis limb from limb for being in league with Branto she'll be just in the mood to take us out.'

'She'll cheer up once she hears that Branto's leaving,' said Nian, and turned the knob of the magistra's door.

'*Get out!*'

Something very heavy had thumped the door closed again before it had opened more than a finger's-width.

'Hm,' said Keer. 'Still not exactly the life and soul of the party, though, is she?' And he stepped back to gesture politely to Nian: *after you*.

Nian gave him a filthy look and inched the door open again.

'Er . . . it's us,' he said, but the magistra was stringing together a stream of words so dense and chewy and lurid that there was never any chance of his being heard.

Keer grinned, and at that Nian's pride flared up inside him. He flung the door wide in a grand confident gesture—but then had a sudden attack of caution and brought down an invisible shield to protect them as he did.

'We're back,' he announced.

The magistra gave them one swift glance of loathing from the pink bed where she was kneeling, and ceased screaming insults long enough to hurl something at them. It burst through Nian's shield like a catapult-fired avalanche, and would have pushed them halfway back down the corridor if Keer hadn't chucked something back that deflected it so that it merely banged into the door frame with a noise like several worlds ending and tore the door half off its hinges.

Nian started speaking as soon as he'd gulped his heart back down.

'We're back,' he said, again, unnecessarily, while the magistra's large chest was still heaving with outrage. 'Branto's leaving, and he's not coming back, ever. We've done everything you wanted.'

Dorcis, who was standing near the wall, cool and grey as a column of water, gave a wintry smile, but the magistra let out a yell of triumph and scorn.

'There!' she shouted, her head jutted fiercely forward so that her coarse black hair hung down like

211

goats' ears. 'There, Dorcis! You see? So you have failed to destroy me and now you are going to die.'

Dorcis shrugged a little, and seemed, if anything, even more bored and weary than she had before.

'If you kill me, you will be even more alone than you are now,' she observed, but not as if she cared very much.

The magistra gave a short sharp scream of contempt.

'But why should I want to be with you?' she demanded. 'You've been plotting to betray me ever since I've been magistra! All you've wanted, all this time, is to take my power for yourself.'

Dorcis looked even wearier.

'That's not quite true,' she said. 'I wanted to help the people of the Mirelands, as well. People are being murdered, or chased away, and soon you will be really, literally alone, unless you let me help you to use your powers to help people. Alone, Pella: think what it will be like. Alone in all this great desolate mire.'

The magistra hissed at her.

'Oh no,' she said.

She turned to Nian and Keer and she smiled a wide white insane smile.

'You see, I have other friends, now,' she went on. 'And they are going to stay with me here for ever.'

30

'Told you so,' said Keer, while Nian's brain was still grasping weakly at this betrayal.

'But . . . of course we're going home,' Nian said. 'The whole point of us getting rid of Branto for you was so we could go home.'

'No it wasn't,' the magistra told him. 'I never meant to let you go. Why should I?'

At least three different things collided in Nian's throat and came near to strangling him.

'But I *must* go home because your owlmen will attack, soon, and all my friends—'

'—are going to die, blah blah blah,' agreed Pella, rather bored.

'You see?' said Dorcis, in a sort of bitter triumph.

Nian struggled on through his bafflement and frustration.

'They are good people,' he said, whilst knowing she wouldn't care. He thought about Derig, whose brain might already be destroyed; about Tarq; even about good old Snorer, who, whatever he deserved it was not to die horribly in a fight in the dark with a monster with no heart.

'You could at least stop the owlmen,' he said; then hated himself for sounding so weak.

The magistra only shrugged her hefty bare shoulders. 'The owlmen are just shadows. I've made them to lie in wait, and then kill everybody, but they aren't alive. I can't call them off as if they were dogs. No, they'll attack. There's nothing I can do about it, even if I could be bothered.'

Keer shifted in his place by the wall.

'We'd *best* stay here, then,' he said to Nian. 'There's no point in going back to the House if all those bogging owlmen are going to start carving everybody up.'

Nian wanted to scream and stamp his feet; it was only the knowledge of how stupid it had made the magistra look that stopped him doing it.

'That's right,' said the magistra. 'They're going to attack anyone with a scent of blood about them.'

'Yeah, they've gone for a couple of people already,' said Keer, but with no more than a scientific interest. 'Hey, but why did they attack so soon? I thought they were still supposed to be lurking.'

The magistra made a face at him.

'There are bound to be one or two malformed amongst so many,' she said, scathingly. 'I expect some of them will last more than a day after they've come to life, too.'

'Given your skills, some of them will probably last a *hundred*,' muttered Dorcis.

Nian found himself distracted even as he was balling his fist to thump her. *One or two malformed* . . . The magistra had the most extraordinary, terrifying

214

powers, but she was not very skilled in their use. Not really.

It must be possible to defeat the owlmen if Pella had made them. It must be.

But only, but only, but only *if he were there*.

Nian came to a decision.

He was going to get back through that passageway, or else he was going to perish in the attempt. He couldn't undo the magistra's weaving that was holding it closed, but he could fight the magistra and force her to undo it herself.

He could try, anyway.

Nian took a deep breath of the clammy air of the shrine, and readied himself for a fight to the death.

31

Nian stood and faced the magistra.

'Open the gate,' he said, very steadily. 'I'm going home.'

Keer gave him a perishing look.

'Oh, for bog's sake,' he muttered. 'What's the point in risking our lives to get home just so that we can get sliced up?'

'He's full of power. He'll manage somehow,' said Dorcis. 'And if he defeats the magistra then soon the Mirelands will be safe again.'

'Oh, well, that's brilliant, then,' muttered Keer, savagely. 'Yip-bogging-pee.'

Pella shot Dorcis a look of freezing blue loathing, but when she spoke it was to Nian.

'But why do you want to get back to a world where you are alone?' she asked. 'Where no one understands what it's like to have so much power fighting inside you, or how it churns about so that sometimes it's hard even to breathe, let alone sleep. Power that's never quite under control because it's growing and swelling and changing all the time, so that using your powers is like trying to parcel up the air that leaves your lungs.'

Nian tried to keep a barrier between them, so he could fight her; although she was dangerous and selfish, he couldn't help but recognize that in some ways she was the best friend he could ever have.

'Remember what it's like to have everyone afraid of you,' said the magistra, and now she was almost pleading.

'If you gave your power to me, Pella, then you need not be lonely any more,' put in Dorcis.

'Yes,' said Nian, clutching eagerly at this solution. 'You could do that.'

Keer snorted.

'Come off it,' he said. 'You can't want Dorcis to be magistra! Pits, Nian, these people here are worse than the ones at home. You really can't trust *anyone*.'

'Well, I'm going to have to trust you, Keer,' said Nian, but without taking his eyes off the magistra for a second.

But Keer shook his head.

'Nah,' he said. 'You'd have to be mad to do a thing like that. I'm completely untrustworthy, I am. Nothing personal, but I've learnt the hard way. I'm only on the lookout for the main chance.'

'Well, this is your main chance,' said Nian. 'We get back, you get money, remember? You stay here, you get nothing; and that's looking on the bright side, because I'm still expecting the worlds to start falling to bits.'

Keer waggled his head from side to side, considering. 'Yeah,' he admitted, putting his hand thoughtfully up to his chin. 'Well, in that case perhaps—'

Keer swung out his hand hard in a back-handed slash, and one of the magistra's stuffed animals exploded with a dull thump.

The magistra said *oomph*, overbalanced, and fell over backwards right off the bed.

Nian wondered for an insane fraction of a second about going over to help her up, but one look at the snarl on her face made him forget it. He dived into cover on the other side of the great pink bed. Keer was already there, cursing quietly and continuously.

'Just don't expect much from me,' he muttered. 'I'm only the shape-changer, remember. You're the one with the talent for destruction.'

Nian made a face. He hadn't got a talent for destruction at all: destruction was what happened when he lost his temper.

'We've got to be careful,' Nian said. 'If we go and kill her we'll never—'

The great pink bulk of the bed shot upwards as he was speaking and Nian found himself gazing straight at the lesser pink bulk of the magistra. She showed her teeth in a snarl and flicked a pink fingernail in his direction. He ducked, realized after a puzzled second that she hadn't actually thrown anything, found the room was suddenly much darker, and discovered that the bed was falling down on him.

He flung up a hand: this would have done no good at all if Keer hadn't chucked up another small stuffed animal that exploded powerfully enough to deflect the bed. It flipped sideways just a fraction of a second before it broke their necks, crashed lop-sidedly into the wall, and then, amidst a rustle of descending satin, flopped over to land on its back with its legs in the air.

Nian tried not to think about how nearly that had just come to killing them both.

'Thanks,' he gasped to Keer, as he scuttled round to the other side of the bed and into cover again.

'I'm only doing it for the money,' said Keer, close behind him.

They lay together with their heads down against the mildew-smelling rug and panted.

And there was silence. Nothing moved apart from dust. Dorcis sniffed.

'I've been telling you for weeks that this place needs a good clean,' she said, but the magistra's chest was heaving with the effort of hurling the great bed about, and fortunately hadn't any breath spare to reply.

'Well, go on!' muttered Keer, savagely.

'Go on what?' muttered Nian back.

'*Go on, get the bogging magistra*, what do you think? Hit her really hard before she does for both of us!'

Nian tried to think of something to throw at her that wouldn't actually blow her head off, but now there was a distracting rumbling from somewhere outside. And it was getting louder. And louder.

And louder.

'*Pits!*'

The last word came out very squashed because Nian and Keer were rolling out of the way of the massive marble sphere that was smashing its way through the doorway. Nian threw himself into a neat forward roll and onto his feet, because if that thing got them it'd squash them as flat as ox-grot.

He was just about to blast a pit in the floor to swallow up the bogging thing when the magistra let out a crag-crow screech of rage, and when Nian looked he saw that the marble sphere was indeed so enormous that it had *got stuck between the twin pillars of the doorway.*

He repressed a mad cackle of glee and ducked down quickly behind the chest of drawers.

Keer spoke from a window ledge.

'For bog's sake, don't just squat there, you grotting idiot? *Scrag* her!'

'How?' muttered Nian, breathlessly, on the lookout for the next attack.

'What? Oh, for pits' sake, you're the one who pulled down nigh on half the House, aren't you? The one who destroyed the Lords' powers?'

'Yes, but—'

'But what? Oh grot, she's doing something else, now. I can feel her doing it.'

Nian could, too. He could feel it in the increased coldness of the chilly room, and the ice-mint tingling of the air.

'For truth's sake,' said Keer, exasperated. 'I think she's going to . . . *woomph*!'

Nian just caught a glimpse of a movement on the floor, and then something was shooting up at his face.

He threw himself out of the way, but the thing was small and quick and it got under his guard. And now there was something hairy scrabbling at his face, and two round mad eyes staring into his own, and he *couldn't breathe*. He went to yell, but then didn't dare open his mouth because the hairy thing was trying to push itself between his lips.

Nian went over backwards against the cold wall. It was so utterly horrible and disgusting that he sort of forgot to fight the thing until someone hacked him on the shin. Keer was rolling round on the floor, kicking and squirming, and one of the magistra's little dead animals had its paws pushed against his mouth and nostrils.

The sheer horrific inventiveness of this shocked Nian's brain clear. He dug his fingers hard into the furry body of the animal on his own face, and he twisted. The thing wasn't alive, but it shivered and squawked and its blue glass eyes bulged . . .

. . . and then there came a grinding and crunching of little bones under Nian's fingers, and a moment later there was a soft double thump as the thing's head and body bounced separately down onto the floor and away.

Nian spat away the foul taste of animal paws and lunged over to help Keer.

Keer's glare, when he was free, was almost as bulging and vicious as the stuffed animals'.

'That does it,' he said, spitting in his turn. 'If she's going to be that sick then I'm getting out of here.'

'No!' said Nian, urgently. 'I need you! And we mustn't get separ—'

But he found himself talking to the empty air.

32

Nian looked around the magistra's room, alone and utterly betrayed. Keer must be pretending to be a pot of face cream or something.

Don't trust me! Keer had told him that, but Nian could still hardly believe that Keer would leave him to face Pella alone.

The shock of it stopped him dithering. He was summoning up a sort of power-sack to ram down over Pella's fat head when something from behind him grabbed his throat.

He thought at first that it might be a snake: he felt it hastily, dreading the bite of fangs, and found a knot. No snake, but one of the cunningly-plaited curtain ropes. It was the work of a moment to call in a hundred years of rot to disintegrate it to threads.

'Grot!' said the magistra, crossly, and made a sharp punching gesture that exploded the one remaining window into a thousand glittering pieces.

Nian turned to face the thousand blades that were whirling towards him, and the sight of those blade-edged triangles of glass reminded Nian of the schoolroom. Of Grodan and Derig. And he remembered he was angry.

The shards of glass fractured the lamplight into hundreds of minute flashes and rainbows. For half a heartbeat Nian didn't know what to do, but . . . yes, there'd been a hundred occasions when something had come spinning through space towards him and catching it had been desperately important.

A small voice, Keer's, reached him: *Cheat, you grotting bogger!* it said, and Nian scooped up his powers and concentrated absolutely, just as he had at pockle just a couple of days ago.

And, just as it had then, the world slowed down so that the shards of glass began to wheel towards him in a grand and swirling spiral. But there were a thousand of them, and there wasn't, wasn't, *wasn't time* to catch them all.

Oh, for grot's sake! whispered a low, exasperated voice in his ear. *Make a screen, make a screen!*

Nian rocked back on his heels. He slammed a screen across in front of him with such haste it took two layers of skin off his nose. The glittering glass slammed into the screen with a noise like gravel in a bucket.

'Grot!' said the magistra, again. 'Stop fighting me!'

'You can hardly expect him to stand there and let you cut him to shreds,' put in Dorcis, drily. 'I should give in if I were you, Pella. The boy is powerful, and he's angry, now.'

'Yes,' said Nian, with his heart thumping. 'I don't want to hurt you—'

'—yes you do,' said the voices of Dorcis and Keer, together.

But he didn't. Not really. He'd have happily thumped

223

her, but not with his powers, which were so large and strange and dangerous.

The magistra frowned, and the gleam in the blue depths of her eyes was almost as sharp as a knife itself. But she was still alone, really alone; Nian understood that so very well.

The magistra began to rub the finger-tips of one hand together as if she were spinning, and at once a thin thread began to form under her fingers, fine as gossamer, tough as wire.

'Watch out!' exclaimed Dorcis, sharply.

'*Do something!*' whispered Keer's frantic voice. '*Or she'll wrap you up like a spider's lunch!*'

Nian focused his steely attention on the end of the silver thread. With a flick of his mind he caught it, and as he did he was struck by some memory from home, his first home at the farm. Yes, a memory from the springtime when the waters were tumbling and foaming. He had stood beside Father and waited for the silver fish to leap.

Yes. Yes!

The magistra hissed and whirled the thread up so it spun like a top, ready to drop down on Nian in a funnel of sticky silver that would shrink until it had him pinned and helpless.

But Nian had watched Father cast a fishing line so that it landed three fingers from a fish's hungry mouth. Nian snapped his wrist and sent the thread forward in an arc that stalled and fell, as light as a fur stole, round the magistra's shoulders.

He yanked on it as hard as he could. The magistra

tried to dive out of the way, but her arms were trapped against her body and she couldn't wriggle free.

Nian ducked under the thread and leant his weight back on it, and all the magistra could do was flap like a newly-hatched duckling.

'All right. You've lost,' said Nian, breathlessly. 'I've won. Give up.'

The magistra swore at him, but Nian was concentrating on turning the thread to iron, and widening it to a span-wide strap. This was not only fireproof and rotproof, but rather less likely to cut the magistra's arms off.

The magistra was struggling to push her powers towards the iron band—but she didn't know how to do it. Nian felt grateful and pitying at the same time, for even the Lords could have done that.

And here was Keer again, sliding down one of the walls from the ceiling.

'Is that where you were?' demanded Nian, so surprised that for a second he forgot that things were desperate. 'I thought you were disguised as a cockroach, not just sitting on the chandelier!'

Keer looked at Nian as if he was mad, and stupid with it.

'Of course I couldn't disguise myself as a cockroach,' he said, with contempt. 'I'm about a thousand times bigger than a cockroach, aren't I? Unless you have eight-span cockroaches in the country, farm boy.'

'Let me go!' screeched Pella, still struggling. 'Let me go!'

225

Dorcis had both her hands flat against the wall behind her.

'So what comes now?' she muttered. 'The magistra is caught, but she's still the magistra.'

'Open the gateway so that we can go home,' Nian said to Pella, ignoring this, holding the end of the iron band as she fought and butted against it.

She screamed a furious word of defiance that made even Keer wince.

'Oh come on,' he said, annoyed. 'That's not very nice, is it? Look, you've lost, all right? It happens to all of us in the end unless we're very careful about picking our opponents. So you'd better just open the gateway, and then the farm boy here, who's soft as goose-grot, will untie you, and everything will be back to how they were before Branto showed up.'

But Pella only struggled even more violently and swore some more. Nian checked the strength of the iron band; it'd hold fast against a lot more than she was throwing at it.

'But why do you want us to stay?' he asked, though he understood quite well. 'You can't expect us to be friends, can you, not when you've just tried to drop a bed on our heads.'

But the only answer the magistra gave was to charge at him, head down. Nian side-stepped neatly, and she might have broken her neck running into the wall if he hadn't hauled her round to a halt.

'Stop it,' he said, but only irritably. 'Stop it, or you'll hurt yourself. Look, all you have to do is open that gate. That's all. We'll deal with the owlmen ourselves as best we can if we have to, but we just *have* to go back.'

A gold sandal lashed out and had slashed away a strip of Nian's shin before he could get out of the way. He said a word quite as bad as anything the magistra had come up with, and if he hadn't been fully occupied hopping round in a circle clutching at his damaged leg he might very easily have chucked a wall at her.

'What did you do that for?' he gasped, at last, blinking back tears of anguish.

Keer was regarding her sourly from his corner.

'Try tightening that band a bit,' he suggested. 'She'll probably start being a bit more reasonable once she hears her ribs creaking.'

The magistra insulted several members of Nian's family.

'I shall never do as you ask!' she spat. 'Not if you were to go down on your knees and shower me with rose petals and kiss my feet and write me poetry!'

Nian spent a mad second working out if he actually could do all these things simultaneously, but then Dorcis spoke.

'You must take away her powers,' she said. 'Pass them to me and I will unlock the passageway for you. *I* certainly don't want you here.'

Dorcis had been asking Nian to do this all along, but Nian hadn't taken much notice because surely such a thing wasn't possible. Surely your powers were part of you, like the way you liked jam, or pockle, or had smelly feet. Giving away your powers would be like

227

cutting off your hand, or like an eagle plucking out its flight feathers.

But now Nian pushed his own powers towards the magistra. He had known that her powers were different from his own, and . . . yes. They were not really part of her at all, except in the way that the air was part of her. Nian looked carefully at the bonds that tied the magistra's power to her body and mind.

Pella plunged at him like a teased bull, distracting him.

'Hold her,' said Nian, curtly, trying to concentrate.

'*Ow!*' said Keer, as he grasped her arm. 'Boggit, she's grotting *cold*!'

But Nian ignored this. He was close to the magistra, now. It was terrifying to be so close to anyone, but Nian gathered his courage and dived down through the layers and layers of her mind, through the years of life and power and aloneness and fear.

Fear? That was unexpected. Fear of . . .

. . . fear of the dark, of the echoes of the room, of the fiery streamers and the shadow of the great bed, of everyone, everyone, because they were all strangers and Mother had gone away for ever, and this power was like a vulture that took you soaring above the ground, high, so high that you could grasp the stars, perhaps, unless they were hot like the shining lamps or sharp like shining knives and what if the vulture opened its great talons and let her fall . . .

. . . Nian felt the dizzy tipping inside the girl as the powers rolled nauseatingly around inside her . . .

. . . and each day went on for so long for there was

no bedtime and no breakfast time so it was as if she were cartwheeling very slowly over and over until at last at last at last she glimpsed a way out through her powers and touched the world again . . .

There!

Yes, if she wanted something, really wanted it specially, it would come. Not always exactly the right thing, but something, something.

Shiny sequins, highest heels, shiny shiny knives (real ones at first, but then sharper, cleverer ones that could cut through . . . anything).

And then one day Branto came, terrifying Branto who had long ago killed Grandfather and Trun.

Knives and owls and shadows . . . enough to make an army. Lots and lots, marching off on their long scissor legs, hunters, sharp-beaked and ready for battle against everyone, everyone, for no one was to be trusted.

And then . . .

Nian leapt with a great effort out of the magistra's mind and back into his own. The magistra was there, still bound in front of him, and he felt a stab of real distaste which was aimed largely at himself.

Dorcis was saying something to him, and he knew it had already been said several times.

'Can you do it? Can you extract her powers?'

And now Nian had looked at the magistra properly, at Pella, it would be easy.

'Yes,' he said.

33

The magistra let out a scream of rage and fear and threw herself into a struggle so violent that a little stain of blood began to spread itself along the warp and weft of her silken bodice. Nian, in pity, went to loosen it, but a fist of power batted him away.

'Haven't you learned yet?' said Keer, exasperated. '*Don't trust anyone!*'

But Nian hadn't learned, and he hoped with all his heart he never would.

'Quick!' said Keer. 'Nian, she'll be free in a minute, I can feel her doing it. Quick. Quick! *Do it!*'

'Yes,' gasped Dorcis, putting back her fine grey head. 'I'm ready.'

And Nian was close to Pella, so close, and getting closer, until his lungs were moving with hers and his heart was echoing to the same beat.

And his blood had turned thinner and more bitter, and there were men coming, men, bad men, and she had to hide . . . Grandfather was the wisest, bravest person in the world, but they'd killed him.

Remember there are worse things, much worse things, than being alone.

Keep the power tight so that the bad men . . .

. . . *trust no one*. If anyone comes, lash out, lash out!

Nian clutched hold of his own mind again and took the time to steady himself.

Pella.

He understood, now. He understood he could never trust her, that she needed him to look after her.

That he shouldn't leave her, ever.

But the owlmen were coming, and soon Derig and the others would all be dead.

He made his choice.

He tugged with his powers, and saw something coming out of the magistra's body. It was like a thin trail of silver smoke to start with, but it quickly thickened to a shining river that swept into the room.

'*No!*' screamed Pella.

It was so thick he could hardly see her, now, though her scream was going on and on, and becoming shriller, and thinner, until it was like the cry of an owl far far away.

And now the strands were whirling away across the room and Nian could see Pella again. She was crouching with her hands held as though they were trying to grasp at the silver stream, but the strands of power still swept away from her.

And Nian was as appalled and revolted as if he were watching her bleed to death.

He let go of the band that joined them, and then it all stopped, quite suddenly, while the strands of power were still as thick and heavy as a unicorn's tail.

231

'No!' said Dorcis's voice, from over by the wall, but louder, stronger, than Nian had heard it before. 'How dare you?'

Keer's eyes were glinting with surprise, and a little amusement.

'Nice,' he said, appreciatively. 'Yeah, there's no point in pulling all that power out of one maniac only to give it to another one. *Don't trust anyone.* Yeah, you've got the hang of that all right. It's just like professional pockle, really,' he went on, musingly. 'Where you have three teams playing at the same time. The only way to win is to keep both other teams equally weak.'

Nian stood between them all and wished he were still a trusting innocent. A country bumpkin. In fact, a farm boy, as Keer so often said.

He flicked a finger at the magistra—no, at *Pella*—so the iron band round her burst undone.

'Will you open the gateway to my world, now?' he asked Dorcis. She mused a little.

'You've given me half of Pella's powers . . . or rather, not quite half.' She raised a finely-formed eyebrow at Nian. 'Why not half?' she asked.

It had been little more than an accident, but Keer grinned.

'Because you're cleverer than Pella is,' he said. 'Nian's evened things up.'

Dorcis nodded to acknowledge the compliment.

'So we rule together or not at all,' she said. 'Yes, I see. And I will open the gateway.'

Pella was still crouched on the floor, unmoving.

There were huge spaces inside her that until recently had been filled with power. Being Pella at this moment was like being suddenly blind on the top of a maze of cliffs.

'What am I to do?' she whispered. 'If I'm no longer the magistra, what am I to do?'

'Anything,' said Dorcis, crisply. 'You're not the magistra, but you are . . . someone else. And there are millions of someone elses. The choice is much, much wider than it was before.'

Pella felt her way up the cold marble of the wall to her feet.

'I still have power,' she said, through gritted teeth. 'Enough to fight you, Dorcis.'

'Yes, Pella,' agreed Dorcis. 'But not enough to win.'

'Yeah, you can forget that,' said Keer, 'unless you want to grapple with Dorcis for the rest of your life. And I can't say I'd fancy it myself.'

A silvery packet of power, about as dangerous as the dead fish it resembled, flipped through the air from Dorcis towards Keer and he ducked it at the very last moment. Nian gave Dorcis half a smile.

'What will you do now?' he asked.

She came as near to smiling back as made no difference.

'I intend to make life very difficult for men like Branto. Yes, I shall sprinkle some justice here and there. It's badly needed.'

'But what about me?' gasped Pella. She was leaning against the wall as if its support was the only thing stopping her from falling to pieces. 'What can I do?'

233

Dorcis looked at her without much warmth, but with a little pity.

'Almost anything,' she said, drily. 'As long as it doesn't annoy me.'

Pella made a face at her, but then wavered and blinked, as if the world was still inclined to sway around her.

'You wait till I'm strong again,' she said, and there was a hint of the old fierceness in her voice already. 'Because exactly the same goes for you.'

Nian looked from one to the other of them. Would they squabble endlessly and for ever in this sunless place? Or would they rule together in friendship? But it was up to them. He had his own world to care for and his own life to lead.

His own life? But he still hadn't worked out what that was supposed to be.

'How can I destroy the owlmen before they go on the attack?' he asked Pella.

'You can't,' she said, rubbing at her arms where the strap had been. 'At least, no one ever has yet. They've been very useful if someone's being annoying.'

Keer let out a whistle of surprise and respect. 'Bogging pits,' he said. 'Even I've never actually *killed* anyone.'

'Well,' snapped Pella, glaring. 'I suppose you've never had to.'

Keer scratched his head.

'Well, I think it's more that I've always gone for the quieter option,' he said. 'Lying and cheating and thieving and that. Though of course,' he finished up, 'that does take intelligence.'

234

Dorcis smiled grimly and began to move her hands in the air as if she were undoing knots in a piece of string. 'What a bungle you've made of this, Pella,' she remarked, as she snagged a nail on what seemed to be a particularly tight knot.

'It was enough to stop these two,' sniffed Pella. '*And* it was done in a hurry. *And* by someone self-taught.'

Keer was walking restlessly round the room as if taking farewell of the place before the journey back through the abyss.

'Hey,' said Nian, suddenly taking proper notice. 'Put all that stuff back!'

Keer shot him a glance, of surprise as much as resentment.

'You're learning,' he said, almost with approval. 'I thought you were too innocent and high-minded to notice I was nicking stuff.'

'I was,' said Nian, 'but then I met you. So put it back, all right? Anything that ends up in the wrong world weakens the whole system.' Keer sighed heavily, fished inside his tunic, and brought out a string of pearls.

'And the rest,' said Nian, grimly.

Keer rolled his eyes, but brought out several more pieces of jewellery, a mirror, two pairs of scissors, and a cut-glass bottle.

Nian folded his arms.

Keer had two brooches tucked up one sleeve, and a set of hairbrushes up the other. Tucked down the side of his shoe was a comb carved from some green stone.

Nian started tapping his foot.

Keer's other shoe was full of coins.

'You wouldn't have been able to *spend* those in your world,' pointed out Pella, with scorn.

'Gold's gold, isn't it?' said Keer. 'I know a man who'd soon get that melted down. He makes good-health amulets from the metal—once he's mixed in a good bit of lead, obviously. Does a good trade in them.'

Nian sighed.

'Don't you know *anyone* who isn't a thief or a cheat?' he asked. 'Or both.'

'Course not. Not until I came to the bogging House, I didn't, anyway. I spent the first couple of days trying to work out what scam you were all running . . . and then I finally worked out that you weren't running a scam at all. I mean, you were all *genuine*.' He shook his head. 'I still can't really get my head round that.'

Nian opened his mouth to explain—but then couldn't quite be bothered.

'It's just simpler,' he said.

Dorcis made a tugging motion in the air. There was a succession of tiny popping noises as if something had ripped open and Nian felt the gate yawn wide.

'Come on,' Nian said to Keer, over his shoulder.

'But you can't go!' cried Pella. 'Don't leave me here on my own!'

'You won't be,' Dorcis told her. 'We've got a lot of battles to fight, Pella. I should imagine you'll rather enjoy it.'

'Come on,' said Nian, again, to Keer.

Keer sighed, but came.

'I can't imagine why you're in such a hurry to get back to the place where the owlmen are about to murder us,' he muttered.

'Nian,' said Pella, pathetically, 'you can't leave me.'

But he couldn't stay; not when every second brought the moment nearer when the murdering owlmen would step out of their walls.

'Live well,' he told her.

'But I don't know *how*!' she exclaimed. 'I don't even know what I want!'

'A purpose,' said Nian, rapidly, as time sped through the worlds. 'Friends.'

'But how can I have them? Where do I start?'

'Here. Where you must always be.'

Nian was grabbing Keer's sleeve as he spoke and heading towards the bright pink wall.

'Not *here*!' called Pella, desperately, after him. 'Not always! Not in this cold place!'

But there was no time, no time, not when all his friends were in such danger.

'I must go to my own cold place,' he said.

And together he and Keer stepped off the edge of the vast cliff into the abyss.

34

They went down, down, into nothing, and the great darkness of the void swept up and swallowed them. Through Keer's palm Nian could sense the scream that hung formless around them as they fell.

And now it was cold, even colder than the shrine they were leaving behind, although the darkness was growing speckles that became pinpricks of light.

And now, slapping through his face, were visions: a tile-red desert, an emerald grasshopper, a pink ancient tower, and . . . and . . . and . . . and—but now they were coming at him so fast that they had blurred into a flurry like a vividly-hued snowstorm.

But here, swiftly, was a tunnel of greenness shooting up towards him fast, ever so fast, and bigger and wider until it slammed into the soles of Nian's shoes and sent him staggering forward and blundering into the block of stone that marked the centre of the garden of the House of Truth and the point, also, at which Nian's world touched, ever so gently and delicately, the millions of others that spun through the void.

Nian grasped the rough stone and gasped and gasped, and beside him Keer heaved in breath until he had air to mutter a stream of words to make the sky blush.

And when Nian looked, he found that the sky *was* blushing, faintly, but that was with with the approaching dusk.

Keer wiped his nose on his sleeve.

'Grot,' he muttered. 'Grot grot grot grot grottety grottety grot.'

And Nian couldn't have put it better himself.

Keer pushed himself upright and turned right round.

'No,' he said, almost in a moan. 'That's not right. Oh boggit, that's not right!'

'What isn't?'

'The suns. Oh struth, what's going on now? It shouldn't be sunset, should it?'

Nian took one more breath and managed to speak.

'It is. So it must be supposed to be.'

Keer grabbed the hair at the back of his neck.

'Look, but . . . '

'No,' said Nian. 'It's not like that. We've been in another world and we don't know how long their days are. You've no way of knowing how long we've been away.'

Keer blew out his lips.

'So what day—which sunset is it?' he asked.

Nian shook his head. That didn't matter; at least, many things mattered more.

Whether Derig was still alive. That mattered, mattered terribly.

Whether the owlmen—he felt his insides contract at

the thought of them—whether the owlmen had begun to move.

Nian turned to head for the door to the House. He knew much more about the owlmen than he had when he'd left the House, but he still didn't know how to destroy them.

What he did know was that the owlmen were out to murder every living creature within its walls.

As soon as Nian stepped across the threshold he felt the fear that filled the House. He looked one way and then the other along the pale corridor; nothing moved save dust.

Keer, behind him, shivered.

'I don't know what you're going in there for,' he muttered. 'It's getting dark. Those owlmen may come to life at any minute.'

'I know,' said Nian, as with every heartbeat the fear dug more deeply into him. It was eating its way through him and turning him to ice.

'So come on,' urged Keer. 'Look, no one knows we're back. We can get away through the garden. There's no point in us being killed, is there.'

Nian hesitated, with the garden growing blue behind him and the pale corridor dulling in the twilight.

'That's true,' he agreed.

'Yeah,' said Keer. 'We'll go together. It doesn't even have to be to the city, we can go anywhere you like. Your valley, even. I mean, there's nothing easier than living off farm boys—they'll give you their life-savings and then thank you kindly for it, master. They're so stupid I sometimes wonder how they remember to breathe.'

Keer turned and took a few steps back out into the garden.

'Let's cover as much distance as we can before it gets properly dark.'

Nian would have followed, except that his hand was grasping the doorpost and somehow it wouldn't let go. It was stupid, because his heart was pounding inside him and with every double thump the time grew closer when the owlmen would step out of the wall and walk on scissor-legs towards . . .

. . . towards Hani. And Snorer. And Rago . . .

Nian had three flashing glimpses of the future: Hani ducking and falling, his teeth still bared in his wild pockle-playing smile; Snorer, clasped arms raised to deal a massive downwards blow, staring in amazement at the blood spurting from his chest; Rago, spitting spiteful Thought as the shadow of an owlman folded impossibly in front of him.

The fear inside Nian was still mounting. It was screaming inside his head *run! run! run!*

But somehow he didn't run.

One little part of his mind, the part that was not filled with terrible pictures, or screaming, was running along as smoothly as a spinning-wheel.

I'm the Truth Sayer. I'll be the best at fighting them. Pella made them, and she doesn't know much.

There must be some way . . .

'Don't be a complete grotting moron,' said Keer, behind him.

That annoyed Nian very much indeed, for he was thinking, or trying to think, as hard as he possibly could. He thought about the world he had just left— of the coldness of the wind and ice and, most of all, the distrust the people.

If he went away with Keer he would take a little of that coldness with him. Perhaps it would fade and be soon forgotten; perhaps it would lodge in his throat like a grindlenut.

If he went with Keer . . .

He looked back. Behind Keer was the garden and the enormous sky and beyond it a thousand worlds full of wonders.

And Keer was alone in all that space and time.

'Warn everybody at the inn,' said Nian. 'Tell them to get out of there.'

And then he stepped swiftly into the House of Truth and along the darkening corridor.

35

Nian hurried along the corridor. It was quiet, as usual, except for his noisy heart, which was beating even faster than his footsteps.

He went along the long slow corridor and the twilight became bluer, richer, and with each star that pierced the sky the hour of the owlmen moved closer.

And there, at last, was someone. A bulky figure standing on guard by the door to the Council Chamber.

It looked at Nian, and then looked again, and took a quick step towards him.

'Truth Sayer!' it said in Snorer's voice. 'Where in the name of grot have you been?'

'Another world,' said Nian, but Snorer's eyes were going past him to search the dimness behind him.

'You've not found the beggar-boy,' he said.

'Yes, I did,' said Nian. 'He's all right. He's gone down to the inn.'

Snorer let out a sudden noise like an exasperated ox. 'Oh, well, that's all right, then. Fine. As long as you both enjoyed your trip . . . Have you any idea how worried we've been? We've been been up all night searching everywhere for you. The Lord Tarq must have aged a decade since yesterday. Boggit, he looks a hundred and twenty, now. And young Hani's nearly driven himself mad trying to locate things you'd have had with you, like your comb, or your socks. Just what the *grot* did you think you were doing going off like that?'

Snorer's heavy brows shielded all but the sharpest points of light in his eyes, and his thick fingers kept twitching as if he wanted very much to hit someone.

Somehow, despite all his desperate hurry and the desperate danger, Nian was very glad to be home.

'Long story,' he said. 'Where are the others?'

Snorer grunted.

'We've got a big guard on the owlmen's cellar,' he said. 'The rest of the lads are doing sentry round the corridor. Waste of time, as there's no way we can stop the bogging things, but what else can we do?'

Nian frowned. Good question. What else could they do?

'Where are the Lords?'

'Thinking,' growled Snorer. 'And I hope to pits it helps, because nothing else is going to.'

'All right,' said Nian. 'I'm going to find the Lords. You get that guard away from the cellar. Right away, do you understand? And close every door you can.'

Snorer glowered at him, baffled and angry.

'Those bogging things can cut through wood,' he pointed out. 'They can cut through glass, metal, even. Anything. Closing doors won't help, we can't keep them pent up, whatever we do.'

Nian would have hit him over the large dense head if he thought it might have knocked some sense into it.

'Do it anyway,' he said. 'It'll slow them up. But get everyone right away. Bring them all to . . . '

Where? There was nowhere safe. Nian felt the fear of the owlmen afresh, threatening to stifle him. He needed space to breathe, to think, perhaps to fight. Space for his brain and body to work smoothly together. Yes, there was somewhere: where was it?

Yes.

' . . . to the pockle ground.'

Snorer scratched his head.

'But . . . '

'Just do it!' snapped Nian, and turned and ran on down the corridor.

Nian's feet found their way to a room where a tiny withered man sat blank-faced on his mat.

'Lord!' said Nian.

Tarq's skull-like face came back to consciousness gradually, like someone rising from deep water. And then he smiled.

'You have returned,' he said, as if he could now be content. 'This gives me hope, my son.'

The old man was not fully back in the world, or he would not have said *son*, but Nian couldn't bring himself to resent it.

'The owlmen are going to attack tonight,' he said.

Tarq regarded him quietly for a moment, and then nodded.

'Well, I have lived long enough,' he said. 'Though most of the others, I fear, have not been so fortunate.'

But then his smile widened and he came as near as Nian had known to laughing.

'I could wish I were not such a small lean creature,' he went on, 'and then perhaps the owlmen might sate themselves on me.' He felt a forearm with a rueful hand. 'There is hardly flesh enough on me to satisfy a bush-rat. Not, at any rate, if it were hungry.'

Nian found himself smiling, too, for whatever happened at least he would not be alone.

'I've come from the world of the owlmen,' he said. 'But I still don't know how we can fight them.'

Tarq blinked his pale eyes kindly at Nian.

'Being Truth Sayer means you see deeper and straighter into the heart of things than anyone else, but that does not mean that you will always understand what you see, and there is no reason at all that you should be able to defeat it. Being the Truth Sayer, your talents are not chiefly for destruction.'

He got up from his mat slowly and carefully, but without any of the lurchings or wincings of old age.

'Come,' he said. 'The House is full of minds, and as many different talents, and perhaps together we will be able to solve this problem.'

'Do you really think there's a chance we'll be able to?' asked Nian.

'I know we won't unless we try,' replied the old man, and led the way out of the room.

36

Hani was the first of the boys to see them.

'Hey!' he shouted over his shoulder. 'Hey, you lot! He's back!'

Immediately there was a crowd of silhouettes jostling and pushing behind him in the sleeping room door.

Nian looked at the tallest and gawkiest of them.

'How's Derig?' he asked Gow, with his heart in his mouth.

'No worse,' came the answer.

If Derig had been worse he would have been dead; at least he was not dead. Nian took what courage he could.

'And Keer,' asked Alin. 'Did you find him?'

'Keer's safe,' said Nian. 'Come on.'

'Where are we going?' asked Hani. 'Are we leaving the House?'

The owlmen's long legs would cover the ground fast. They would march down, a swinging lethal blackness, and catch the hindermost of them. And they would all be trapped and slaughtered on the narrow path.

Nian winced away from the word slaughtered,

though at the same time there was just something about it that felt important.

'We're going to the pockle ground,' he told them.

'But what's the point of that?' demanded Alin. 'At least we can put a wall at our back if we stay in the House.'

'The owlmen can walk through walls. We need space,' said Nian, and hurried on.

By the time they got to the pockle ground the place was shifting with black figures. Most of them were Tarhun, and couldn't see a thing in the darkness. It was quite hard to remember to steer them a wide berth to avoid being elbowed in the earhole or having your foot trodden on by a big flat Tarhun boot. Ranger the master builder was walking round in circles muttering, 'What *should* we do? What *should* we do?' But then he'd been doing that pretty much ever since he'd arrived in the House.

No one trod on or elbowed Rago, for his cracked voice rose spikily above the murmuring and jostling of the crowd. 'Very well, very well, here I am!' he was saying. 'I have left the House, as I have been asked. And now what do you want me to do? It is a long time since I played pockle, but I shall flip those owlmen with very good spirit, I assure you, if that's what is required. But I can tell you this, if by any chance I survive this night, then I shall turn my flipper on whoever is responsible for turning me out into the night air. If I can catch him before pneumonia sets in, at any rate.'

It wasn't actually very cold at all. The clouds were streaming across to cover the stars and hasten on the night, but they were bringing no breath of freshness with them.

And here was the Lord Firn pottering up.

'I'm afraid I haven't been given my orders,' he said, plaintively. 'I was told to report here, but no one has told me what I am to do. Because, if there is nothing I can help with, then I think I would like to go back to the library. I do not like to leave it alone while those owlmen are in the House.'

Nian wondered weakly what Firn thought he might be able to do against a hundred striding murderous figures.

'Is the Lord Grodan here?' he asked. 'And Derig?'

'Here, Lord,' said Snorer's voice, and sure enough there were two stretchers arriving, each borne by a pair of beefy Tarhun figures.

And now Grodan's voice could be heard.

'Just here, just here. That's it. Gently, men, gently! All right, all right, that will do. Now, where is the Truth Sayer? I heard he was back from his latest escapade. Tell him I wish to speak to him immediately!'

Nian dodged away into the crowd. The clouds were still advancing and turning more and more of the sky to the colour of lead.

If the owlmen stepped out of their walls at that moment then they were going to be killed. All of them. Nian found himself breathing very fast. He'd walked right up to the end of the pockle ground, where the drey hung emptily from the trunk of its tree.

Nian looked up at it and wished for a pock, so he could practise. He could do that. One small simple task where failure didn't matter all that much—or, at least, it only really mattered to him.

Behind was a crowd of dark murmuring figures, and gradually more and more of them were saying the same thing. *Truth Sayer,* they were saying, and as more people said it, it grew into a soft hump of sound. *Where's the Truth Sayer?* If he had been Keer, he could have changed into something else—into the form of one of the owlmen, perhaps: would that be safe? Or into a cockroach, pushing its way into the leaf-litter.

(But, hang on, what had the magistra said? *They'll go for anything with a trace of blood about it.* So perhaps a cockroach wouldn't be safe. Did they have blood, or what the owlmen would count as blood?)

Keer would be safe, anyway. He was cunning. Surely Keer would find a way to survive. Except . . .

'*Of course I couldn't turn into a cockroach,*' Keer had said, with contempt. '*I'm about a thousand times bigger than a cockroach, aren't I? Unless you have eight span cockroaches in the country, farm boy.*'

And at that something fell into place in Nian's head. *Chunk,* it went. He turned round and shouldered his way back through the great milling figures of the Tarhun until he found Tarq.

'I know why the owlmen haven't been setting off earthquakes, even though they've come from another world,' he said, and suddenly he was hoping that this small fact might be the first pebble that started an avalanche of discovery. 'It's because they're so small!'

Behind Tarq, Alin and Gow exchanged puzzled

glances. 'They're taller than a man, Nian,' pointed out Gow, frowning.

'And there are more than a hundred of them,' said Alin.

'Yes,' agreed Nian. 'They do look big, but they aren't, really. That's why they keep seeming to wink in and out of reality.'

Hani scratched his head.

'I don't get it,' he said, and Nian found himself grinning at him in a sort of triumph.

'They're pictures on the walls,' said Nian. 'That's why they only exist head-on. Think about it! You can't see a picture sideways on, can you? And a picture doesn't weigh anything. You could have hundreds of pictures, and they'd only add up to the weight of the paint . . . and the owlmen aren't even made of paint!'

The end of Rago's withered nose poked aggressively out of the shadows.

'Nonsense, nonsense! Tarq, the boy speaks twaddle, as he so often does. How could a picture do the damage we have seen? Wood and glass and stone sliced into slivers. Well? Well?'

Tarq listened, and nodded.

'Of course it could not,' he agreed. 'Not if it were merely a picture. But it would explain why there have been no disturbances of the earth.'

'But it would not explain the evil I felt when they attacked me,' said Grodan, from his stretcher. 'They were malicious. I felt a mind behind them.'

Nian could not deny this, for he had felt it himself.

'And that was no painting that attacked me, either,

251

Truth Sayer,' put in Snorer, growling, but a little apologetic. 'It was stronger than any man.'

More and more people were joining their group as the discussion went on, anxious to hear what was said—or perhaps merely anxious.

'There *was* a mind behind them,' Nian said, groping his way through the arguments that were forming all around him. 'The magistra made them, and sent them here to do a particular task. But she's always been in her own world. She hasn't had any connection with them since they've been here.'

'*She?*' echoed Emmec, with a shudder. 'You mean those bogging—' he coughed hurriedly, to swallow the word, 'those *blasted* owlmen were sent by a woman?'

'Ha!' snapped Rago. 'That explains much!'

But Firn shifted, and fussed, and spluttered weakly, and said:

'But . . . my mother was a woman!'

'What a coincidence,' said Grodan, in his driest tones.

But luckily here was Gow's voice.

'If they are so thin, it explains why they are so sharp,' he said. 'They can pass between the fibres of a thing and meet no resistance.'

People all around were nodding at that.

'That's clever, that is,' said Ranger's voice, quivering with anxious energy. 'Really clever. But it's not going to help us when the owlmen step out of the walls, is it, knowing how easily they're going to slice us up.'

The circle winced. But Tarq only said, mildly:

'It might help us, my friend. Knowing what they are may give us the key to stopping them.'

'Yes,' said Nian. 'That's what the Lords have been trained to do, isn't it: to stop things from being what they are.'

Rago snorted.

'At last, at last, some gleam of light has penetrated the boy's thick head! Yes, Truth Sayer, that is what the Lords are trained to do. And once we understand these creatures, or images, or shadows, or whatever they are, then we may well have some means towards destroying them.'

A huge round silhouette spoke up diffidently.

'When I fought one of those things, it was like hitting a sheet of metal,' said Snorer's voice.

'Humph,' said Grodan. 'Well, I suppose that tells us something.'

'Yes,' said Nian. 'And the girl who created them was very fond of knives. I think these owlmen might be quite like blades.'

Caul spoke for the first time.

'A knife could be blunted,' he suggested, tentatively.

'Not if the thing does not exist properly sideways on!' snapped Rago.

'But still,' said Tarq, 'a blade is not indestructible. Not to rust, for instance.'

'Might a magnet help?' suggested Emmec, thoughtfully.

In the darkness, Nian was aware of the Lords exchanging glances. Firn began to bob up and down, preparing himself for the effort of speaking.

'We might make a mind-current to bear these creatures away,' he said. 'That would act very much like a magnet. Perhaps we could encourage the owlmen to go back to their own world.'

Nian sent his powers towards the statue that marked the touching place of the worlds, but shook his head.

'The way's been shut off,' he said. 'If the owlmen go through they'll most probably end up in some other world.'

Reeklet grunted.

'But if it's them or us—'

'Then it must be us,' said Tarq, mildly, but unanswerably.

Rago's harsh voice spoke up:

'We could lure the owlmen in the direction of the precipice, though.'

'Perhaps we could,' said Grodan. 'If we had more time.'

'Would an ordinary magnet work?' asked Snorer, diffidently. 'All the Tarhun carry lodestones,' he explained, to a murmur of agreement from the circle of huge silhouettes.

And then Nian, quite suddenly, remembered something else.

'But we all carry owlmen lodestones,' he said. 'All of us. It's *blood* that attracts the owlmen, and we all carry plenty of that around.'

A murmur of dismay ran round the circle, but Caul shook his head.

'It can't be only blood,' he said. 'For in that case, why was the schoolroom destroyed?'

'Because Nian and I had that fight,' said Alin, suddenly. 'We spilled quite a lot of blood over the place. I expect one of the owlmen took the place apart trying to find the source of it.'

That made sense, but . . .

'What about the poisoning of the Lords' dinner?' asked Grodan, though his tone was not as sarcastic as usual. 'If the owlmen are little more than machines, then why should they do such a thing?'

There was a blank pause, and then Ranger spoke.

'Snerk is a genius of a cook,' he said. 'No one could resist Snerk's food.'

'Wurrrr,' said an even more enormous hump of darkness. 'Wurrr-urrr. Durrrr. Murrr'n'murrrr. Cukk!'

'That's true!' said Snorer, with the light of revelation in his voice. 'That stew was full of blood, wasn't it?'

'Blood?' echoed Firn, in dismay.

'Course. Rich meaty blood. Moles', in that case, as Snerk says. In a rat-based jus. Irresistible.'

All the Lords seemed to be momentarily frozen with horror, but Alin said:

'But the owlmen didn't eat the stuff, or even slice it up, did they? They poisoned it with quicksilver.'

And then, with a feeling as if all his insides were made of tumbling blocks, everything came together and Nian understood.

'Quicksilver,' he echoed. 'That wasn't poison, that was the owlman itself! The things are made of *quicksilver*.'

A stir ran round the whole group.

'It might be so,' said Grodan. 'At least, largely. In which case we could act upon them.'

'If there was time,' said Caul, pulling at his chin. 'And if they came at us one by one. But it seems unlikely that they will form an orderly queue, ready for extermination.'

'Unlikely?' spat Rago. 'Impossible!'

Snorer made a great throat-clearing noise.

'We Tarhun are not without skills,' he said. 'We can fight. We can't beat those things, but we might be able to hold them up so they did not arrive all at once.'

Tarq bowed his head.

'That must help,' he said.

'Aye, for the short period before we are killed!' said Rago, bitingly. 'This is folly, to talk of fighting a thing that can turn itself so nearly out of existence. It would be a simpler matter to fight a cloud.'

Gow was rubbing at his beaky nose with his most earnest and pedantic air.

'But what about the stew?' he said. 'The stew destroyed the owlman. There must have been something about it that was fatal to them.'

'Wurrrrr. Wurrrr. Murrr-murrr-murr. Boggoff!'

'No, no,' said Snorer, pacifically. 'No one's suggesting that it was unwholesome, of course not—except to that murdering devil of an owlman.'

'Nian,' said Caul, suddenly. 'What was the world like that the owlman came from?'

Nian tried to sum up a thousand impressions.

'Damp,' he said, 'and perishing. Freezing. The whole

256

place was made of marble, but it might as well have been blocks of ice. And it was even more freezing outside, once the wind got at you. And there were no suns—or none that we saw, anyway.'

'So the blood in the stew drew the owlman to it,' said Caul, his usually pale face flushed with excitement. 'But then—'

'The heat!' exclaimed Gow. 'Yes, the heat of the stew might have done it. If the place they came from is always cold, then the owlman wouldn't have been constructed to cope with any sort of heat.'

Nian felt a flicker of hope.

'Even the food was cold,' he said. 'And there were no fires anywhere that I saw.'

The Lord Firn started bobbing and blinking.

'But we used heat on the owlman in the corridor,' he pointed out, apologetically.

Caul nodded.

'But perhaps they aren't affected until they come to life,' he said.

'But then—'

'Yes!' said Grodan. 'And that explains why the owlman did not finish killing me or Derig. The heat of our blood dissolved it.'

There was a stirring round the circle, as their minds moved from confusion and terror to teeth-gritted determination.

'We could light fires,' suggested Alin.

'That would protect us,' agreed Tarq. 'At least, while we could keep them lit.'

'We can generate heat with our powers,' said Caul.

'Especially if we use them in the old way, as we did before the Truth Sayer came.'

Rago made a noise like a stool scraping over a stone floor.

'But it is no good just to keep the foul things away,' he said. 'And the fuel from the garden, or from our powers, will not last long. What will happen then?'

'I suppose the heat of the day might destroy them,' quavered Firn but Rago snarled at him.

'The dawn will bring cold rain.'

'And we *must* destroy them,' said Nian. 'Because once they've finished with us they'll go off somewhere else, most probably. Keer's gone down to warn the tourists, but no one without powers will stand a chance.'

'Murrrr,' said a growly voice. 'Burrrr. Nurrrr nurrr, n-nurrr nr!'

Snorer punched his fist into the air.

'Yes!' he exclaimed. 'We could do that! Snerk's just made a man'sweight of spiced haggises ready for the winter. If we used them as decoys that would help split those bogging owlmen up so we could deal with them.'

'Murrr. Slurrr-slurr-slup!'

'Yes, they certainly are,' agreed Snorer, with huge enthusiasm. '*Much* better eating than one of the scrawny old . . . er . . . than any of us.'

'Good!' said a hoarse voice: and the shock of the Lord Rago's approving of *anything* gave them all an accession of energy and hope. 'You boys,' Rago continued. 'Don't just stand there! You waste enough time running around in circles trying to play pockle, now run to the kitchens and bring as many of those haggises as you can back here! And hurry!'

Nian was halfway to the House when he felt something twitch inside him. A feeling as though his skin had shivered away from his flesh. A feeling as cold as ice, but sharper, darker, fiercer.

And he knew that the owlmen were stirring.

37

The kitchen was red in the light of the great fire. Against the glow, strings of haggises were hung up to dry like hop-wreaths at harvest time.

The boys, Nian, Emmec, Hani, Gow, and Alin, jumped up to catch the strings and haul them down. There must have been dozens of long strings and hundreds of small plump haggises.

'Hurry up, hurry up,' muttered Emmec, as Gow found the end of one of his strings caught up in a basket of spiky things which might have been thistles, if thistles could possibly have had any place in a kitchen.

'I'm trying,' said Gow. 'Oh grot, it's really stuck. What shall I do?'

Nian threw his strings at Alin and boosted himself lightly up the fifteen spans to the shelf the thistles were on.

'Struth!' breathed Emmec, gazing up at him. 'I always forget you can do that. Can you untangle it?'

'Here.'

Nian threw down the string of haggises, and Emmec caught it neatly, left-handed, like the skilled pockle-player he was.

'That's it,' said Hani, suddenly. *'Pockle!* That's what we need. If we had our flippers we could send these haggises all round the place and really confuse the owlmen.'

'But our flippers are all in the cupboard by the garden door,' said Nian. 'And the owlmen are already beginning to move. It's too risky.'

Hani swallowed hard and painfully, as if he had something stuck in his throat.

'It'll make a real difference if we can get them, though,' he said. 'Anyway, with my powers being what they are, you won't be missing much if they get me. See you in the garden!' and he dived out of the door.

Nian half went to go after him, but gave up. Hani was running straight towards danger, but there were lots of people out in the garden that would soon be in a danger just as great. And the Truth Sayer's powers might make a real difference.

'Oh come on, come on,' he muttered, half-appalled and half-savage, and he led the others back the other way and out to join the rest.

Derig lay, still unconscious, on the rough grass and Grodan lay propped up on one elbow beside him.

'Go!' he said testily, waving Nian away. 'Go and see to the others. We shall be all right.'

'But . . . you're not strong,' said Nian. Grodan gave him a perishing glance.

'I still have my powers. Not as many as I had before you came along, it's true, but I can make heat enough

261

to stave off a few owlmen.'

Nian still hesitated.

'I shall look after your friend,' Grodan went on, more quietly. 'No one will be more carefully guarded, I promise you.'

Nian felt a huge surge of gratitude—but a sharp call came from the direction of the House.

'Someone's coming!'

Nian heard the sharp intake of breath from everybody present, but he was already sending out his powers to see who was coming. He saw at once that it was someone smaller than the owlmen, and more solid. And . . .

'Hoy!' called Hani. 'I've got them! Who wants a flipper to play haggis pockle with?'

And all round voices were answering him.

'Me!'

'Me!'

By the time Nian reached him Hani was almost surrounded by people reaching eagerly to take a flipper, or swishing it experimentally through the air once they'd got one.

Hani grinned bluely through the gloom.

'There were dozens of flippers in that cupboard,' he reported. 'Probably practically every boy who's ever come to the House must have brought one with him. Some of them are pretty cracked, but I reckon they'll hold together for a while.'

'Did you see any sign of the owlmen?'

Hani carried on handing flippers out to avid hands.

'I heard them,' he answered. 'A lot of scratching,

and sort of whispering. I think they're slashing their way through the walls.'

A withered hand shot over Nian's shoulder and snatched an old flipper that Hani had been about to give to one of the Tarhun.

'Give that to me, give that to me!'

Rago's eyes were shining with a sort of glee.

'Ha! It's a long time since I held a flipper, but I trust I won't have lost all my skill.'

'You used to play *pockle*?' asked Hani, in so much amazement that he forgot to say *Lord*, and only added it hastily and at the last moment before Rago clouted him round the head with the flipper.

'Of course I did, boy, of course I did! I was not always a Lord of Truth, as you of all people should realize! Yes,' he went on, weighing the cracked leather of the flipper thoughtfully in his hand. 'I remember, when I used to play for United—'

Hani's eyes nearly fell out.

'*You used to play for United?*' he whispered, in complete shock.

Raga's eyes shot out a fierce gleam of pride and satisfaction.

'Certainly I did. I was the youngest boy ever to gain a scholar's contract with them, I'll have you know. *And* the youngest to score a hat-trick in a junior match against City!'

He bustled away, as bent and bad-tempered as ever, and everyone fell back in awe and respect.

'*Bogging pits*,' murmured Hani, quite dazed. 'To think . . . '

Nian felt nearly the same—and *he* didn't even support United.

'Well,' he said, gulping down his amazement. 'The owlmen will have no chance now, with skills like that ranged against them.'

There were grins all round; then a rending, splintering sound.

Everybody turned sharply towards the noise, although only those with powers could see the black shape that was tearing down the remains of the door.

Behind it was a jagged darkness. It consisted of more owlmen than any of them could count.

38

The silence lasted only for a second. Then there came through the mountain air a sound like shears through grass. It was a home-like sound, but it sent shivers of dread down every back.

The owlmen were striding, and they were following the scent of blood.

Nian found his mind accelerating almost to scorching-point. Some of them had powers: they would be safe unless they were surrounded, for they could make fireballs that would melt the owlmen to a spot of poison. The decoys, the round haggises, would help, but it would still be a blundering fight in the dark for the Tarhun, poor fools.

Nian cast his powers over the shifting crowd on the pockle ground. The Tarhun had shouldered their way bravely past the tiny Lords to form a wall of protective bone and blubber. That was brave, but against the owlmen it was all wrong, all wrong, all wrong.

Nian pitched his voice high so it could be heard above the scissor-sound of the owlmen's striding.

'Tarhun!' he called, and he made his voice louder, too, louder than it could have been without his powers to strengthen it. 'Tarhun, let the Lords through! They can make heat with the power of their minds. Protect their backs!'

But there was not time for that. Nian saw this within a few seconds. Everyone saw the sense of what he'd said, but in the darkness the Tarhun couldn't even find the Lords amongst the great shoulders and bellies of their comrades.

Light. That was what they needed more than anything else. Nian looked around. And there was something: a tiny point of light shining steadily quite near the ground.

A glow-worm, that was all. But it was something. Nian whisked it up with half a Thought and placed it gently on the edge of the pockle drey above him. He could not make the glow-worm any bigger because its skeleton limited its size, but he brought together from all over the garden the chemicals that were mixing themselves in the glow-worm's small abdomen, and he pushed them together into a little bubble of space.

The light was flat and green. It turned the people of the House into an army of lumbering ogres and wizened goblins.

Even in the light the owlmen were no more than silhouettes, but at least they showed up against the hideous slime-green of the walls. Their feet showed clearly against the glowing grass, but above that the shapes of the owlmen merged into a mass of darkness, and it was only at the edges that the outline of a long-fingered hand, or a feathered ruff, or a sharp little hooked beak, showed momentarily.

But even this outline was untrustworthy, for the

owlmen could fold or bend themselves like sheets of hartskin. Whenever a hand or arm turned edge-on it disappeared, so that the edges of the darkness seemed always to be flickering, and it was hard to believe that the darkness was solid, and the light was not.

Nian boosted himself high up into the open arms of a holm-tree. The owlmen had spread themselves out into a wall. It was no thicker than a span's breadth, but when he looked closely Nian saw to his horror that it was a span packed closely, layer upon layer, like the walls of a tiger-bee nest.

Not a hundred owlmen, but a thousand; maybe more than that. They could easily have been hidden amongst the rafters of the roof, or in further cellars, undiscovered. Or each of them might have been a dozen, layered one on top of the other against the wall, which is why the owlman in the corridor could melt into the Lords' stew and yet still be on the wall.

A ball of fire shot golden and spitting out of the ranks of the people of the House. It burned its way swiftly through the air and straight into the barrier of darkness that was the wall of the owlmen. Nian heard the *shunk!* as it whammed home, and then the angry sizzling as it was quenched.

But the wall still advanced. That fireball might have killed a dozen owlmen, but it didn't matter because behind it were dozens, hundreds, more.

There must be thousands of the things, Nian realized, with a terrible qualm. He fought an impulse to turn his head against a massive branch of the holm-tree and give up all hope.

'Hani!' he called, and an anxious green face turned up in his direction. 'Hani, see if you can lure some of them away!'

Hani showed his teeth in a flash of ghastly green, and Nian heard the Thought Hani flung at him, an exasperated screech of almost-despair. *Boggit! You want me to draw attention to myself?*

But Hani was already leading a group of boys and Tarhun off to the right of the main body.

'Here, Lord,' called a trotting green-streaked mound of Tarhun. Ranger. That was Ranger. 'I can throw furthest!'

Hani didn't argue. He slapped a haggis hastily into the Tarhun's great paw; it was at that moment Nian realized how completely terrified Hani was. How completely terrified all of them were: boys, Tarhun, and probably the Lords, too.

'Spread out, then, spread out!' came Rago's cracked voice, as he hastened after them. 'Let's see some passing skills, here. You, boy, Alin, take the left wing with Gow, and the Tarhun can cover the mid-field. That's it! Come, then, Tarhun, flip-off!'

If the worst came to the worst—and how could things not come to the worst?—then Nian could, literally, fly. But the others were stuck on the ground with the owlmen, *a thousand bogging owlmen.*

Ranger drew back a huge arm and threw. The haggis flew through the air in a wide slow arc, spinning a little in the emerald light. And a hundred sharp hooked beaks turned to follow it.

'That's it!' shouted Nian, as a layer of darkness

turned, vanished momentarily, and then began to stalk after it on scissor-legs.

But there were still so many, so many. The owlmen's eyes were invisible, but the malice of their gaze was tangible, threatening, as if needles were stabbing out of the darkness.

The ranks of the House of Truth were giving ground before them: that was all they could do.

But what was that that had been left behind?

Two shapes: two people. One small and still, and the other . . .

Nian cursed. Grodan. That was Grodan down there, with Derig; and somehow no one had thought to help them.

Grodan was pushing himself up on his elbow, and lifting a fist to throw something at the owlmen.

Grodan's powers had never been for fire, and he was weaker even than usual. The fireball thumped into an owlman and might have killed it, but then it fizzled out and there were more owlmen behind, more, and more and more.

Nian's feet hit the ground, and he didn't know whether he was more relieved he'd found the courage to jump down, or in a state of utter terror.

And then he felt the eyes in the dark wall that loomed just a few reaches away from him, and he knew.

Grodan looked round and nodded.

'Truth Sayer,' he said, calmly. 'Good. Take the boy. You'll have to drag him on his stretcher. You can do that, I'm sure, for he's lost weight since he was attacked. It will jolt him, but he won't know anything of it.'

'But you'll be—' began Nian; then could not face the thought of what was going to happen to Grodan.

But Grodan's face remained composed.

'Better one than both,' he said. 'And it will be quick. Go.'

The wall of black was only five seconds away. Nian bent down to grasp the handles of Derig's stretcher, and as he did the haggises he had stuffed down the front of his tunic flopped forward and back against his chest.

And he realized there was one other thing he could do.

So he did it.

He took out one of Snerk's haggises and then threw it with all his might straight into the black wall of the owlmen.

The fireballs had made little impression on the owlmen, but the haggis did. It hit the wall with no more than a soft thump, but it dented the wall—or perhaps the wall curved round it, like the fingers of a grasping black hand.

All this only took a couple of seconds.

'I said, go!' snapped Grodan as the wall curved further into a hundred delicate layers, like the wings of some monstrous vulture.

And here, with a great heaving of breath and galloping feet, was Ranger, back again.

'Quick,' he gasped. 'I'll take the old man, and you take the boy. Now go go go!'

Nian grasped the handles of the stretcher again and yanked on them hard. The thing moved with a great jerk, and Derig's head flopped sickeningly from side to side, but Nian wasn't strong enough to get the thing moving smoothly; all he could do was to heave at the thing with a mighty effort, and then heave again.

Ranger grabbed the Lord Grodan, hauled him to his feet, flung him unceremoniously over one huge shoulder, and went off into the green darkness using the curious gliding footsteps of a dancer.

Nian followed as fast as he could, but that wasn't fast. He was most desperately afraid of the moment the shadow of the owlmen would fall on him, because he knew that when it did he was going to turn and run like a hornbuck.

Each heaving effort pulled the stretcher a couple of spans across the rough grass of the pockle ground. Where were the owlmen?

He didn't want to look, but he'd done it before he could stop himself.

And he found himself looking up at a towering whirlwind of black feathers.

39

Nian didn't understand what he was looking at to start with. He looked round. There was a group of Lords at each side of the owlman wall which extended from either side of the great whirling funnel that had appeared in front of him. The Lords were not throwing fireballs, but sitting quietly in Thought. There was a sort of glow around them as they sent out their powers.

And now two silver arcs were growing from each group. They were delicate things no thicker than wires, but they spat sparks as they grew, piercing the green-black of the sky.

Nian understood that, at least. The arcs from each group would meet in the air to form two arches, and then the Lords would lower them to make a ring enclosing the owlmen.

And then the Lords would straighten the sparkling wires and cut each owlman in two.

(What would happen then? Would there be owlman legs scissoring over the garden, or owl screeches echoing maddeningly off the walls of the House? But no one knew.)

But as if everything wasn't already complicated

enough, over there was a jagged group of stately owl-men striding towards the gap in the wall, heading for a crowd of strangers with faces yellow and grey in the light of their blazing torches.

They were being rescued, thought Nian, even more confused. But who would come here, to the House?

A mighty hand slicked with green hairs grabbed his sleeve, and he jumped half out of his skin.

'Get out of here, you bogging idiot!' gasped Ranger's voice, rough with something close to panic.

'Go, go!' shouted someone else. And here was Reeklet's nasty moustache snarling at Nian round wet green lips.

'Derig,' Nian gasped, his hands still clutched to the handles of the stretcher.

The green on Reeklet's face flicked up and ran lumi-nous squiggling worms across his forehead.

'Ranger'll take him,' he snapped. 'Come on!'

Someone elbowed Nian out of the way, and Nian stumbled, turned like an eel, and ran.

'Grot!' someone was saying. 'There's more of those bogging owlmen peeling off. They've scented the grot-ting tourists!'

Tourists. That was who they were. Keer had warned them, but instead of running away they'd come up to help.

'At least that'll relieve the pressure on young Hani and the boys for a bit. And those torches should stop the owlmen escaping for a little while.'

'A little while,' said another voice. 'But struth! What's going on with the bogging wall of the owlmen!'

The great whirlwind had curved round until it had become a vast feathery ball. Nian, not sure whether it was more terrifying to know or be ignorant, bent his powers on it.

'*Bogging pits!*' he said.

Reeklet turned little black eyes on him.

'What is it?' he demanded.

'They've turned on each other,' said Nian, shaken by the ferocity of it. 'They're slashing each other into shreds. But why in all the worlds . . . '

The Lord's silver wires had formed their arches, now: the silver lines were opening like some vast flower bud and coming down on either side of the huge ball of bloodthirsty owlmen.

'What did you throw at them?' demanded Ranger's voice. 'That was what started them off.'

'Only a haggis,' said Nian.

'Murrrr,' said another voice from the darkness. 'Nurrr. Nurrrr nurrr. Burrrr.'

Nian, with a slightly wild feeling that one more problem didn't actually make a lot of difference, dived into Snerk's mind and pulled out his meaning.

'But that's it!' he said, in amazement, hope springing up inside him. 'That's it! The owlmen slashed that haggis into a thousand pieces, and all the bits have gone everywhere—over all of them—and so they're all tainted with blood and so *now they're attacking each other*!'

'Murrrr,' said Snerk, but in such a satisfied tone that it needed no translation.

Ranger punched the air.

'And that'll do our work for us if we let it!' he exclaimed.

'We must tell Hani,' said Nian, but Ranger pulled him back.

'No. You go to the tourists. They'll all get slashed to shreds as soon as their torches go out. Have you got any more haggises on you?'

'Three,' said Nian, checking. 'That'll do.'

'All right, I'll go to Hani, and Snerk will keep an eye on these two injured ones. Now go.'

Nian ran through the black-and-green garden, all the time alert for the shadow that was really an owl-man; but still he didn't see it until too late.

A thin black arm slashed down at him. Nian dropped to the ground, rolled, and tried to get up again, but his tunic was snagged on the thorns of a bramble, and for a crucial few seconds all he could do was kick out at the darkness.

His foot hit something as solid as iron—but the black shape above Nian that was only half tree only swayed a little, and the twigs at the end of a branch flicked out long fingers. And everything was happening so fast that Nian had no time to do anything but panic because any moment now . . .

. . . something thumped massively into the ground just beside him and threw bits of earth up into Nian's face. Nian jumped so violently that he turned round in mid-air and landed staring at a great axe embedded halfway to the shaft in the damp earth.

Something grabbed him, and he nearly threw up with sheer terror.

'This way, quick!'

A woman—that was a woman's voice (but how and why and what on earth . . .)—but the owlman was still there, there, and it was going to . . .

. . . Nian had thrown a fireball at it before he'd finished thinking. It hit the owlman squarely and bounced off, sending several figures ducking.

But the owlman had stopped fighting. It was swaying slightly, and folding its cut-out arms over the hole that had appeared in its belly. Then it turned its vicious eyes on Nian—jutted its beak forward—and carried on leaning, and leaning, until with a screech that iced the air it bent into a V shape with its head and feet on the ground, and stiffened, and stopped moving.

'Quick, lad,' said the woman's voice. 'They're all over the place. Quick.'

Nian pushed himself to his feet and stumbled after her. There was a jumble of tourists over here. Nian looked at their staves and walking sticks and determined faces and didn't know whether to laugh or cry.

'All get into a group,' he said. 'And then I'll have the best chance of being able to protect you.'

But one of the largest of the tourists shook her head.

'Nay, lad,' she said. 'We've run halfway up the mountain to help, and help we will.'

Nian turned to scan the garden. The Lords were lowering their double arch the last few feet to contain the main body of the owlmen. Hani and the boys were skilfully occupying a whole phalanx of other owlmen by flipping a haggis to and fro, and Ranger was charging across to them waving his arms and shouting.

But there were owlmen everywhere, a dozen or so stalking implacably, large owl-eyes gleaming with hatred, towards the tourists.

The large woman settled a hand firmly round a pair of fire-tongs.

'I'll soon see to this lot,' she muttered; and for that moment she sounded so completely like Mother that Nian was shot through with hope and even a sort of joy.

'It's my turn now,' he told her. 'After all, you've just saved my life.'

'Foul things,' she sniffed. 'To be going after children and holy men, and in the House of Truth, as well!'

'Hang on,' said someone else—a thin man whose ears stuck out hugely against the green glowing walls. 'Haven't I seen you before? Yes, you were playing pockle with the other lads. Why, you're the Truth Sayer, aren't you?' Several people gave out small screams of shock or excitement, but Nian was looking round to make sure of the position of every stray owlman. Yes. If he flipped one of Snerk's fat fragrant haggises just . . . *there* . . . that should lure all these owlmen into attacking each other.

He must have lost a couple of haggises when the owlman attacked him. He got out his last one. He had lost his flipper, too, somewhere in one of the last several crises, but he didn't have to get the haggis very far.

'What is he doing?' whispered someone, but with as much respect as bewilderment.

Nian was weighing the haggis in his hand. The

timing and positioning were critical. All the owlmen had to arrive at the haggis at more or less the same moment, so that the slices would fly up and splatter them all.

Yes, he could do that, and he could do it best without his powers. He pulled back his arm, and threw.

He knew he'd done it perfectly as soon as the haggis left his hand. It wasn't easy to keep sight of it as it sailed through the stripes and jags of the shadows, but one after another the owlmen's wafer-thin heads flicked out of sight for a moment as they turned to follow it.

'Bogging pits,' murmured the man with the ears, beside him.

Several owlmen were converging with long scissor-strides on the spinning haggis and there! There, with a whizz of arms that turned the owlmen to blurs, was the attack.

The haggis almost exploded. Bits of it flew everywhere . . . and in an instant the focus of the owlmen's attack changed. They turned towards each other and began a grotesque and stately dance of destruction.

It was truly horrible, but Nian was held in a sort of fascinated admiration by their skill and sudden focused speed. He could not but see that they had a certain beauty about them, a spareness of line.

He suddenly remembered the girl who had sent them. The flolloping beribboned mass of her; the litter of gaudy tat that had covered the tables and bed and floor of her room. But there had been something in her that had called these things into being. Something savage, perhaps, but also a beauty as hard and sharp as a diamond.

Nian was the Truth Sayer: but he hadn't realized that, until now.

The owlmen had become a flickering ball of blackness. Sometimes fragments would fly out from the centre of it, but only Nian with his strong powers could distinguish a severed, long-fingered hand, or a fall of feathers. Behind him people were cheering, but Nian stood, pierced with a great sadness, as the last fight of the owlmen failed, and the flurrying ball settled to a hump and then to hardly more than a heap of black flakes, like ashes.

Nian looked round the garden. There was a lot of cheering, now. The Lords' double arches had contracted into a single rope, and the silver of it shone on a great puddle of black on the grass beneath. Caul, at one end of the rope, was flinging it into the air in triumph, and at the other end the Lord Firn's face was irradiated by a quite astonishing and most definitely unholy grin.

And there were Hani and Alin and the others jumping up and down, hooting like swing gibbons—and in the centre of the pockle ground a mass of bulky green-streaked Tarhun silhouettes were knocking fists together in the ritual of victory.

But over there was someone who was not celebrating. It was one of the Tarhun. Snorer. He was kneeling quietly on the ground beside . . .

Nian felt everything fall coldly away from him.

He began to walk, and then to run.

40

Nian came to a halt a pace away from Snorer's great fat back.

The figure on the ground in front of him was vaster even than Snorer was. In the green light it lay darkly like some vast butchered carcass.

Which was what it was.

Snorer blindly reached out a flapping arm and clutched hold of Nian's tunic. And Nian, in pity, stepped closer to him, put a hand on his broad shoulder.

One of the Tarhun.

There were bound to have been casualties. And Nian didn't even know all the Tarhun by name. After all, they were greedy, dishonest, quarrelsome, cheating, filthy, useless . . .

. . . the word *useless* made Nian's heart lurch in his chest. He turned his powers on to the huge figure on the ground and he saw what he already knew.

Ranger. It was Ranger, caught and cut down by the owlmen as he charged across the garden.

Nian threw himself down onto the ground beside him and began to search, search through every fibre for some life, just a spark of it, that he might be able to fan into flames and back into existence.

Snorer gave a great shuddering gasp, and then another.

'Is there . . . some hope?' he blurted out, softly.

Nian opened his mouth to say *there is always hope*. But that wasn't true.

Sometimes things happen and there is no going back. He knew that. Every day things happened. You were forced to take turnings, and sometimes they turned away from where you wanted to be. Sometimes where you wanted to be ended up across such a huge divide of time and space that you could never breach it. Never.

Nian suddenly had a vision of his life, and it was branched like the cold veins that he was exploring in Ranger's great body.

This man is dead, his brain said, but he still searched and searched for something, anything that might be warmed into life and begin to stretch itself and grow.

Around him the silence was growing outwards like a pool until it covered the whole of the garden and everyone inside it.

No one moved, and though most of them could not know what was happening, somehow the awfulness of it was chilling every heart.

Please, thought Nian, though he didn't know who he was speaking to. *Please, let there be something*.

The cold of the great figure was increasing, was beginning to make him shiver, but still he searched, more and more minutely.

Someone was moving behind him, now. Nian was

only slightly aware of it until a hand came to rest on his shoulder.

'My friend,' said Tarq, quietly. 'Come, you must rest, now.'

Beside him, Snorer was suddenly crying, except that it was not Snorer at all, but someone closer. Much closer. Nian wiped his face on his sleeve.

'I cannot rest,' he said. 'I am the Truth Sayer.'

'And you have saved many lives,' said Tarq.

Nian shook his head angrily.

'That's not enough. I want this one, too.'

Tarq nodded quietly.

'Yes,' he said. 'I understand. But what is the Truth, my friend?'

And once more it was as if Nian was on the edge of the gulf that separated the worlds. He looked down into the blackness, further and further, for the twinkling stars, for a glimpse of a shining green stone, for the many-hued flutterings that might crystallize into another world. But however far he looked there was nothing . . .

. . . except . . .

. . . perhaps there was something, but however hard he strained his powers he couldn't quite make it out. He was about to cast himself off into the gulf so he could get nearer to it, but at that moment he heard a voice.

Friend? it said, in a whisper.

That was not Ranger's voice, but it distracted Nian long enough for the abyss to disappear and for his feet to fall down down down to the cruelly trampled earth of the garden once more.

'What is the Truth?' someone was asking, again.

'Ranger is dead,' said Nian. But even as he said it, there was a new, different hope beginning to sing inside him.

He got up and bowed to Ranger's empty body, and then he went in search of the person who had spoken to him from the abyss.

Grodan was lying propped up beside Derig. Grodan's face was so yellow and gaunt and papery that seeing him made Nian realize how long he himself had been without rest. But he would be able to rest soon.

One last effort.

Grodan looked up.

'Well, he is still alive,' he said; he was too exhausted even to be sarcastic.

Nian felt a great warmth towards the man.

'Yes,' he said. 'You have saved him, Lord. And I know where he is, now.'

He stood beside Derig, and once more he sought the edge of the abyss that was, as he understood, now, not the abyss in which the worlds spun, but somewhere even stranger and darker and further away.

He stood there, and he looked as far as he could into the almost nothing. He sent long gentle ribbons of his mind out, out, into the darkness.

Here I am, he said, though without speaking. *I have come to show you the way home.*

There was no answer, but the darkness might have moved just a little, like the sea in the wake of a far-away ship. *I am here*, Nian said again. He would have called Derig's name, but somehow he knew that names did not belong here in the abyss, but were tied to brighter places.

And then he caught a whisper, not from one particular place, but from the whole infinity of blackness in front of him.

Here.

It was only the faintest vibration, but he called out to it in welcome.

This way, he said, as he curled his toes round the edge of the abyss so he should not topple down, and down, and become lost himself. *Here is the place where you belong, friend. Here is your place. Here.*

But there was a hesitation, almost a resistance, and so he reached out further, to gather up the delicate thing and draw it to him.

And it came because he was the Truth Sayer and had powers beyond those that anyone else had ever had. But as it came closer, as it accelerated and began to grow more solid or scented or flavoured or coloured or sonorous or none of those things, it left behind it trails of regret; almost of fear.

I am here, Nian breathed, but still it quivered with shafts of sadness as it came in obedience to his call. And here it was, in front of him. He took it, stepped back from the abyss, and it vanished.

But as he opened his eyes to the multitudinous garden, Derig opened his eyes, too. And they were wide and dark and full of sorrow. And Nian wept.

41

Nian awoke much later. The suns were long up, and the sleeping room was empty but for a neat row of rolled mats. Nian lay for a few minutes and listened to the unaccustomed patter of feet and the bustling busyness in the garden. He felt weighed down by something, but he couldn't remember what it was . . . perhaps something to do with Derig, except he couldn't really remember very much about what had happened, except that Derig was going to get better.

Nian got up and wandered out to find out what was going on.

'Hey, Nian's up!' shouted someone as soon as he showed his face at the garden door, and a general stampeding heralded the arrival of Alin and Emmec and Hani and Gow, grinning all over their faces. Nian looked around at them and found himself grinning back.

'What are you lot doing out here?' he asked. 'How did you manage to get out of lessons?'

Emmec laughed.

'We're working,' he told Nian. 'Those owlmen melted down to pure quicksilver, and we're searching it out and picking it up before it sinks into the ground and poisons the whole place.'

'Look,' said Hani, thrusting a cup towards him. At the bottom of the cup was a rounded hummock of shining liquid that managed to be both as bright as silver and as dark as charcoal.

'Is that all you've got?' scoffed Alin. 'Look. I've got twice as much.'

The glistening dome of the surface of the quicksilver showed strange reflections of the sky and trees . . . at least, was that the sky? The shadows moving across it were surely moving swifter than any cloud.

And those two dark patches . . . yes, they were eyes, and, now, Nian could see a face around it, and dark hair tumbling around that. And sparks, flying all around, as if Pella were in the middle of some great cataclysm or fight. Fight, he decided, was the most likely.

He peered more closely still.

There, bent by the concave surface of the metal, was a long column of grey. Dorcis. Yes, there she was; lots of the sparks were coming from her fingers. And Pella . . . Nian wasn't quite sure what was happening, because Pella seemed to be ducking and diving away from them and . . . and laughing. Yes, really laughing, as she caught the sparks and tossed them back to Dorcis.

And there were men in the background, tiny as ants, running in a jumbling rabble over the hills and far . . .

But people were talking round him, and the surface of the quicksilver dome was fading back to grey.

'Yeah, well, you've been searching under where the main owlman wall was,' pointed out Hani. 'I've been tracking the stuff through the undergrowth. That's *miles* more difficult.'

Gow rubbed hard at the side of his beaky nose.

'Actually, Hani's right,' he agreed. 'He *is* really good at it. Much better than any of the rest of us.'

Hani wriggled about a bit in embarrassment, but seemed pleased.

'Well, it's easy, finding little things like spots of quicksilver,' he said.

'No it's not,' said everyone else, in chorus.

'That's why we always let you fetch pockle cones that go into the bushes,' pointed out Nian.

'Yeah,' said Alin. 'Hey, Hani, perhaps you're not a complete moron, after all.'

Hani looked a bit confused.

'No, I think I am,' he said. 'I'm sure I must be. I mean, I always have been.'

'Oh, don't worry,' said Emmec. 'It's nothing to do with your brain. You've just got the nose of a dog, that's all.'

'Bog off,' said Hani, though he seemed quite relieved. 'Better a dog's nose than dog's breath, anyway, like you lot.'

Emmec made as if to throw his bucket of quicksilver over him, and Hani dodged away, squealing.

'Hey, Nian,' said Alin, 'talking of dog-breath, we asked Rago if he'd give us some pockle coaching, and he said we were a bunch of ham-fisted incompetents who certainly needed it. So I think that meant he might.'

'Yeah,' said Emmec, with a reverent, far-away look. 'Just think of being coached by someone who used to be in the *United* squad.'

'Hey! You boys!' came Caul's voice from somewhere not too far away. 'Am I to take it that you've got time to spend the next couple of hours in silent Thought?'

The boys exchanged rueful glances and tiptoed back to look for the tiny shining spheres that were all that was left of the melted owlmen. Nian helped for a while, until he came across Snorer sitting watching a small bonfire. There was a metal bucket hanging over it, and members of the Tarhun were prowling up carrying shovels heaped with flakes of stuff as fine as ashes but as tough as beetle-wings. The stuff went into the bucket with a hiss like a frying snake, and melted with a whiff of greenish smoke and the scent of damp marble.

Snorer gave Nian a swift look from his piggy little eyes, and then went back to poking the contents of the bucket with a stick.

'The Lord Tarq says that he will go over the ground with a mind-straw and suck up the last bits of the owlmen,' he told Nian. 'But we're clearing away as much as we can ourselves, to make sure there aren't enough left-over bits to come together and make another owlman. Not that they're likely to fuse together again, but we don't fancy risking it.'

'I'm sorry about Ranger,' said Nian.

Snorer gave him another swift look, and then nodded.

'Yes. Yes, I'll miss him. Still, it was a fine way to

go, wasn't it? Fighting? The best way. Oh, Ranger will have been well pleased with that.' Snorer sighed hugely, his paunch wobbling against his fat thighs. 'The Lords are saying that perhaps we'll not bother about rebuilding the walls of the House, after all, to commemorate the help the Tourists gave us in the fight. And that'll be a sort of tribute to Ranger, too, of course.'

'Really?' asked Nian.

'Yes, good old Ranger,' went on Snorer, fondly. 'He should have joined the Tarhun when he was young, really, like I did, but Auntie Mallie, she was his mother, she insisted he got a proper trade. Yes, it was only when Auntie died that he gave it all up and came up here, and then of course he was a natural. Why, he was such a cunning liar he even managed to persuade the Lords to give him the contract for rebuilding the walls of the House!'

Nian couldn't see what was so cunning about that.

'But why shouldn't he have got it?' he asked. 'He was a builder, wasn't he?'

Snorer looked slightly shifty.

'Well, not exactly,' he admitted, poking the contents of the bucket. 'Not as such, no. Though he did make a very nice rocking chair for my grandad, once. Beautiful, it was. Made entirely of ox-bones. Ah, it was a wonderful thing, until we had that bad winter and the dog ate it. But a work of genius!'

'But . . . Ranger had never built anything?' said Nian. 'No actual . . . buildings?'

'Well, not as such, no,' Snorer admitted. 'But then,

his trade kept him on the move the whole time. I'm sure he would have done, if he'd had the opportunity.'

'So what was his trade?' asked Nian.

'Oh,' said Snorer, shrugging his huge round shoulders. 'He had a job herding oxen.'

Nian blinked with shock.

'You mean . . . '

Snorer sighed.

'Yes,' he said. 'He wasn't really a master builder. He was a cowboy.'

42

Snerk was guarding the entrance to his kitchen.

'Nurrrr,' he growled, pointing fiercely with a ladle to a bowl of hot water that steamed on a table by the door. 'Gurrrr!'

'Oh,' said Nian. 'All right, then.'

He dipped his hands in the bowl.

'Burrrr-burr! Gurrrr! Guk!'

'Oh, yes, of course,' said Nian, meekly, and picked up the bar of snot-coloured soap that lurked next to the bowl on a grimy saucer. He washed his hands thoroughly to remove every trace of owlman quicksilver.

'Hurrr,' said Snerk, appeased. 'Nurr, boggoff!'

'Fair enough. Thanks,' said Nian.

And did.

The Lord Firn was bobbing along the corridor in a quite worrying amount of excitement.

'Ah yes, Truth Sayer,' he said, blinking his little eyes at Nian. 'I have been thinking about the owlman wall. It was made up of many layers packed together, and I was thinking that instead of rolling up our manuscripts in scrolls, we might try cutting them into squares, and sewing them together. They would take up much less space, and they would be less susceptible, I believe, to damage.'

Nian tried to imagine how such a thing might work, and failed completely.

'Tarhun Reeklet might be a help,' he suggested. 'He's keen on sewing.'

'Is he, is he,' muttered Firn, trembling with enthusiasm. 'Then I must seek him out.'

And he pottered away as fast as his ancient legs would take him.

Derig and Grodan were sitting quietly together in a small room near the Council Chamber. Grodan was helping Derig to eat something that Nian might have thought was porridge, except that Snerk's kitchen never produced anything quite as straightforward as that. Grodan had got back the sarcastic twist to his mouth, but Derig, propped up with a bedding-roll, still looked frail and exhausted.

Nian bowed to Grodan, whose face darkened into his customary scowl.

'I hope you're going to smarten yourself up before you let anyone from the outside see you,' Grodan snarled. 'Your tunic's hardly fit for a dish-rag. What will people think if they see you like that?'

'They'll probably think that I've been fighting in two separate worlds to save all our lives,' replied Nian, stung.

Grodan grunted.

'Then I can only hope that at some point you will learn *to think*, Truth Sayer, rather than relying on all this scrapping and brawling.'

Nian, outraged, drew in a deep breath . . . and saw something unexpected in Grodan's eye. A spark of something. It would be ridiculous to call it warmth, for Grodan was surely incapable of feeling anything for anyone; although there he was, patiently helping Derig to eat.

Nian changed his mind about what he was going to say.

'How is Derig?' he asked.

'Weak,' said Grodan.

'Is there anything I can do to help?'

Grodan gave him a filthy look.

'I think you've done enough. The way you've chosen to cure him isn't making his recovery very fast.'

'No,' said Nian. 'But this way there'll be no scarring in his voice-box.'

Grodan's face was sharp, but with interest, for once, rather than contempt.

'You hardly used your powers on his voice-box at all,' he said.

Nian considered. He hadn't thought about it like that, but it made sense to let Derig's own body do most of the work, for generally it had more knowledge and wisdom than he ever would.

'Humph,' went on Grodan. 'Well, it's possible, I suppose, that there's some merit in that way of working.'

Nian felt as surprised and pleased as if Grodan had clapped him on the back, or smiled, or something.

And now Derig's lips were moving.

Nian had to put his ear very close to Derig's lips to hear what he was saying.

'I was a long way away when you came,' he whispered, with difficulty. 'But it wasn't so bad.'

Nian thought of the abyss from which he had pulled Derig. It had terrified him—but perhaps that was because he had been clinging to the edge, to life, with all his strength.

But still, he found he understood.

'Yes,' he said. 'In the end, there's nothing to be afraid of.'

And Derig, smiling, closed his eyes.

The Mirelands

Dorcis pointed a powerful white arm, and something began to stir amongst the tufts of bronze grass.

'What is it?' asked Pella.

Dorcis was concentrating and made no reply, but soon a furred crest bobbed into view.

'A *springer*,' murmured Pella, puzzled.

It was a young one, too foolish even to be scared by the pull of Dorcis's powers. It let Dorcis pick it up without even struggling.

Dorcis gave it to Pella.

'When is it going to die?' Pella asked, cradling it against her.

'Not for years, if you look after it properly.'

Pella stroked the honey-coloured fur. Then, suddenly, she looked up at Dorcis.

'I know everything I make turns out mad and vicious,' she said. 'But it still might be a help with sorting out the bandits. An army of . . . of ferocious nutcrackers, perhaps. That'd be fun.'

Dorcis threw back her head and laughed.

'I can't see any of those bare-kneed bandits arguing with those,' she agreed.

43

Nian hurried on. He needed to walk all round the corridor: the House had been in danger for so long that it was hard to believe that it was safe.

'Hey, farm boy!'

Keer was standing by the sleeping room. He had his sleeping mat strapped to his back, and his pockets were bulging with things that must certainly be stolen. Nian used his powers to investigate. At least Keer hadn't taken anything that mattered personally to anyone, contenting himself with pinching various bits of gold and silver that had been donated to the House over the centuries, and all the money he could lay his hands on.

'You're going back to the city,' Nian said.

Keer nodded.

'Yeah. Course.'

'But why?'

Keer shrugged.

'Well, I've found out all I needed to, haven't I?' he said. 'I was only playing with my powers, before, but now I'll be able to move in and clean up. Yeah. I reckon I'll be rich in two years, if I live that long.'

Nian could believe it.

'So there's just the slight problem that anyone who leaves the House has to promise not to use their powers to hurt anybody,' he pointed out, rather apologetically.

'Do they?' said Keer, with complete indifference. 'Yeah, well, I'll only be using my powers on the other grotters, won't I? And not exactly to hurt them—unless it's them or me, obviously—just as a matter of business. I mean, *someone's* got to be stinking rich, so why shouldn't it be me? I mean, it's not even as if you're going to give me that money you owe me, is it?'

Nian made a face.

'I will,' he said. 'It's just that . . . well, I haven't actually got it just at the moment.'

Keer nodded.

'Yeah, yeah. And when will you have it?'

Nian scratched his fair head.

'Well . . . if we do well with the afternoon teas, then I suppose . . . '

'Come off it!' Keer said. But then his eyes brightened. 'Hang on, though, what about your family's farm? You're the elder son, aren't you? Hey, how's your dad been keeping?'

And Nian couldn't help but laugh.

'Sorry, but that's no good,' he said. 'I gave all my inheritance to my little brother.'

Keer shook his head regretfully.

'Well, I can't say I'm surprised,' he admitted. 'And I bet you were glad to be shot of it, too, weren't you?'

'Yes,' agreed Nian. 'Yes, I was.'

'Bogging moron,' said Keer, but without bad-feeling. 'A fortune like that dropped into your lap, and you give it away for the chance to live like a peasant and to be first in the firing line whenever anything dangerous turns up.'

And to be lonely, thought Nian, but he only held out his hand.

'Live well,' he said.

Keer shot him a suspicious look.

'Yeah, well, that'll come once I've got the money and stuff, won't it.'

'Perhaps,' said Nian.

And Keer frowned, but then he seemed to shrug all that away. He just touched Nian's hand.

'Don't forget you'll be welcome if you ever come back,' Nian told him; Keer only snorted.

'What, after all the stuff I've just nicked?' he asked. 'Come off it!'

'No, that's all right, we knew you were a cheat and a thief, anyway, and we're still a long way in your debt. I couldn't have managed without your help in the Mirelands—or if you hadn't brought the Tourists up to the House, either.'

'Oh, that was an accident,' said Keer. 'I was just going to scarper, but one of the Tourists caught me stealing one of their ponies, and they sort of assumed I'd come to lead them into battle. Embarrassing, really.'

'Yes,' said Nian. 'I didn't think you'd have done anyone a good turn like that except by accident.'

Keer grinned at the compliment.

'There's a silk merchant called Varn in the city,'

Nian went on. 'If you tell him you're my friend, he'll help you. But don't try stealing from him, whatever you do. He's very clever and powerful.'

'Oh, I'll be all right,' said Keer. 'I like fending for myself: fighting, and using my wits, and all that. I'd be bored here, being safe and organized. Still, thanks for having me. Say goodbye to people, and all that sort of thing. Good luck . . . and live well, Truth Sayer.'

Keer ducked his head in farewell, and turned and walked quickly and purposefully away through the door that led to the Outer House.

His figure was silhouetted for a second against the white walls, and then he was gone.

Tarq was in the schoolroom. An outsider might have thought that he was sitting doing nothing.

He looked up as Nian came in, and he smiled.

'My friend,' he said, in welcome.

Nian came and sat in front of him.

'I'm lonely,' he said. 'I know I have you, and the other Lords, and the boys, and the Tarhun, and I know they are all my friends—but I'm still lonely.'

Tarq was listening, but he didn't make any reply.

'And . . . there's nothing that can be done about it, is there,' said Nian. 'Because I'm the Truth Sayer, and I'm the only one, and there's no one anywhere in the world who can understand.'

And still Tarq said nothing.

'It's mostly all right while I'm doing things,' Nian went on. 'It doesn't matter much what, studying, or using my powers or just playing pockle. As long as I'm doing something, then it's all right. But when everything stops . . . I sort of remember there's no hope.'

'My friend,' began Tarq, but Nian shook his head.

'I know that doesn't make any difference,' he said. 'I mean, I don't *have* to be happy or anything. All I have to do is to keep on and on. Doing stuff. And if I keep doing stuff as hard as I can, then things won't ever stop. But it's difficult, sometimes, because I still sort of don't know what I'm supposed to be doing.'

'My friend,' said Tarq, again, very gently, 'I think you know what you are supposed to be doing very well indeed. Consider. If you had not gone to the world of the owlmen, then we would probably all be dead.'

Nian looked at him uncertainly.

'But going to another world . . . '

' . . . was necessary, for us, and for the worlds,' said Tarq. 'Wasn't it?'

Nian blinked, and tried to ignore the sudden hope that had sprouted inside him.

'But I mustn't go into other worlds because it's much too dangerous,' he pointed out. 'That's what you and the other Lords have always said.'

'Come, now,' said Tarq, his eyes sparking with something that in someone seventy years younger might have been called mischief. 'It is not kind, Truth Sayer, to remind your elders of all the foolish things we've said.'

Nian got to his feet and began walking backwards and forwards.

'There are thousands of worlds,' he said. 'You wouldn't believe how different they are: forests, cities, lakes, deserts . . . I just can't imagine what it'd be like to be in a desert: somewhere so bare, and so hot.'

'Well,' said Tarq, patiently, 'perhaps that's where your fate will draw you next.'

'I'll tell you something,' went on Nian, hardly listening. 'The quicksilver from the owlmen—that's going to make a link through the abyss between the worlds. I've already seen things in it. So I could sort of keep an eye on it, couldn't I, and if I saw something interesting . . .'

'Nian! *Nian!*'

Footsteps pelted along the corridor and Hani skidded at full tilt through the schoolroom doorway and only avoided falling over Tarq by making a wild leap right over him.

'Is there some emergency, my friend?' asked Tarq, mildly.

Hani unravelled himself.

'No, Lord,' he said, apologetically. 'At least, it's just that we've finished clearing the quicksilver from the pockle ground and Rago—the Lord Rago—came out to inspect it, and, I don't know, we were talking about those haggises last night and one thing led to another and he's sent me in to find some flippers so he can show us how they should really be used. So I thought that Nian—'

'*Really?*'

Hani grinned. 'He's going to give us a coaching session!'

301

Nian had got halfway to the door before he remembered he was in the middle of a difficult and important discussion with Tarq about the fate of the worlds. And stuff.

He looked back.

'Go, go,' said Tarq, pacifically. 'It will give me a chance for Thought, and it's plain I must seize every chance for that.'

Nian turned and ran at full speed down the corridor towards the garden door.

Outside, the suns were breaking through the cloud. Nian leapt to clear a log and let his powers take him up in a high exultant arc ten reaches across the garden.

Voices from other worlds seemed to sound round him as he went.

Live well, they said.

A Guide to the Pronunciation of Foreign Words

Alin	A-lin (a as in *hat*)	Pella	PELLa (a as in *about*)
Branto	BRANT-o (o as in *go*)	pirt-pu	PEE-ert-POO
Bulls-Eye	BULLZ-ei (ei as in *eider*)	pockle	PO-k'l (o as in *got*)
		Rago	RARG-o (o as in *go*)
Caul	KORL	Ranger	RAYN-ja (ay as in *say*, a as in *about*)
Derig	DE-rig (e as in *leg*)		
Dorcis	DOR-kiss	Reeklet	REEK-lit
Emmec	EM-ek (e as in *leg*)	Rik	RIK
Firn	FERN	rutnips	RUTT-nipz
Gow	GOW (G as in *go*, ow as in *now*)	sirrom	SI-r'm (i as in *sit*)
		Snerk	SNERK (er as in *jerk*)
Grandy	GRAND-ee	Snorer	SNOR-a (a as in *about*)
Grodan	GRO-dan (o as in *go*)	Tan	TAN
grohl	grol (o as in *go*)	Tarhun	TAR-h'n
Hani	HAN-ee (a as in *hat*)	Tarq	TARK
Keer	KEER	Thian	THEI-n (th as in *think*, ei as in *eider*)
Mallie	MALLee (a as in *hat*)		
Mirelands	MEIr-landz (ei as in *eider*)	Trun	TRUN (u as in *run*)
		Vanna	VANN-a (first a as in *hat*, second a as in *about*)
Mirelandic	MEIr-LAND-ik (ei as in *eider*)		
Miri	MI-ree (i as in *sit*)	Varn	VARN
mouselets	MOWSS-litz (ow as in *now*)	Wiglana Squimp	wigLARNa SKWIMP (a as in *about*)
Nian	NEE-n		
Peggary	PEG-aree (a as in *about*)		

Sally Prue first started making up stories as a teenager, when she realized that designing someone else's adventures was almost as satisfying as having her own. After leaving school Sally joined practically all the rest of her family working at the nearby paper mill. She now teaches recorder and piano and enjoys walking, painting, day-dreaming, reading, and gardening. *Cold Tom*, Sally's first book, won the Bramford Boase Award and the Smarties Prize Silver Award. Sally has two daughters and lives with her husband in Hertfordshire. *The Truth Sayer March of the Owlmen* is Sally's sixth novel for Oxford University Press.

HOW IT ALL BEGAN...

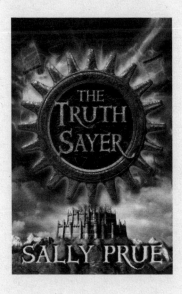

Nian is a boy with a destiny. Taken from his home and family to live in the House of Truth, he must practise his skills of mind-reading, weather lore and manipulation of matter. Once he has achieved mastery, he will become one of the elect, a Lord of Truth.

There's only one problem. Nian doesn't want to become a Lord of Truth. He just wants to get away.
But his only means of escape is to step into another world.
To be precise, into Jacob's front room.
In Essex. Just before tea time.

Nian doesn't speak English, he doesn't know what to do with a toaster, and he's got no idea what those roaring lumps of metal speeding down the road are.

The truth is, this is going to be interesting...

AND CONTINUED...

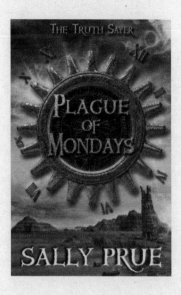

It's Monday morning, but already everyone in
the House of Truth is exhausted. And that's
before Tan turns up with news that something's gone
wrong with the worlds. Only Nian can solve it,
but he needs a good night's sleep before he can
work out what to do. Except that when Nian
wakes up, it's Monday morning again...
and Tan hasn't arrived yet.

Meanwhile, far away in another world, an ancient
monument is about to be opened up for the first time
in generations. But inside lurks a deadly menace.

Only Nian has a chance of averting disaster.
And he'll get right on to it.
In the morning, as soon as Monday's over...

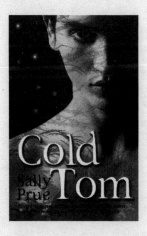

ISBN 978-0-19-272765-6

Tom had never been to the city of the demons before, and it smelt of death. He stood and shivered by the bridge over the river, his skin prickling with danger. It was madness to cross— but then he was in danger if he stayed, too.

Tom is one of the Tribe. But he is not like the others—he is clumsy and heavy, and the Tribe drive him away into the demon city. But Tom can't live with demons either—they are so hot, so foul, and he knows they are trying to enslave his mind.

But there is nowhere else to run. Between the savage Tribe and the stifling demons, is there any way out for Tom?

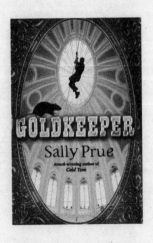

ISBN 978-0-19-272764-0

When Sebastian is chosen as the High Priest's apprentice
at the Temple of Ora, everyone's shocked.

But Sebastian soon discovers that as apprentice, he can
have anything he wants ... limitless creamcakes, training
sessions with Golden United, even zip-wires and donkeys to
liven up ceremonies at the Temple. He can pass entertaining
new laws to annoy teachers, as well.

But then there are strange explosions, falling objects,
whispered threats. Sebastian realizes the Temple, with its
all-seeing golden statue, holds many secrets.

Can he ignore it all? Or should Sebastian and his pet rat,
Gerald, risking life and whisker, try to out-fox the most
powerful mob in the city?

ISBN 978-0-19-275310-6

'impressive ambition and psychological complexity'
The Telegraph

'I'd like to suggest you read this without pausing for breath'
The Bookseller

'Scary and thrilling, and quite impossible to put down'
Irish Post

Stevie wants to do something bad. That's the only
way he'll impress the gang. But doing bad things takes
a bit of daring, a bit of skill.
Stevie needs help.

That's when he finds the devil's toenail on the beach.
It's just what he needs – he can feel a strange power
coming from it, giving him a new strength . . .

And when he's learned to use that power, then everything
will be better for him. Won't it?

Ryland's
Footsteps

SALLY PRUE

Cold Tom   Branford
Boaw Award   Nestlé Smarties Silver Award

ISBN 978-0-19-275339-7

Rye had been prepared for most things on the colony – for the rain, and the warmth, and the metal-box houses – but he hadn't really been prepared for Dad's being Governor . . . for his being so absolutely in charge . . .

There are other things that take Rye by surprise as he gets to know the island – the lizards that burn you if you touch them; the secret caves; the gods and their magic; the underground prison and the prisoner's daughter. And all the time people keep telling him how like his father he is.

Rye makes friends with Kris, an island boy, and together they explore the colony and try to find out its secrets, and the reasons behind all the disasters that are putting the very existence of the colony in jeopardy.

But in facing up to the greatest threat of all, Rye has to choose where his loyalties lie, and discovers that being so like his father may not be such a bad thing after all.